WHERE IS MY DAUGHTER?

LOUISE BRODERICK

ISBN 978-1-7393049-0-4

Published 2023 By Lavender and White Publishing.

Copyright © Louise Broderick /Lavender and White Publishing 2023

The right of Louise Broderick to be identified as the author of this work has been asserted by her in accordance with the Copyright, Designs and Patents Act 1988.

Typesetting, layout and design Lavender and White Publishing.

A CIP catalogue record for this book is available from the British Library.

www.lavenderandwhite.co.uk

Thank you for taking the time to read this book. I hope you enjoyed it, I certainly enjoyed writing it. Each time I sit down to write – and that is every day – I realise just how lucky I am this is my job. I can only keep this job because people like you enjoy my books and buy them. No words can express how grateful I am for that.

If you would like to find out more about my other books, please visit my web site.

www.louisebroderick.com

I love to hear from readers so please feel free to contact me on via my Facebook page or email. The details of these are all on my web site.

I hope you enjoyed this book and would like to help me carry on living the dream, writing for a living. If you would like to help, please take the time to leave a book review on Amazon. Positive reviews really do help to sell a book, so if you would do that for me you are helping me to continue creating my books and continuing as a fulltime writer.

Can I just say a huge thank you in advance to anyone who takes the time to do this for me. I know very well how precious time is and am hugely grateful for anyone who cares enough to spend some of their valuable time helping me. Thank you.

Dedication

To my three brilliant children for all their love and support.

Acknowledgments

As always, this book got finished because of my amazing support team. While I might put in the hard slog of moving my hands over the keyboard, it is the work of my editor, Ruairi and critique team, Stephen, Katie, Barbara and Bill who have knocked the manuscript into shape.

After long months of work, it is such a relief to hand the book over to my production team who as always have done a wonderful job. Thank you to Liz and Les for their hard work and creativity.

While the book is set in my favourite county, Cornwall, I have taken huge liberties with the setting, the towns and cities. While some of the places are real, others exist only in my imagination. A big thank you goes to my dear friend Claire for her help in establishing just when the Truro branch of Tesco first opened.

My Other Books:

Writing as Louise Broderick
Trainers
Winners
Millionaires Are A Girl's Best Friend
After – Sometimes The End Is Just The Beginning
Plot. Write. Sell.

Writing as Jacqui Broderick
Pony For Free
The Unwanted Pony
The Cat's Whiskers

Contents

Chapter One

1989

She was used to pain. But not like this. He took pleasure in its creation, the anticipation of watching her endure the slow build-up of discomfort as he turned it unhurriedly to torment. She'd learned how to twist her body, to ease her muscles to gain some relief. She'd discovered how to deceive him, crying out, pleading before it was unbearable.

This, though, was relentless, bands of fire, agonising, gripped her body. 'Nan, help me.' Glanna shifted her position so she could see the older woman. Even she seemed to take no pleasure in watching Glanna's pain. Nan flung herself out of the wooden chair beside the bed and began to pace the room.

'Glanna. Do you want water?' Nan dabbed restlessly at Glanna's sweat drenched forehead with a damp cloth. The fabric was cool, giving momentary respite from the furnace which seemed to burn beneath her skin.

Glanna grunted a denial, the animal-like sound expelled through teeth that chattered against one another.

'Could be a long time yet.'

Glanna's head rocked from side to side against the stained fabric of the pillow.

Nan drew the cloth over Glanna's exposed skin. The chain, holding her wrist to the top of the bed rattled a rapid rhythm in time with the tremors that racked her limbs.

Glanna writhed again as another torturous wave took hold of her. There seemed to be no beginning to it, nowhere she could ease the pain, and no end to it. There were, she was vaguely aware, brief respites when the pain seemed to retreat slightly before surging forwards in a tide which left her senseless.

When he was there, teasing at her body with the tools he laid out with such precision, she had learned to let her mind free. Her physical presence remained, the chains cutting into her wrists and ankles, while mentally she left the dank room, the soiled mattress, the creaking bedframe, and returned to the life she had once taken so much for granted. In her imagination she once more walked the rooms of her home, rested in the security of her family, laughed as she ran with her sisters along the golden stretch of beach near the house, she had grown up in. He could control everything she did, but not that. He could never reach her there.

But this pain was something she could not escape from, it held her captive. Had Nan removed the chain from her wrist, opened the door and told her to leave she could not.

Glanna took a gasping breath, aware of the need to force air into her lungs. An image of home drifted ghostlike in front of her. She pictured herself curled with her sisters on the vast expanse of battered sofa which had dominated the lounge. A bowl, overflowing with popcorn moments before, spinning across the room, the yellow kernels spilling onto the floor. Morwenna, the oldest of the three of them had caught it with a foot as they had pushed themselves back away from the television, in horror and disgust at the programme they were watching. On the screen a woman writhed and swore as, red and bawling, a wrinkled baby emerged from her. The girls had hidden their faces in their hands, feigned vomiting noises, before descending into fits of giggles.

The vision evaporated, frail strands Glanna could not keep hold of. She screamed; a noise she was only dimly conscious of as the pain ripped through her once more. She fought it pushing her heels into the damp sheets to try to straighten her body.

'Don't you try anything,' Nan's voice cut into the haze of pain. Glanna let her arm drop to her side, freed from the chain that had kept it bound to one end of the bed. The pins and needles that swept through from her elbow to her numb fingers were a minute distraction.

'Fuck off,' Glanna panted.

She was aware now of another sensation, a base instinct deep within herself. The need to push, to expel the child.

'Help me.'

Nan, beside Glanna twined her fingers compulsively into one another, her fear palpable. She who had watched and taken pleasure in Glanna's torment, flailing now in the face of the younger woman's pain and terror.

He was there. She knew instinctively. Glanna had become vigilant of his presence, her senses tuned to his approach. The long months of captivity had made her aware of him, of his needs, his moods. She'd learned to sense his arrival, to brace herself for what he would do, to let the innermost part of her being go free where he could not touch it. In between the horror, it was almost possible to forget what a monster he was. His smile was disarming, charming even.

Something now, a faint footfall, a shadow crossing the room had made her aware of him. He stood in the corner of the room, watching. His face, impassive as always beneath his dark hair. He had come to watch, to see the birth of the child he had planted in her unwilling body.

'How long will it be?' His voice, normally deceptively soft, had a tense edge.

'Eddie, how should I know?' Nan snapped.

'Help me,' Glanna groaned. She moved her head and met his eyes.

'Take me to the hospital. Please.'

Eddie shook his head. 'It's just a baby. The animals give birth on their own all the time.'

Glanna screamed again, a shriek of pure anguish and panic.

'If she dies, you'll deal with it, Eddie.' Nan crossed the room towards him, hands on hips, her face contorted with rage. 'I'm sick of you. Stupid bastard.'

'Help her then.' His voice had a gentle note Glanna had never heard before.

'It's coming. Help me. Please.'

In the dim light of the cellar Glanna saw Eddie blink slowly as if to blank out the sight. His eyes when they opened again had a compassion she had never seen. Not for her, she knew, but for the child inside her. A small human they had created some time during the long months she had been his prisoner. Stuck in the dank, darkness of the cellar, he her only human contact.

'I don't know what to do,' Nan's voice filled with irritation.

'Haven't you brought enough calves and lambs into the world? What's the difference?'

Nan, for all her bulk, could move swiftly when she needed to. She crossed the dirt encrusted floor in two strides, fists raised she rained blows on Eddie. Glanna, despite her pain, watched him cower away from his mother. 'This is your fault. Stupid, filthy animal. You can't leave them alone can you?' Nan taunted.

Shoulders hunched to fend off her attack he backed out of the room.

'You like this don't you?' As the pain diminished momentarily Glanna met Nan's eyes, 'Watching me scream.' Glanna whispered, her voice weak with pain and exhaustion.

The older woman dropped her eyes first.

Glanna gasped as another wave hit her. She couldn't remember how long she had endured the agony. Had it begun this morning, when the first shafts of light began to illuminate the dingy cellar? Or yesterday? Time seemed to have lost all meaning.

At first, when she had come round, in the cellar, her face cut and bruised, she'd tried to keep count of the days. She'd used part of her hair clip to drag a mark through the yellowing, chipped whitewash that covered the walls. One mark for each time the light began to brighten the tangle of battered furniture in the damp room. She'd fought him so hard each time he opened the door and came into her, received so many punches that had knocked her unconscious that she wasn't sure if she missed days. Waking confused and only dimly aware of his presence.

Gradually she had stopped fighting. There was no point. He took enough pleasure in hurting her in other ways without giving him more reason. She'd tried pleading with him. Telling him about her family, her parents, sisters, her home, the life they had together. He listened impassively. She spoke about the course she was doing at the university in Exeter. She'd been walking home from writing an essay in the library, when he had picked her up. It had been quieter in there than the noisy house she'd shared with three other students.

In the days when she had first found herself in the cellar, she had cursed her stupidity, her naive trust of the man who had stopped his vehicle in front of her and asked for directions, struggling incompetently with the folds of a street map. She'd been engrossed in the map, tracing the streets with her finger to show him how to find the one he had asked for. She didn't remember much of his attack, a short, ferocious rain of blows which had left her reeling and unable to stop him bundling her into the back of his pick-up.

She had a vague memory of a journey, bumping and sliding in the back of the vehicle, her legs and hands bound, a strip of something across her mouth. It had been hard to breathe, let alone fight.

When the bumping finally stopped, he'd pulled her roughly out of the pick-up, shouldering her as if she were nothing more than a sack of animal feed. In the darkness she'd seen the silhouette of a house against the night sky, one single window illuminated, yellow glowing behind the curtains. She'd smelt the familiar tang of the sea and that of farm animals before he'd descended into the depths of a damp smelling building.

And that was where she had stayed. Sometimes chained, others not. The marks on the wall, painstakingly made with her hair clip became too many to count. It had been cold in the cellar, the only light and warmth coming from the sunlight when it penetrated the small oval window set high up the wall.

He'd thought of everything. There was a bed, a small table and chair, a litter of yellowing paperback books, their pages damp and curling. He'd even installed a small bathroom behind a bright, plastic shower curtain, adorned with frolicking dolphins. Food was brought regularly, along with mugs of coffee which were always cold by the time he had finished with her.

Months, she knew, had passed before she'd noticed changes to her body, there had been no choice but accept the awful truth that part of him was growing inside her. No matter how much she despised him and everything he stood for, it was hard not to feel compassion for the tiny form that moved and kicked inside her. His violence had stopped then and he had treated her with something which resembled reverence, resting a hand on the swell of her belly to wait for the inevitable kicks from within.

Glanna had cried, pleaded with him to let her go, promised not to tell anyone what had happened to her, what he had done. She longed for her mother, who she knew would be beside herself with grief for her missing daughter. She locked those thoughts away, knowing she would go mad with the heartache. She had to get through each day and wait, until one day she might get a chance to escape.

'The head's out.' Nan's voice contained a mixture of excitement and fascination. 'That's it. There's the baby.'

Glanna was aware of a slithering sensation, and the pain receding as if it had never existed. Glanna rested her head against the pillow, conscious now of the chill of the room against her sweat dampened skin and of Nan, wrapping the baby in fabric. Within the folds of the cloth Glanna glimpsed a wrinkled, red face, the tiny button of a nose and small, rosebud lips.

'It's a little girl,' Nan tucked the baby into one arm, cradling her gently. The baby cried briefly and then was silent. Nan moved across the room, rocking the bundle.

'Nan,' Glanna, eased herself onto one arm, swung her legs to the side of the bed and levered herself upright. 'Nan. Is she okay?'

Nan, her head lowered towards the baby, raised her eyes to glare coldly in Glanna's direction before she took a step backwards.

Glanna held out her arms towards Nan. 'She's mine. Give her to me.'

Chapter Two

'**P**lease. Give her to me.'

Nan met Glanna's eyes, the softness when she had looked at the child turning swiftly to the usual distaste. 'Here,' she thrust the bundle towards Glanna. In the moments since she had been born the baby's tiny face had smoothed out, turned from the livid red Glanna had glimpsed, when she had emerged into the world, to a gentle pink. Her eyes, blue in the pale light, searched for and then locked onto Glanna's.

'Hello,' Nothing else existed, not the terrible cellar, the circumstances of being held prisoner, the pain of missing her family. Nothing, except the beauty of this tiny, fragile person. Glanna eased the folds of cloth aside, found and touched her baby's tiny fingers. They were minute replicas of her own, each tipped with a delicate nail. The fingers moved, seeking and then holding onto one of hers with a surprisingly strong grip.

'You're like animals, you and him.' Nan poked at Glanna with a finger. 'Filth.'

'He is. Not me.' Glanna glared at Nan, hunching her shoulders against the expected blow which would always follow any outburst from her. It didn't come. Bravely she continued, 'We need to get her to the hospital.' Wasn't that what they always did on television?

Nan let out a snort of derision. 'No hospital.' She rolled her eyes. 'Stupid bitch, what do you need a hospital for? Women have given birth for thousands of years without doctors.' She spat the last word as if there was something vile in her mouth.

'To check…' Glanna began, faltering beneath the scorn of the older woman. 'On television…'

Nan's lip curled. 'Dumb cunt.'

She took a stride towards Glanna. One of Nan's powerful shoulders slammed into her, shoving her easily out of the way. 'Move,' she snapped, beginning to haul at the bloodied threadbare sheets. With deft movements she gathered up the fabric, bunching it into a ball and throwing it violently across the room where it hit the wall and then fell. The bundle opened, the bloodstained material pooling across the floor.

'There you are,' Nan turned to glare at Eddie who stood watching from the doorway. 'See what you've done, with your filth.'

He was silent, his eyes dropped to the vast slate slab beneath his feet.

'You clean that up.' Nan gestured towards the pile of sheets. 'Filth.' She pushed past him on her way out of the room, her movement stirring the musty air. He jerked his shoulder out of the way to avoid contact with his mother.

Glanna pulled the baby closer to her. Slowly his shoulder moved back. His presence brooding and malevolent.

'You had the baby.'

'Yes.' In another life she would have made a smart retort in reply. Not now. She spoke only when necessary. Obedient, passive. Whatever it took to avoid angering him.

He stood uncertainly, a new chapter in their dysfunctional

relationship. As if he felt the power to give birth gave her some new authority. 'I'll get sheets.' As he moved across the room Glanna gave an involuntary gasp of fear, drawing away from him in anticipation of a blow, or worse. He glanced at her, releasing a snort of derision at her reaction.

Glanna moved towards the pale light that came in through the semicircle of the single window. Craning her neck upwards she could see the azure blue of the sky, the wispiness of a single pale cloud, in front of which, the branches of a tree swayed gently in the breeze. At its height the sun would cast a single shaft of light through the window, illuminating a dusty band across the floor. Undoubtedly a perfect autumn day. Or perhaps it was early winter. She had lost track of the time passing.

On the days when she was untied Glanna stood in the light, soaking up the warmth of the sun, staring at the dancing tree branches. Locked in the virtual darkness it was impossible to imagine the simple pleasure of standing outside, breathing fresh air, a gentle breeze touching her skin. She watched the clouds for hours, wondering if her parents, her sisters, friends, were looking at the same ones. Apart from the marks she made on the wall, the restricted view through the window showed her the inevitable passing of time. The trees had been bare when she had first looked through the window. She'd watched the first pale green leaves appear, then turn to golden. The branches were bare again now. The seasons marched on relentlessly, as the world went on without her.

Cradling the baby in the crook of her arm she gently pushed the fabric away from her body, letting the warmth of the sun play on the delicate skin. The baby gurgled, a noise Glanna took to signal pleasure.

Eddie bundled the sheets up and tossed them out of the room, closing the door behind them in a gesture she was familiar with. There was no need, she was too exhausted, too sore, too crushed to contemplate trying to escape.

'Can I...?' He came to stand beside her. Glanna stood still, feeling her toes curl with involuntary hatred at his nearness. The slate tiles beneath her feet were sticky with dirt and damp.

Glanna's fingers tightened around the bundle of fabric as Eddie, with a gentleness she hadn't known he possessed, moved the cloth away so he could look at his daughter.

'She's beautiful.' He shook his head as if he couldn't believe what he was seeing. He traced a long finger over the baby's face, the curve of her cheeks, the tiny bud of her nose. 'Like you,' Eddie used his finger to lift the curtain of Glanna's hair. She froze, compliant, shuddering inwardly at his touch. 'I'll get the sheets.' He said, drawing away finally.

As he left, Glanna heard the familiar sound of the key being turned in the lock. She sank slowly on the edge of the bed watching her tears fall on her daughter's face as she hungrily nuzzled her mother.

Glanna slept then, exhausted, curled on the knobbly mattress, the baby tucked beneath her arm.

The sound of the key being turned in the lock woke her. She was instantly wide awake, watchful, fearful of his approach.

'I've brought you some food,' he set down a plate and mug on the table beside her, 'and tea. And clean sheets.' He set down the plastic bag, which had dangled from one hand. 'Nappies and baby clothes.'

He sounded like an excited father coming to visit his wife and their child.

'Thank you.'

'Nan made a stew.'

'Oh.' Glanna was starving, the plate of food smelt delicious, reminding her painfully of her mother's cooking.

Glanna eased herself to the edge of the bed. It was difficult, hampered by the baby and her own sore body.

'I'll take her while you eat.'

Glanna, knew better than to argue with him. Unwillingly she released the baby into his arms. However, much as he might like to hurt her, it was clear from the gentle way he cradled his daughter no harm would come to her from him.

She began to fork up the food, shovelling it into her mouth as fast as she could. All semblance of politeness had long been abandoned. Food, especially warm and nourishing like this, was a rarity. Usually, he brought her a stale sandwich, or toast, with a slick of congealed butter and jam.

'Hi, little one.' He paced, slowly up and down the cellar crooning to the baby, rocking her gently in his arms. 'Who is the most beautiful girl in the whole of Cornwall? The whole of England?' He laughed, a noise of sheer delight.

Glanna, glanced at him in surprise.

'Nah, the whole world.'

She watched as he clumsily, but with infinite gentleness put a nappy on the baby and then eased her kicking limbs into a sleepsuit. He'd been shopping, the clothes were still in their packaging and smelt of new, clean fabric.

'I've finished,' Glanna devoured the last mouthful of food and pushed the plate away. 'Give her back to me.' She stood, emboldened by the gentle way he was handling the baby.

For a long moment he stood, the baby tucked in his arms, as if to defy her. 'She needs to be fed.' Glanna held out her arms, relief coursing through her as he reluctantly relinquished their child.

'What will we call her?' Eddie came to sit on the bed beside her, watching as Glanna began to feed the baby.

'I...' Her voice caught in her throat. He spoke as if they were a normal couple, cooing over their first child, rather than the man who held her captive and who had watched as her unwilling body grew with the result of their abnormal union. There was no we, no loving partnership, just a repugnant coupling when he demanded it.

'I'm not sure.' Glanna edged away from him, repulsed at the touch of his arm against hers.

'Well, you decide.' He stood, the creak of the bed a familiar sound.

'Thanks.' Glanna, tried and failed to keep the sarcasm out of her voice. If she annoyed him for once he did not react, instead collecting the empty crockery and leaving the cellar.

The door shut firmly behind him and the key turned. A moment later the electric light was extinguished. A pale shaft of moonlight gently illuminated the cellar, softening the edges of the battered bed and chipped furniture.

Glanna, laid her daughter on the mattress while she rummaged beneath the bed. Her fingers found the hair clip. In the moonlight she used all her strength and anger to carve yet another mark on the wall. One more day.

With the last reserves of her energy, Glanna unfurled the fresh sheets and pulled them over herself, cradling the baby in her arm. 'What am I going to call you, baby?' Glanna's voice was soft, filled with wonder. How was it possible, Glanna mused, sleepily, that she could love this child? And yet she did. The tiny baby had been created while her mother was chained spread-eagled on the bed. A child should be made with love, not with roughness and fear. She had expected, throughout her pregnancy, to hate the child, to despise what she represented. Glanna did not want any part of Eddie, not his touch, not his breath on her, his mouth covering hers. Nothing. And yet this small scrap of skin and bones had been made from their bodies. Life was not her fault. She had been no part of the torture and possession. Glanna had wanted to hate her, had wanted to rid her body of the foetus, and yet now she was here, she felt nothing but love for her.

The baby's legs kicked against the fabric she was wrapped in.

'Demelza? Tegan? Rozenwyn?' Glanna listed Cornish names. 'Nah.' She shook her head at the bizarreness of her situation, locked in a dark cellar, her family no doubt assuming she was dead, choosing names for a baby. She angrily wiped at the tears that were falling, it did no good to cry, or scream, or batter against the door. The only person who would ever come was Eddie, and she had learned quickly he was not a person anyone should make angry.

She thought of her mother, her sisters. Perhaps she could call the baby after one of them. She dismissed the idea. It was too painful to be reminded of them.

'You're going to be my princess. How about Elizabeth? Anne? Zara?' In the darkness she gently stroked the baby's cheeks, awed by the softness of the skin beneath her fingers. And then she knew. 'Mia,' Glanna said softly. 'It means mine.'

Chapter Three

'**M**ia.' Glanna spoke her child's name, letting the word roll over her lips. She liked the sound of it. Mine. Nothing to do with the creature who had planted the seed inside her.

Food was brought more regularly after Mia was born. Gone were the stale sandwiches and scraps of bread. They were replaced by proper meals, meat, vegetables, more than often brought to the cellar still hot. She needed the nourishment with Mia to feed. He even brought a small heater that he plugged into a socket behind the cellar door, running the cable through a gap between the wood and the slate floor. The heater spat and stank of burning dust when he first turned it on. It made little difference to the frigid temperature in the room, unless she stood right beside it, but it was, Glanna supposed, a concession on his part. A sign he perhaps saw her as something resembling human.

Mia grew quickly, despite the conditions in the cellar, rapidly outgrowing the sleep suits he had bought. Eddie solicitously replaced them with more. New ones brought in the next county Glanna realised when she found a receipt for a Devonshire shop in one of the bags. Clearly, he didn't want anyone who knew him questioning why he was buying baby clothes.

Mia's presence made the days in the cellar easier. There were moments of pure joy. Her first smile, her eyes, which had turned rapidly from blue to brown, locking onto her mothers, her mouth curving into a broad smile of recognition. Her eyes were his, Glanna had soon realised. Somehow, she found the strength to ignore the fact he was anything to do with her miraculous child. Mia's eyes were her eyes, not his.

The joy was tempered with times of abject misery. Times when Glanna allowed herself to think about her old life. How must it be for her family, wondering what had become of her? Did they think she was dead? Or that she had callously walked out of her life, made a new one without even a backwards glance?

Glanna changed Mia's nappy, throwing the old one packaged with the soiled baby wipes into the far corner of the room. Let him pick them up, like the piece of shit he was.

'Your granny would love you.' Glanna tickled Mia's soft belly with a gentle finger. The baby gurgled with delight, kicking with her strong legs. 'Your granny will love you.' Glanna corrected herself. She must never give up. Never think that one day she wouldn't go home. With Mia. She held tightly to a vision of running up the garden path, Mia in her arms, into the waiting embrace of her parents. One day she would get free. One day. She just had to wait.

She froze, hearing footsteps outside the cellar door. Him. Now the baby was older, he'd started doing *that* again. He'd appeared one day with a large box and began to erect a cot for Mia, complete with a plastic mattress and blankets, still in their wrapping. All brand new. Nothing, it seemed, was too good for Mia. Glanna hadn't realised at first what the cot had meant. She soon did. The child could be put in the cot, rather than lying in her mother's arms. He didn't even need to cover Glanna's mouth. She wouldn't shout or scream for fear of frightening Mia.

'I need to clean this floor. The baby is starting to move around. Get me a brush.' Glanna forced a flat note into her voice. She wanted to rage at him, let go of the hatred she felt, but that only served to anger him.

He grunted in agreement. 'I've got something for you.' His voice held an excited note.

She was silent, watchful as he dug into the back pocket of his jeans. Had he come up with some new way to torment her?

'Here.' he shyly held out a small, red box towards her. 'Take it.' He thrust the box forwards, suddenly impatient.

Despising her hand for trembling, Glanna reached forwards and took the box. It was light in her fingers, something moved and rattled inside.

Under his attentive gaze Glanna opened the box. Inside was a silver bracelet, a rope of silver, three stands twisted together. 'It's for you.' He repeated when she looked at him questioningly. She flinched involuntarily as he took hold of her wrist. She watched silently as he fumbled clumsily with the clasp, his head bent over her limb, intent on his task. He was so engrossed she could have, had she had the nerve and the weapon, bashed his head in. The opportunity was there, but there was nothing in the room she could have used, even if she were brave enough to try.

Finally, he succeeded in fastening the strands around her wrist. 'Pretty. Do you like it?' As he released her wrist, she let her arm fall, the silver strand resting against the scared skin where his chains had cut into the flesh.

Glanna made a noise, a cross between a sob and a snort of hysterical laughter. He'd brought her a present. Like a partner giving her a gift to symbolise his love. The irony of the gesture twisted into a knot in her stomach. 'Thank you. It's lovely. You're very kind.' It seemed the only thing she could say, that would not antagonise him.

A smile of delight split his face. He hovered, uncertainly, as if unsure of his imagined new slant on their relationship. He took Mia and walked the room with her, boosting her upwards with a gentleness Glanna had not imagined he could be capable of. Mia giggled in delight, the noise strange in the tension.

After he had handed Mia back to her and left, carefully locking the door behind him Glanna, remained standing in the centre of the room, immobile since he had put the bracelet on her wrist. She stood until she heard his footsteps retreating. Only then did she rush to the stained toilet bowl and vomit.

* * * * *

It had been Nan who had decided Glanna should be allowed into the house. So Glanna, who was responsible for feeding and caring for the baby, was brought from the cellar to the farmhouse during the day. Somewhere, beneath the violence and rage that simmered inside her was a tiny grain of compassion. That, Glanna knew was reserved solely for Mia. The cellar, Nan had told Eddie was not a suitable place for the child to be. They took great care, though, Nan and Eddie, to make sure the doors were always locked, that she was never unwatched. Eddie's grip on her arm, as he escorted her from the dankness of the cellar into the daylight left more dark bruises on her flesh. She knew, if he could have prevented the pleasure from feeling the sun on her face and breathing fresh air, during that short journey, he would have done.

Mia, in a brand-new dress which flared out over her nappy-clad behind, shuffled her way around the farmhouse kitchen. 'She'll be walking before long.' Nan's voice had held a note of pride as she watched her granddaughter, fingers gripping onto the fabric of the sofa, legs buckling occasionally with the effort of keeping herself upright.

'Yes,' Glanna nodded, her voice deliberately impassive. Soon Mia would be a year old. She leant forwards to hold out her hands for her daughter to fall into. Pulling Mia into her arms she glanced out of the kitchen window, beyond which the bare branches of the trees danced wildly in the autumn storm that lashed against the house. The sea, she knew, would be crashing onto the beach close to her home. She pictured the expanse of sand, the rocky outcrops, the wildness of the sea, churned brown and grey by the storm. Glanna forced her eyes back to her daughter. So much time had passed, while she had been trapped here. It did no good to think of the past. Or the future. All that existed was each day, each hour, getting through that. Waiting. Waiting for the one moment she knew would come. Eventually.

'I need to feed her.' Glanna picked Mia up, rocking her gently as she began to grizzle, an irritable, demanding sound, food the only way to pacify her.

'Up there. Don't be long.' Nan jerked her head in the direction of the stairs. She crossed the room her face inches away from Glanna's, her mouth twisted into a sadistic smile as her fingers tickled Mia's chin. 'She won't need you much longer.'

'I'll be quick,' Glanna whispered obediently. She tore her eyes away from Nan's, heaved Mia onto her hip and made her way up the stairs.

In the upper story of the house were three rooms and a bathroom. The doors were always closed, bar one, which she had assumed to be Nan's. Glanna sank down on the edge of the ancient looking bedstead which almost filled the room. One tiny window let in the only light. 'You won't get out of there.' Nan had commented casually the first time Glanna had been allowed to feed Mia upstairs. 'Try anything and I'll hurt you so much you'll beg me to kill you.'

As Mia fed, Glanna moved to the window. It was too small to get out of. There would hardly be enough room to get her head out of it, let alone her body and that of Mia as well. There was no point in trying to shout out of it either. The house, she could see, was surrounded by fields and woodland which went on interminably into the far distance. No one ever visited either, so there was never any chance of alerting anyone.

She winced as Mia suckled roughly. Soon it would be time to stop feeding her. Mia had begun to eat solid foods, sitting in the highchair Eddie had bought for her, but she still seemed to want her mother's milk too. 'Your granny would love you,' Glanna whispered to Mia, watching as her child fixed her eyes solemnly on her mother's face. 'Your real granny, not that one.'

It was hard to contain the rage that burned inside her. The pain of being kept, a prisoner with no way to escape. She daren't let herself think about her home, all that she missed, the agony was too much. Yet sometimes, in bleak moments, she let her mind wander, imagining her mother, the delight she would take in Mia. There was so much she wanted to ask her about being a mother. Nan certainly wasn't forthcoming with conversation, let alone help. While she was gentle with Mia, Nan took every opportunity to hurt Glanna seeming to take great pleasure in seeing her trying to stifle the cries of pain to avoid frightening Mia.

Glanna let her hand stray to her belly, flat again after Mia had been born. Was another child already growing inside her? He'd left her alone after Mia had been born. But not for long. At least with Mia close by he was less rough, as if he took less pleasure in hurting her.

Later, they'd eaten dinner together. A scene Glanna would have laughed hysterically at had she not been filled with fear. Eddie sat beside Mia, in her highchair, as she attempted to eat a bowl of mashed potato. More of it seemed to go on the floor than found its way into Mia's mouth, but he dealt with each spill with infinite patience, wiping the floor and praising her when the spoon did find its way to her mouth.

Nan sat the other side, glowering at Glanna, who ate quickly and quietly, not wanting to antagonise either of them.

'Time she went back.' Nan announced, as Glanna swallowed the last mouthful of food. Eddie obediently pushed back his chair, his own meal unfinished. As Glanna got to her feet Nan seized her plate and threw it roughly into the sink.

'Animal.' Nan hissed as Eddie, Mia balanced on his side, took Glanna's arm and led her out of the kitchen. 'Filth, you're a pathetic waste of a human. How did I ever raise something like you? I wish I'd drowned you when you were born.' Her tirade followed them across the yard. Glanna stole a look at his face, shadowed in the powerful arc lights positioned around the buildings. He was expressionless, as if he could not hear his mother. As they began to descend into the cellar his fingers tightened on Glanna's arm. Away from his mother's loathing he could finally assert his power.

He sat on the edge of Glanna's bed, watching silently as she undressed Mia, put on her nightclothes, and settled her into the cot. Mia stood, holding on the bars of the cot, chattering, her words as yet unintelligible.

'I've made a bedroom for her in the house.' Eddie said, his words cutting across the childish babbling. 'Mia is going to sleep there.'

'No don't. Please.' Glanna looked at him in panic. Mia was the only thing that made her life worthwhile. That, and the hope one day she would get to go home.

'Soon.' Eddie said firmly. He stood, unbuckling his belt. 'Be nice and I'll let her stay with you a while longer.'

Chapter Four

As the key turned in the lock Glanna pulled the covers over herself, curled in a tight ball and finally let the tears fall. Beside her, disturbed by her mother's sobbing Mia stirred, pulling herself upright against the cot bars to stand, staring solemnly at her mother.

'It's okay my lovely,' Glanna wiped her eyes with a corner of one of her rough blankets.

'Mammmaaa,' Mia waved a pudgy arm through the bars of her cot.

'Come here,' Glanna eased herself out of bed. The cellar, in near darkness now, was sufficed with the red glow of the heater. 'I might be a prisoner, but you're not going to be.'

She lifted Mia out of the cot, feeling the warmth of her small body through her sleep suit. 'Come on, sleep with me.' Glanna huddled down beneath the blankets once more, Mia curled against her belly. Placated by the presence of her mother the cellar was soon filled with the gentle sound of Mia's breathing.

Glanna lay awake, watching her daughter's small perfect face. The oval shape and button nose reminded Glanna of her sister, Morwenna. She could see nothing of Eddie, except for the colour of his eyes. She stroked the wisps of soft hair in a distracted gesture while her mind raced. What was going to happen when Eddie decided Mia was to sleep in the house? Would she just stay in the cellar again, something to be used whenever Eddie felt the urge? That day was coming soon. What would happen to Mia without her to look after her? She forced her thoughts away from a life where she was locked away from Mia, where Nan and Eddie were the only people to look after and influence her.

'I want to go home. Mia,' Glanna whispered, bending to kiss her daughter's forehead. She stirred in her sleep, murmuring softly. 'I want my mum. My dad. My sisters.' Her voice cracked as her throat tightened with grief. One moment, that was all she needed, one second when their attention wavered. Mia moved, sprawling onto her back, her body, small and delicate was still heavy, solid. It wouldn't be much longer before Glanna wouldn't be able to carry her, if she got the chance to run. Could she attack Nan? Or Eddie? Glanna eased Mia across the bed, wincing as her aching muscles protested. Whatever plans she pondered during the dark night hours were impossible in reality. Neither Eddie, nor Nan ever failed to watch her movements. But all it would take was one split second of inattention. Just one.

* * * * *

'He's not given you this virus yet then?' Nan whined, moving listlessly around the kitchen, a thick cardigan draped around her shoulders. She wrenched the curtains across the window, shutting out the twilight. 'You take everything else from the dirty bastard. Filthy bitch.'

Glanna glanced at Nan. A sheen of sweat glistened on the older woman's forehead, yet she shivered, despite the heat from the wood burning stove. There was nothing to say in reply, nothing which would pacify Nan while she was in this mood. To open her mouth would just mean an attack from Nan. For a big woman, even one so clearly ill, Nan could still explode in a violent onslaught against Glanna.

'Could have been that little bastard who gave me the flu.' Nan pointed a finger aggressively at Mia who sat on a blanket on the kitchen floor, surrounded by the toys Eddie had bought for her. Mia was still sniffly and feverish from another of the colds she'd been battling on and off for the last few weeks. Glanna dropped her eyes, not wanting to enrage Nan. It was the first time she had heard Nan ever say anything hostile towards Mia.

There was no wonder Mia had succumbed to yet another illness. While sometimes she was allowed to spend time in the warmth of the house, a huge portion of time was spent in the damp, airless cellar. Glanna bit her lip, she dare not remind Nan of the terrible conditions Mia lived in for most of her life. She wanted to keep Mia with her as long as possible. She was sure when Mia was well again Eddie would take the child away, leaving her locked once more in the cellar. Alone.

'Nan na na.' Mia held her pudgy arms out towards Nan.

'Take her away. Go and feed her or something.' Nan pulled her cardigan tighter around her shoulders and shuffled towards the sofa. 'I'm too ill.'

Head lowered Glanna rolled her eyes, enjoying Nan's misery. She did nothing while Glanna suffered, listening to her screams, ignoring what her son was doing. She'd get no sympathy from Glanna.

'Could I take Mia upstairs, give her a bath? The steam might help stop her snuffling.' Glanna tucked Mia onto her hip.

Nan did not reply, instead stretching out on the sofa and lowering her head onto the cushions wearily.

As she turned to go Glanna spotted the bunch of keys Nan usually kept in a pocket, abandoned on the kitchen table, beside Nan's bottle of 'medicinal' whiskey, and an upended pack of flu remedy sachets. Glanna tore her eyes away from the keys. Eddie would be home any minute. She couldn't run. Not now. Nan might be ill, but she was still watchful of Glanna. She'd have no time to grab the keys, get to the door, open it and be gone. Not carrying Mia. Not with Nan in the room. She'd imagined one day Eddie or Nan would forget to lock the door, that she'd find it open and make her escape. Not this. The keys were there merely to taunt her, to show her how much of prisoner she was. She daren't try to escape.

Glanna made her way upstairs, Mia on her hip. She chattered contentedly as Glanna ran the bath and played with her while Mia splashed in the water.

Later as she made her way carefully down the wooden stairs with the newly bathed and changed Mia in her arms, the keys were still on the table. Nan lay stretched on the sofa, her eyes closed, breathing deep and regular. Glanna forced a breath into lungs that seemed to have stopped working. Mia, stupefied by the warm water, rested her head sleepily on Glanna's shoulder. Glanna's head spun with the possibility of escape, tempered by the terror of being caught. If Nan woke and saw the keys had been left within Glanna's reach and she hadn't run perhaps she'd become less suspicious. Perhaps there'd be a better time, when Eddie wasn't due home, when Nan wasn't so close.

Maybe the time would never come. Eddie had made his intentions clear. He was going to separate Glanna from her child. Glanna eased Mia further onto her hip and inched towards the table. Her heart thundered against her ribcage. She closed her fingers around the bunch of keys, slid them noiselessly off the table. They weighed heavily in her hands, the metal cool against the dampness of her fingers. Three strides and she was at the door, listening intently for the sound of Eddie's pick up, for Nan stirring. She knew the key, she'd watched so many times, ready for a moment like this. It turned easily in the lock. Glanna eased the door open, feeling the chilly air from outside.

''Nannnn.' Mia lifted her head and pointed with delight towards Nan. As Glanna looked back in horror, Nan, roused by Mia's voice sat up, her face crumpled from sleep.

Glanna hauled open the front door and ran into the dusk, hearing a chair crashing to the ground as Nan charged after her.

'Naa naaa,' Mia's voice was loud in the silence of the deserted yard. Her delight in this new game obvious.

'Shhhh,' Glanna pleaded, looking desperately for an escape route. She couldn't go down the drive, in case Eddie returned. She had no idea about the layout of the land surrounding the farmhouse and buildings. During the daily journeys from the cellar to the house she had been aware of a tangle of sheds, the presence of animals somewhere.

She shivered as a bitter wind swirled around the old stone buildings. Glanna forced a breath into her lungs, the air carried the salty tang of the sea, overlaid with the smell of farm animals and damp earth. Even in her panic she savoured the freshness after the oppressive air in the house. Somewhere close by animals moved in a field, their hooves sucking and squelching in the mud.

In the dusk the corner of one of the buildings, the furthest away from the house offered a hiding place. Glanna ran, feet sliding on the damp cobbles, her hand covering Mia's mouth to stifle her cries. The child bounced against her hip, heavy and cumbersome.

From her hiding place Glanna could hear Nan moving around the yard. 'Come out you fucking bitch.' Her voice was loud, filled with anger. Glanna crouched in the darkness, her legs quivering with terror beneath her. Mia, confused by the new game, was quiet, awed by the darkness. Her silence wouldn't last long, Glanna knew that. She had to get away from the farmyard, out into the fields where she could run, find safety, but in the darkness, it was impossible to know which way to go.

Glanna stole a glance around the corner of the building, seeing Nan's bulk silhouetted in the doorway of the house. She was going away. Inside. She was going to let Glanna free. Relief flooded over her, until a moment later powerful arc lights illuminated the yard.

'I'm going to find you, and when I do, you'll wish you were dead.' Nan had come back outside and was walking slowly around the yard, pulling open shed doors and snapping on the lights.

Glanna saw Nan go into one of the sheds, she covered her mouth with a free hand to stop herself crying out from terror. From within the building came the sound of banging and clattering, silhouetted against the dusty window she could see Nan frenziedly throwing tools and equipment out of the way in an effort to find where Glanna was hiding.

Knowing Nan would find her if she stayed in the yard Glanna got to her feet and crept slowly away from the shadows. There had to be a way out of the yard, perhaps the gap between the buildings would lead to the fields. Her arm ached with the effort of supporting Mia on her hip. A locked gate barred her way. It was impossible to climb with Mia in her arms. She let out a sob of utter despair.

Close to the gate was another shed. In desperation she made for its shelter. Perhaps Nan would think she had got away. Mia began to sob, a soft whimpering noise. 'Please be quiet,' Glanna pleaded, the noise of her own breathing louder than Mia's cries of fright.

The shed smelled of oil, the floor was sticky beneath her feet. She eased her way past the bulk of a tractor, a spanner, discarded, spinning away as she kicked it, the noise echoing into the darkness.

'I know where you are.' Nan's voice was filled with anticipation.

In desperation Glanna crawled under a work bench, hampered by Mia clinging to her neck, which was wet with the child's tears. Mia, terrified, began to wail, her voice loud in the darkness. She was trapped now, there would be a beating. Eddie, she knew would take great pleasure in punishing her.

'Stupid cunt.' Glanna saw Nan's legs, their approach slow and deliberate. 'Did you think you'd be able to get away?' There was a conversational tone to her voice, as if she and Glanna were discussing the weather.

With a leisurely movement Nan crouched down, reached beneath the workbench and seized a fistful of Glanna's hair, hauling her roughly from her hiding place. Mia, her body banging on the ground screamed in protest. The sticky oil soaked through the knees of her jeans as Glanna began to scramble to her feet. Her head snapped backwards as Nan slammed one of the heavy spanners from the workbench into her. Her fingers grasped Mia instinctively, feeling the child roll from her arms as her body hit the ground.

'Mia...' Glanna reached a hand out towards her child, watching, helplessly as Nan picked up her daughter. Her head felt sticky, she wanted to move, needed to get away, but she could not.

'Come here my darling,' Nan said gently scooping Mia up into her arms. She straightened up slowly, adjusting Mia onto the curve of her belly and rocking her gently, watching Glanna's limbs twitch compulsively as the light faded from her eyes.

Chapter Five

1991

'Mum. I'm eighteen.' Grace Tallis pushed her unruly mane of auburn hair behind her ears and met her mother's steely gaze.

'Grace, I don't care if you are eighteen or twenty-eight, if you're living under my roof and studying for important exams you aren't going out.'

'Come on, this is ridiculous,' Grace tapped one sock clad foot impatiently on the stone tiles of the kitchen floor. 'Katia's parents aren't keeping her in like this.'

'Really?' Eve Tallis rested her hips against the newly installed Belfast sink, folding her arms in what Grace knew was a gesture of firmness. Eve's grey eyes locked onto her daughter's. 'You really think Katia's parents are going to let her go out. To a disco. When she's got important exams coming up any minute. Seriously Grace.'

Grace rolled eyes, a vivid shade of blue, in despair at her mother. 'I know all my stuff, I've only got two exams left. Mum please. It's just the A levels. It's not life and death.'

'Grace, I've said my piece. You're not going and that's final. And if you don't want to study you can help me take the crockery out of these boxes and put them in the cupboards.'

'Fine,' Grace sighed, pushing herself off the chair. 'I'll be in my room.'

'Thought that would persuade you,' Eve's voice held a note of triumph. 'Be glad you've got studying to do, rather than help me put everything back into the kitchen.' Eve circled slowly, extending her arms, 'My new kitchen... All these new units.'

Grace rolled her eyes at her mother's obvious delight at the newly installed fitted kitchen. 'I'll leave you to it.' She closed the kitchen door gently behind herself, longing to slam it hard to rid herself of the pent-up anger inside her. She leant against the wall, listening to the sound of her mother unpacking the crockery and loading it into the cupboards, humming contentedly.

Taking the house telephone from its place on the table beside the front door, Grace sat halfway up the stairs, the cable spooling out in front of her, and dialled Katia's number.

Veronique Wilson answered on the second ring. Grace pictured her slender frame sitting on the elegant velvet sofa, the telephone on the delicate antique table beside her.

'Hello. Mrs Wilson. It's Grace Tallis. Please may I speak to Katia.'

'Of course,' Veronique's voice still held the vague impression of her French origins. 'She's here. Are you studying hard Grace?'

'Yes, I am.' Grace listened as the telephone was handed to Katia, who, from the rustling and banging had left the room and brought the telephone, as she had, out into the privacy of the hall.

'No way.' Katia, sighed, her breath loud in the receiver. 'Mum won't let me go out until the exams are over.'

'Mine neither,' Grace sighed, equally loudly.

'So that's it?'

Grace snorted in amusement. 'When did we ever listen to our parents?'

'You're kidding. Really?'

'I'll be under your bedroom window at nine.'

'You are bad!'

Just before nine Grace clambered down the drainpipe beside her bedroom window, crept across the garden, slid through a gap in the fence and walked slowly across the pristine stretch of lawn in front of Katia's home. The garden was her father's pride and joy and was surrounded by tall rhododendron bushes which had been planted to shield his more delicate flowers from the salty sea breeze. As well as shelter, the bushes provided deep shadows, perfect to hide Grace as she moved towards the house, keeping out of the yellow glow cast by the windows.

'Oh my god,' Katia clung to the helpful branches of the Virginia Creeper which climbed over the wall beneath her bedroom window, her tiny frame belied the strength she possessed. 'I'd forgotten how hard this is.'

She let go and tumbled onto the soft grass, long blonde hair pooling over her shoulders as she landed. The girls stuffed their hands into their mouths to stifle their giggles as they jogged hurriedly out of the garden and onto the lane.

'What did you tell them?' Grace asked, when they reached the main road and slowed their pace. Below them, down the steep hill, the lights of Truro glimmered in the darkness.

'Early night, tired after riding Blackbird and studying for my exams,' Katia, dug her fingers into Grace's arm, lifting her head to look up at the much taller girl, 'Fuck's sake, they'll murder me if they find out.'

'They won't.' Grace poked a teasing finger into Katia's ribs. 'Mine are too busy admiring their new kitchen.' She pulled a bottle of red wine from her coat pocket. 'They won't miss this either.'

'Oh. My. God. You are wicked.' Katia pulled the bottle out of Grace's hand, unscrewed the top and took a long swig of the liquid.

'Who's going tonight?' Grace took the bottle off Katia and swigged from it.

'Dunno.'

'Well, we are, that's all that matters.'

'Grace,' Katia said as they hurried down the steep hill. 'It's too early to go to Discord, there'll be no one there.'

Below them the city lights glittered, their glow pale beside the powerful radiance that illuminated the vast spires of the Cathedral.

Grace took another swig of the stolen wine. 'True.'

They reached the outskirts of Truro, crossed one of the main arterial roads which led out of the city and plunged into the narrow maze of streets. Grace tucked the wine bottle back into her pocket as they wandered slowly up St. Mary's Street past the Cathedral.

'I like that.' Katia stopped to look in window of one of the many craft and boutique clothes shops. 'The blue belt.'

'Yes, it's lovely.' Grace pulled Katia's arm, self-conscious now they were on city streets which were still relatively busy with tourists looking for restaurants and pubs to spend the evening in. It was unlikely they'd be spotted by anyone their parents knew. But still, she felt vulnerable, exposed.

The main part of the small city was quieter, the shops were all closed so there was no reason for any tourists to be there, other than those who were looking for somewhere to eat. An harassed looking couple walked towards them, both hauling suitcases. 'It's down here, I'm sure.' The man said, a fold up map flapping from his hand. Grace gave the young woman a sympathetic smile.

'We could get coffee?' Katia suggested, leading the way up one of the narrow alleyways that led off Boscawen Street. 'Closed,' she sighed a few moments later, looking at the darkened windows of Rosie's Café.

'The river?' Grace suggested as they walked across the open space of Lemon Quay towards the subway beneath the main road. As always Lemon Quay was busy with people standing outside the pubs and restaurants.

'I hate this subway,' Katia shuddered as they walked under the main road, their footsteps echoing in the dim light.

'I'll protect you,' Grace, pulled a scared face as they neared the end of the subway and giggling, ran out into the fresh air. They slowed as they reached the broad expanse of the river and found a bench beside the slow-moving water.

'Peace at last.' Katia pulled the wine bottle out of Grace's pocket and, glancing warily up the path, took a long swig. 'Delicious,' she grinned, wiping a dribble of the liquid from her chin.

'It's not all for you,' Grace pulled the bottle out of her hand.

'Time to go, I think,' Grace said an hour later, getting to her feet. The ground felt unsteady beneath her.

'Yup,' Katia giggled holding out her hand to let Grace pull her upright.

They wandered slowly back towards the city, swaying slightly. Grace fastidiously disposed of the bottle in one of the bins near the Tesco supermarket, before they made their way back through the underpass and into Lemon Quay, weaving their way through the clusters of people who congregated outside the bars.

'Bit of a queue now,' Katia pointed at the line of people waiting to get into Discord.

'Act sensibly,' Grace warned, arranging Katia's hair over one shoulder before leading the way in a determinedly straight line.

'Evening ladies,' the thick-set security guard on the door gave them little more than a quick glance. As they went into the darkness of the building Katia gripped Grace's arm, giggling, 'I can't believe he didn't ask how old we are.'

'Shhhh, Act sensibly.' Grace lifted her head and coolly surveyed the nightclub. 'This is just an everyday thing for us.'

'Yes. Yes. Of course, it is.' Katia swayed beside Grace as they skirted the packed dance floor, 'I'm too sexy for my shirt,' she sang tunelessly to the Right Said Fred track.

Grace found an empty booth and shrugged off her coat, 'Sit down, stop acting like you're a drunk schoolgirl.'

Katie sank down beside her, sighing dramatically. 'Sorry.' She opened her mouth wide, revealing a line of white, even teeth, in a gesture of excitement. 'But that's exactly what I am.'

'It's okay,' Grace drew her finely arched eyebrows together in a scowl, 'just that we don't want to draw attention to ourselves.'

'Nice top,' Katia looked at Grace appreciatively, breaking the momentary frostiness between them.

'Thanks,' Grace smoothed her hands down the front of the sleeveless top, running her fingers along the row of chunky coloured stones sewn along the neckline. 'Mum got it for me.' She pulled a guilty face. The top had been an early present for finishing her exams and working so hard studying. She wasn't supposed to be wearing it yet. Her parents would be so angry and disappointed if they knew what she was doing. 'Is yours new too?' Grace turned her attention to Katia, to block out the guilty thoughts.

'New to me,' Katia opened her mouth in a mock scream of delight. 'It actually belongs to Anna. But what are older sisters for it not to provide an extra source of clothes? Besides, she'll never know. She's still working in London. She won't be home for ages.'

'It's lovely.' The electric blue fabric echoed the colour of Katia's eyes and the rows of tiny beads highlighted her slender figure.

'It's boring sitting down, shall we go and stand at the bar?'

Grace nodded eagerly. 'Let's get wasted.' She put out her hand to haul Katia to her feet and led the way into the throng at the bar.

'Look,' Katia's breath was hot against Grace's cheek, 'It's Rob and he's coming over to us.'

'Try to act cool,' Grace shook Katia's arm to focus her friend.

'Exams all finished?' Rob Dunmore remarked casually, as he eased his way into the crush to stand beside the two girls.

'Yep,' lied Katia.

'Nearly,' confessed Grace, she had to shout over the noise of the music.

'What?'

'Nearly,' she edged closer to Rob, so she could direct her voice into his ear, breathing in the smell of a delicious body wash. The ridiculous earring he'd worn at school was missing, she could see the hole in his lobe where it had been. There was a tiny nick on his cheek where he'd cut himself shaving. She itched to tap the mark and make a comment about learning to shave, but it didn't seem worth the effort to shout over the music.

'Do you want to sit down?' His dark eyes drifted relentlessly past Grace towards Katia.

Katia raised a thumb in agreement.

'Sure,' Grace spotted an empty booth and made her way towards it.

'What are you doing next?' Rob asked as they skirted the dance floor.

Grace eased herself into the seat, rolling her eyes towards Katia at Rob's intrusion, realising it was her who was intruding.

Katia was watching him with something akin to fascination. She'd confessed to Grace while they were at school that she fancied him.

'Exeter,' Grace shouted above the music levels, which seemed to have increased. 'You?'

'Hotel management.' He pushed along the seat as another boy from school slid into the booth.

'Paul,' Grace took a swig of her drink, hoping he wouldn't be able to see the flush that had spread across her cheeks. She chanced a glance at him over the rim of her glass, dropping her eyes abruptly as his dark ones flickered over hers.

'Here's to freedom,' Paul Morris raised his pint glass.

'And adulthood,' Katia grinned clanking her glass against his.

'And to the end of exams.' Grace met Paul's eyes and saw again the naked appreciation she had been aware of at school.

'What are you going to do during the summer?' Rob turned his attention to Katia.

'I'll be busy competing Blackbird and trying to persuade my parents that working with horses is a good career choice. But I have a feeling they'll win and I'll be doing a law degree.'

Grace shot her friend a sympathetic smile. Katia had loved riding for as long as Grace could remember and her battle to work with horses, rather than go to university was something Grace had heard a lot of.

'How about you?' Grace turned to talk to Paul. She fought to keep her face impassive and knew she failed. Paul had that effect on her.

'Exeter. I'm going to do a business degree.' He ran a hand over the close-cropped hair at the back of his head. 'Provided I get the grades.'

'Me too.'

'Looks like we could be seeing a lot of one another.' Paul's wide and infinitely kissable lips split into a broad grin. One tooth was slightly chipped. Grace remembered the rugby match which had damaged it. 'Do you want to dance, leave those two alone?' Paul tilted his head in the direction of Katia and Rob who were deep in conversation.

Grace nodded eagerly and eased her way out of the booth in Paul's wake. He held out his hand to help her out of the seat. After a moment's hesitation Grace took it. His skin was warm against hers, his grip strong as he led the way through the crowds to the dancefloor.

* * * * *

'We really need to go,' Grace caught a glimpse of her watch. Guilt, raw and urgent had shoved its way into her consciousness. It seemed like only moments, not hours since they'd arrived at the disco.

'No don't.' Paul caught Grace by the waist and pulled her towards him. Beneath the cotton shirt he wore she could feel taut muscles. 'I've enjoyed this.'

Grace nodded, 'Me too.'

'So, stay out. You and Katia can come back to mine. My parents are away.'

'We can't.' Grace wriggled out of his grasp. 'We have to go home.' The earlier adult coolness had evaporated, replaced by an ongoing sensation of panic. They had to leave. The two of them still had to get home and climb back in through their bedroom windows. What if their parents had discovered what they had done and were waiting at home, filled with anger, if not fear?

She shoved her way through the dance floor back to the booth. Katia and Rob were oblivious to everything except one another, locked in a passionate embrace.

'Katia,' Grace leant across and touched her friend's arm.

'What?' Katia eased herself out of Rob's embrace. The skin below her bottom lip was stained with lipstick.

'We need to go.'

'Seriously?'

Grace nodded. 'Seriously.'

'Don't,' Paul pleaded, pulling a puppy dog face. 'Come back to my house with us. Just for a while.'

'No.' Grace said firmly. She needed to get out of the disco, get home. Now.

'We can't.' Katia rolled her eyes at Rob. 'We do need to go. I'm sorry.'

'We'll walk you.'

'No, please.' Grace held up her hand to stop Paul. 'We're leaving. On our own.'

Chapter Six

'Come on, let us at least walk with you.' Paul put a hand on Grace's arm. 'Then perhaps we can persuade you to come back to Paul's. I'm staying there. Easier than trying to get a taxi all the way to Baldu.'

Rob asked his hand entwined in Katia's.

'Let's go back with them,' pleaded Katia.

For a moment Grace was swayed. What difference would it make if they crept home at dawn? If their jaunt had been found out they'd be in trouble already, a few more hours wouldn't make any difference. The thought of their parents, frantic with worry brought with it a crashing sense of reality.

'No,' Grace raised her palms. 'We can't. We've got to get home.' She had to know if their parents had found out they were missing from their rooms. She could imagine how frightened they would be, an emotion which would soon turn to anger and disappointment when the girls arrived back.

They must leave. Beneath the haze of alcohol, a knot of tension twisted in the pit of her stomach. The evening, which had been such fun was now a source of anguish.

'Please Katia, we need to go.'

Katia rolled her eyes in annoyance before flinging herself into Rob's arms and kissing him. Grace stood awkwardly beside Paul, wondering if she should do the same. Beside her, he shifted uncomfortably, fingers clenching and unclenching, as if he too were considering what to do.

'I just can't. My exams...'

'I know,' Paul smiled sympathetically. 'I'm glad mine are over.' He shuffled his feet, his eyes meeting Grace's shyly, before he hunched his shoulders and stuffed his hands into his pockets. It seemed to take forever before Katia and Rob eased themselves apart.

'We can do something another night,' Paul, laid a hand on Rob's arm.

'Yes, let's.' Katia agreed eagerly.

'Katia. Please, we need to go.' Grace felt like an angry parent, cajoling a wayward toddler. She was desperate to get home. She knew she would regret not picking up on Paul's invitation, but right now she was consumed by the thought of the row that could be waiting at home.

'I'm coming.' Katia sighed in annoyance before following Grace. 'Bye boys. See you soon,' she half turned, waving and blowing a kiss in Rob's direction.

The city was deserted, bar the occasional drunk weaving slowly up the street and the clusters of ravenous people grouped around the late-night chip shops.

'We should have stayed.' Katia's voice was filled with regret.

'I'm sorry. I just really want to get home. I started to panic about being found out.'

'We aren't going to be found out.'

'Yeah, but what if one of our parents checked up on us.'

'Like they'd suddenly decide they had to tuck us into bed.'

'Hmmm. True.' Grace agreed.

'Or if they had a sudden urge to bring us late night cocoa.'

The image that conjured up was so unlikely a peel of laughter bubbled in Grace's throat, she fought to contain it, to keep the seriousness of the situation. And failed. None of their parents would check up on them. They were undoubtedly sleeping soundly, completely unaware of the mischief their daughters were getting up too.

'Stop it.' Grace stopped in the centre of the deserted road to give rein to a fit of giggles. 'You know if they'd said we could go out we probably wouldn't have bothered.'

'Do you think those old buildings are spooky,' Katia whispered a while later as they made their way down the narrow street past the cathedral. 'Think of all of the funerals and sad things that happened there.'

'There are nice things too. Weddings, Christenings.'

'We'll be having our funerals there if your mum finds out you're not in your room!'

'Stop it,' Grace sighed. 'She'd kill me.'

'Mine too.' Katia giggled. 'They'd kill us after they thought we'd been killed.'

'Exactly.' Grace bit her lip, increasing her pace, their momentary cavalier attitude replaced by an urgent need to get home. The whole idea had been madness. When she had suggested going out she had pictured an adventure, a few drinks and then heading home. The reality was so different. They had stayed out too long. She regretted persuading Katia. Both of them should have been at home studying, not out on this mad jaunt to spite both sets of their parents.

'My mum would be so scared if she went into my room and found I'd gone.' Grace's imagination whirled, picturing her mother's face, peering around the bedroom door, her concerned expression when she realised her daughter was missing. She could picture her hurrying down the stairs, making the announcement to Grace's father, their annoyance turning to fear as they contemplated the horrific scenarios of what could have happened to her.

Ahead of them a mist had rolled into the city outskirts off the river, in the darkness it swirled, damp tendrils shrouding the buildings.

'They'd picture us kidnapped, murdered, our young bodies dumped…' Katia's voice at first filled with amusement faded into silence.

'Yes,' Grace increased her pace again, plunging into the mist. Above them the glimmer from the streetlights was blurred, the mist drifting lazily on the slight breeze. It cloaked their hair in cold droplets, muffled any noise, as if just the two of them existed.

Katia's fingers tightened on Grace's arm. 'I don't like this.'

'It's okay, it's just while we are close to the water. Once we start going up the hill we'll be above it.'

They left the city and began to walk up the hill towards their homes. In the mist the suburban streets, familiar to the girls, had a strange, unearthly air. The houses at either side of the road were vague, hazy shapes. The lights, still on in some of the houses, were blurred, faded into a pale yellow.

Even the road surface, its variances well known to the girls, seemed unrecognisable. Katia stumbled over a patch of tar where the road had been repaired. 'I don't like this. Everything looks so creepy.' Her voice had an edge of fear.

'Don't worry, it's just fog, we'll soon be home.' Grace hoped her voice did not betray the uncertainty she felt. The giddiness of the earlier evening had evaporated, she felt sober now, tired and scared.

'The mist's clearing a bit,' Grace said, breaking the silence, after they had walked further up the hill. She wasn't sure that it was, in the glow from the occasional streetlight it swirled thickly.

'Thank fuck for that.' Katia sighed, released a long breath. 'What's that…?' She froze, staring into the thick darkness the sparse streetlamps barely penetrated.

'It's okay,' Grace spoke with more calmness than she felt.

As they watched, a girl, little more than their age, shouldering a rucksack came towards them out of the gloom.

'Oh, thank goodness,' the girl said, when she was within earshot of the friends. 'I'm so lost. Can you help me?'

'Where are you looking for?'

The girl came closer, pulling off a baseball cap to release a tangle of long hair, red, in the pale glow of the streetlights. 'It's a bed and breakfast. I followed the directions I'd been given… Well, I thought I had,' she dumped her rucksack on the pavement beside her before rummaging beneath a long, baggy sweater and slipping a hand into her jeans pocket. 'Here,' she unearthed a crumpled slip of paper, 'Penzance Road.'

Grace peered at the scrap of paper. 'It's near here. You aren't far away. There's a load of bed and breakfast places on that road.'

'That's right. Someone at the train station gave me the number. I've called and they're expecting me. It's a bit scary floundering around in the mist.' The girl replaced her baseball cap, pulling a thick hank of hair through the band at the back. 'Serves me right for not making any proper plans.' She shrugged. 'A friend told me Truro was a great city.'

'It's a fabulous place.' Katia finally found her voice. 'Some brilliant pubs, we've just been in Discord. One of the nightclubs. You should go sometime.'

'Maybe.' The girl heaved her rucksack onto one shoulder. 'I'm a geology student. I really want to get out and see the landscape. I probably won't stay in the city for long. I plan to walk some of the coast path.'

'Cool.' Katia tried and failed to keep the awed note out of her voice.

'So, how do I get here?' She waved the paper. 'Hopefully they're still waiting for me. I've been wandering around for ages.'

'So…,' Grace turned to face back down the hill. 'Take a right there, just past the streetlight. Second left, then it's the…,' she waved a hand airily, 'third right.'

'Ok, got that,' the girl said uncertainly. 'Right here, then second left, third right.'

'Yes,' Grace nodded. 'That's it.'

'Can't go wrong.'

'Honestly, its easy,' Grace told her.

'It's all just residential streets there. Well-marked. You'll be fine.'

Katia took Grace's arm, 'I want to go home.' She was shivering now they had stopped moving.

'Cheers then,' the girl waved a farewell and set off easing her bag further onto her shoulder.

'Should we have gone with her?' Katia asked as they watched the girl walk slowly down the hill towards the city where in the mist a few bright lights shone through the gloom.

'Maybe?' Grace felt guilty at not helping more. Perhaps they should have accompanied the girl. She was a stranger, alone, late at night. 'She'll be fine,' Grace said, decisively, more to reassure herself. They watched as the girl turned the corner beside the streetlamp, waving a thanks to them as she vanished.

'Of course, she will.'

'Come on, let's get home.' Grace tugged at Katia's sleeve to get her attention.

They drew into the side of the road as a vehicle came up behind them. It emerged from the mist, large and bulky, headlights on full beam.

'Dip your lights asshole,' Grace covered her forehead with a hand to shield her eyes from the brightness.

The pick-up, a single cab with an open back, slowed as it neared them, the driver changing down the gears, as if he needed the extra power to propel the vehicle up the steep hill. There was a loud clunking as the driver missed a gear and then the engine note changed, slowing further.

As the pick-up drew close to them the driver slowed it to a snail's pace.

'Come on.' Grace felt a dart of panic at the driver's actions. Side by side they walked on in silence; throats constricted with an instinctive fear that made speech impossible. The pick-up drew level with them.

'Keep walking,' Grace urged, turning to glare at the driver with as much aggression as she could muster. In the darkness of the interior all she could make out was the silhouette of a man. The engine revved as the driver changed down another gear to keep pace with them.

'What's he doing?' Katia found her voice.

'Just being a tosser,' As they moved into the glow from a streetlight Grace could see more of the driver, his face, turned towards them was in shadow, but his presence was more than intimidating. Grace took comfort in the fact there was one of him and two of them. 'Don't worry.'

'Don't worry?' Katia gulped, close to tears. 'What if…'

'We're nearly home.' Grace gave Katia's hand a reassuring squeeze. 'You come to my house and duck under the fence at the back of my garden into yours.'

'What if he…', Katia was close to panic.

'We'll run!' Grace tried to make light of the situation.

'Thank god,' Katia breathed as the driver, seeming to get bored by his game, accelerated away up the road.

Their relief was short lived. A short distance further on the pick-up drew into the side of the road and waited, its engine running.

Fear gripped Grace. The road, although lined with houses, was deserted. Each of the houses were set back from the road behind high hedges. There was no one to help them. She slowed her pace, unsure of what to do.

'Grace, I'm scared. Why didn't we let Rob and Paul walk us home?'

'Just keep walking. We'll cross over where he's parked. I won't let anyone hurt you, don't worry.'

Beside her Katia sniffed, wiping anxiously at the tears that were spilling down her cheeks.

'He's turning around!' Katia's voice was filled with panic.

As they watched the man drove at a leisurely pace out into the centre of the road and then reversed back again, before heading back in their direction. As he passed them once more, in the pale glow from one of the streetlamps Grace met the driver's eyes. He was looking intently at them. It was impossible to get any idea of how old he was, or what he looked like, but the malevolence felt very clear.

'In here, quickly.' Grace pulled Katia into the driveway of a house. The driver revved his engine angrily as they hurried away from the road. Ahead of them the house was in complete darkness.

'What if he follows us?'

'He won't,' Grace said with more determination than she felt. They stood, uncertainly half-way up the house drive, not wanting to go further in case they alerted the owners and not wanting to retreat to the road for fear he was waiting.

From the road they heard the engine revving and then the noise faded.

'He's driving away.' Grace's legs trembled uncontrollably. 'I want to go home,' Katia stifled a sob. After what felt like hours but was in reality only minutes, Grace gently touched Katia's arm. 'He's definitely gone.' It was hard to hear anything above the pounding of her heart and the noise of their loud, panicked breathing, but she was sure the man had driven away.

They stood, side by side, intensely aware of faint noises in the undergrowth around the garden. Katia whimpered as an owl, vast wings outstretched, flew above them, silhouetted against the night sky. 'It's okay. Just an owl.' Grace laid a hand on Katia's arm, trying to fill her voice with more reassurance than she felt.

Katia, her face an eerie shade in the pale light, turned wide eyes to look at Grace as a single piercing shriek echoed through the mist. 'Oh God, what's that?'

The girls froze listening intently.

'The owl must have caught something.' Grace forced herself to speak through a tightly constricted throat. 'Just some poor animal.' They had to calm down, stop their imaginations running wild, spooked by being glared at by the creep in the pick-up.

'What if that man is still there?' Katia was crying now, tears glittering in her eyes. 'Please Grace. I want to go home.'

'We'll go back to the road. If he's still there we'll wake these people up. Get help.'

'We can't,' pleaded Katia. 'My parents will go mad if they find out what where I've been.'

They made their way back to the road, their footsteps crunching loudly on the gravel driveway, despite their best efforts to remain quiet, expecting at any second for lights to go on in the house and for angry shouts to echo around the garden. But there was nothing. The house remained silent and dark.

The road when they reached it was deserted. There was no sign of the pick-up and the driver who had spooked them so badly.

Grace looked up and down the road. 'He's gone.'

Chapter Seven

'**N**early home.' Grace's words were to reassure herself as much as Katia.

The soft padding of their shoes against the pavement was the only sound as they crossed the road and hurried towards their homes.

'Will you come with me?' Katia asked as they reached the driveway to her house.

'Course I will. Come on.'

A single upstairs light burned in Katia's home. 'We always leave the landing light on.' Katia explained as Grace pointed fearfully at the light.

Grace puffed out her cheeks and let out a long sigh of relief. 'I thought someone had noticed you'd gone and were up waiting.'

'I doubt it. Give me a boost up, will you?' Katia pushed her foot into Grace's cupped hands and bounced once before hauling herself up the vine like branches of the Virginia Creeper beneath her bedroom window. Grace watched as Katia pulled open the window and eased herself silently inside. A moment later she waved at Grace, eased the window closed and was gone.

Grace stood for a moment, listening to the silence, alert to any strange noise. There was nothing. Cajoling herself for being so fearful, she jogged across the expanse of lawn, ducking under the bushes at the far end of the garden to the fence that led into her parent's property.

Beneath the bushes it was pitch black. She took a deep breath, forcing herself onwards. The air smelt of damp earth and fermenting lawn cuttings. The path through the bushes was well used and by experience alone she navigated through the darkness, crawling under overhanging branches before emerging at the boundary fence.

With deliberate slowness she felt for and then found the loose planks, pushed them to the side and slipped through into her own garden. A moment later she was hauling herself up the drainpipe, feet scrambling for the footholds she knew were there and then into the silent safety of her bedroom.

Once there she stood in the centre of her room, listening for any sounds which might alert her to the fact her parents were awake. There was nothing, the silence of the house broken only by the leisurely snores of her father.

Dreading the thought of being caught if one of her parents should wake and for any bizarre reason come into her room, Grace hastily stripped off her clothes, shoved her limbs into her night clothes and scrambled beneath her duvet.

Relief washed over her. The night had been fun, until the pick-up had scared them. It had been madness to go out, to defy both sets of their parents and go to the nightclub. They had done it many times before; being told they couldn't go out was too much of a challenge to ignore. The row, had they been caught, would have been awful.

Stretching out Grace rolled onto her back, tucking her hands beneath her head, watching the shadows on her bedroom ceiling, cast by the branches of the trees. Apart from the deception it had been a fun night, apart from the driver who had scared them so much.

The bell in the tower of the local church at the far end of the road chimed. Grace counted its familiar tone as each hour was marked off. Three. Six hours since they had left their houses and gone into the city. It felt like a lifetime ago. What had the pick-up driver been up too? What had he wanted? She thought of his shadowed face turning towards them and remembered the sharp stab of fear.

Grace turned onto her side, curling her legs into her belly. She was safe. She forced her thoughts away from the weirdo in the pick-up. Paul. She pictured his face. She'd always fancied him, ever since she became aware of the feeling of attraction towards him when she'd become a teenager. Quite clearly, he'd fancied her. He'd always been chatty and friendly at school, seemingly unaware of the blush that spread over her cheeks whenever he was around, or the way she descended into a tongue-tied silence when he spoke to her.

It was different now, school was over. Almost. Two more exams and it would be finished for good. No more chance for the merciless teasing that went on when an attraction was noticed.

Grace turned onto her back, pushing her hands beneath her head and stared at the flickering shadows. She winced, remembering how abrupt she had been with Paul. What an idiot he must think she was. Grace groaned, she had been desperate to get home, panicked by the thought of their evening jaunt being discovered. She'd like to see him again. Would he want to see her, would the sparks she had felt still be there? Perhaps she could engineer a meeting, bump into him and Rob accidently while she was in Truro with Katia. Or she could just phone his house and ask to speak to him. The possibilities were endless. Maybe next time she should let him walk her home, with Katia and Rob. What fool she had been.

Grace rolled onto her side again. Had they heard a noise? A scream? They had been so frightened, their senses so heightened, any noise would sound terrifying. The night was full of sounds, animals, drunks messing around.

The thought wouldn't leave her. She spent the night tossing fitfully, her imagination flitting fretfully over the events of the previous hours.

The fabulous night with Paul, the fun she'd had with Katia, balanced against the fear of the man in the pick-up and the horrible thought that maybe the noise hadn't been that of the owl swooping on some poor animal and maybe there had been a scream.

The sound of her parents moving around downstairs was a welcome relief. Grace got up and headed downstairs to the kitchen.

'Morning love. Slept well?' Grace's mother poured a mug of tea from the pot she'd have on the go most of the day.

'Yes. Thanks,' Grace took the mug, cupping her hands around its warmth.

'Nearly done.' Her father ruffled Grace's hair as he headed out through the door to work. Richard's voice faded into the distance as he went towards the car, still talking to Grace. 'Exams will soon be over and then you'll be a proper adult. Bet you can't wait. Everyone says it but you'll find your schooldays are the best days of your life.'

'Yes, Dad. So you keep saying.' Grace leant in the open doorway, watching as her father got into his car and then drove away, tyres scattering the gravel.

'Studying again today?' Eve deftly pulled hot toast from beneath the grill. Grace winced, her mother had an uncanny ability to handle scalding heat and freezing items with equal dexterity.

Grace took the plate of toast from her mother. 'Yep. I might go over to Katia's to study with her later. We've both got Maths next. That's her last one.'

'Perfect. I'll be here anyway. I'll be in the garden, trying to tame some of the wilderness.'

Grace followed her mother's eyes, looking out into the garden. It didn't look anything like the wilderness Eve constantly joked about. The large expanse of neatly mown lawns and carefully tended flower beds were her mother's pride and joy.

Still in her nightclothes, Grace took the mug of tea and plate of toast upstairs, leaving them on the bedside table while she opened one of her textbooks. A few moments later she pushed them away with a sigh. The words were blurring before her eyes, nothing made sense.

What had the man in the pick-up wanted? Why had he slowed down? Grace shuddered at the memory. What if one of them had been on their own? Where had he gone after they'd run away and hidden? It had sounded as if he'd driven away. But the girl they'd spoken too… Surely, she'd gone onto the side streets by the time the man in the pick-up had driven past them. She'd have been at the bed and breakfast by the time the pick-up had appeared. Safe. He wouldn't have driven onto the side streets anyway, unquestionably he'd have gone down the hill towards the city.

Grace nibbled on the edge of a slice of toast and forced her eyes back to the text. If anything had happened, it would have been on the news. Her parents would have been shocked and frightened. They'd have been discussing it. There'd been nothing. She turned the page and began to read. She had to stop letting her imagination run wild.

* * * * *

'One more exam and it's over.' Katia lay back on her bed. 'I can't believe I'll never have to go to school again after tomorrow.'

'University might be quite challenging,' Grace flicked slowly though Katia's notes.

'But it's not school though is it?'

'True.'

'No one telling us when we can go out.' Katia sat up suddenly, bending her knees up to so she could rest her chin on them. 'Parties. Romances. Paul. And Rob.' Katia sighed blissfully.

'True again.'

'He's so gorgeous,' Katia said dreamily. 'Last night when we were dancing…'

'About last night,' Grace interrupted.

'What about it?'

'The man. The one in the pick-up that was acting weird.'

Katia put her hands over her ears. 'I don't want to even think about him. He was so scary. I thought…'

Grace sat beside Katia and gently eased her hands away from her ears. 'So did I. Whatever he was doing it frightened the life out of me.'

'Fucking weirdo.'

'Listen, Katia. I think we should tell the police. Report him for prowling or whatever.'

'No!' Katia jumped to her feet and crossed her bedroom, looking with frightened eyes towards Grace. 'We can't report him. Please Grace. My parents would absolutely freak out if they knew I was out.'

'But he could have...'

'No. Grace. Please. Don't. If my parents found out...'

'But...' Grace met Katia's eyes. 'That girl. The one we gave directions to. What if we did hear a scream? What if it was her?'

Katia shook her head vehemently, her voice quivered as she spoke. 'Grace, we didn't. It was just an animal like you thought.'

'I don't know. I can't get the whole thing out of my head.' Grace crossed the room to stand beside Katia. Beyond the window her parent's neat garden spread to the thick hedge that formed its roadside boundary. The road they had walked on the night before. 'He was just so frightening. The way he looked at us.'

'Grace, please don't tell anyone. If they found out my parents would never forgive me. Us.'

Grace shook her head, 'I think we should. Honestly.'

'It was just someone weird in a pick-up,' Katia's voice held an odd note, as if she were trying to convince herself. 'Nothing happened. Is there anything on the news about anyone being hurt last night?'

Grace shook her head.

'Well then. We were panicked by the man in the pick-up because we were so hyped up, with the lads, as well as deceiving our parents.' Katia lifted a strand of auburn hair from Grace's cheek, gently tilting her chin.

'Okay.' Grace met Katia's eyes, saw the imploring look in them.

'We heard some animal yelping. We freaked out. The guy in the pick-up could have been someone's dad, driving around looking for them.'

Grace nodded. Katia's explanation made sense. They had been on edge, walking home, spooked by the mist, worrying about getting found out, disappointed at having to leave Rob and Paul. Perhaps the man had just been looking for someone, like Katia had suggested. 'You're right. I should forget the whole thing.'

Chapter Eight

' I wondered when you'd wake up.'

Ayla, jolted into awareness by the unfamiliar voice, sat up. Every muscle in her body seemed to hurt, the worst of all being the taut muscles in her neck. Wincing, she eased open her eyes, bringing a hand to her forehead to ease the pounding sensation.

'You've been asleep for a long time.'

'Where am I?' She was fully awake now. Gingerly she straightened up, feeling each ligament protest at the movement.

He was watching her from a chair beside a dusty window, the daylight coming through emitted the only light. A vast wooden table occupied most of the space in the room.

She swallowed, the noise loud in the silence, wondering if he could hear her heart beating. It thumped uncomfortably against her rib cage, fast, adrenaline coursing through her veins. When he made no reply, she looked around the room. A kitchen, of sorts. Bare stone walls, a slate floor, an old-fashioned range occupying the space beneath a vast chimneybreast. There was a sink beneath the window beside which he sat.

She let her gaze rove over him, not daring to meet his eyes, yet horribly aware of his presence. His handsome face was terrifyingly at odds with his cold expression. At either side of the sink stood an assortment of battered wooden furniture. Ayla tilted her head, glimpsing more of the room, a wooden staircase, an assortment of battered looking armchairs, and an incongruous leather sofa which appeared to be brand new.

'Where am I?' she repeated, hearing the fear in her voice.

'Don't you remember?' his voice was flat, almost conversational. His teeth when he spoke were white, set in a neat, even row.

Ayla shook her head. 'I...' She remembered the train, a long, tiring journey, her rucksack pressed up against her legs in the crowded carriage. Eating the sandwich, she'd bought hours previously, as the train rattled along a track beside the sea. The waves had been brown, boiling angrily onto the beach below.

The carriage had emptied gradually until, by the time it had pulled into Truro, it had been almost empty.

Ayla ran a hand over her forehead. Her fingers felt clammy against the iciness of her skin. Why had she been in Truro?

'I wanted to walk.' She whispered, reminding herself. Someone at university had mentioned the beauty of the path which stretched around the coastline. She'd intended to walk some of it, stay in Truro, and then hike around to Penzance, St Ives too, maybe, if there was time. She'd wanted to study the geology of the area, and to clear her head after the chaos of her exams.

The friend had told her there was a bus which would take her back to the station in Penzance, the end of the line. From there she'd planned take the train back to Exeter, collect her belongings and then travel on to Scotland to visit her parents in their new home for the remainder of the summer.

'You were lost,' he spoke finally.

Ayla nodded her head, remembering. There'd been two girls. They'd given her directions.

'The girls gave me directions. I couldn't find the street.'

He pushed himself abruptly from the seat in front of the window and crossed the room, coming to stand close to her.

'Girls?' She could see him properly now, he was tall, not muscular, but not skinny either. Normal looking.

Ayla met his eyes, they were brown. Kind looking, set in a handsome face, a movie star face, as her university classmate, Catherine Bell, would say.

'Yes, I met them on the road, they gave me directions.' Ayla watched a shadow pass over his face.

The girls had been drunk, swaying as they made their way out of the fog towards her. She'd been frightened at first, the panic at being lost in an unfamiliar city beginning to set in. The fact that they were two young women of a similar age to herself had reassured her.

'They told me how to get to the place where I was staying.' Ayla pictured the two girls, their seriousness as they'd stood on the pavement, the taller one, with the long mane of wavy red hair, gesticulating as she recounted the way to the house.

She'd been aware of them watching her walk away, exhausted after her long day, the straps of her rucksack digging painfully into her shoulders.

Her rucksack. Ayla glanced around the room, relieved to see her bag propped up beside the table at the far side of the room.

'I'd say they lived close by,' Ayla said, irritated now by their drunkenness. The directions had been wrong. The road the red-headed girl had spoken about was not where she had been guided too.

Right, left, right, she'd done exactly as the girl had said, but the road she had found herself on was a residential one, consisting of large bungalows set back from the road. There hadn't been a bed and breakfast sign anywhere. Desperation prickling in the pit of her stomach she'd begun to make her way back to the road where she had met the girls, intending to walk down the hill towards the hazy glow of the city lights.

Tears of frustration and exhaustion prickling at the back of her eyes she'd retraced her steps, trudging across the road. The headlights had seemed to come out of nowhere. Conscious of being in the middle of the road, right in the path of the vehicle, she had run towards the pavement. There had been a squeal of brakes, the protesting sound of tyres against the tarmac. And then she'd stumbled, crying out in panic.

Ayla glanced at her hand. There was a red patch where she'd hit the tarmac, but nothing else. The fall hadn't been heavy, the rucksack spinning from her shoulder having cushioned her.

'You stopped to help me.' The memory of the previous night was hazy, as if she'd been out drinking like the two stupid girls.

He crouched beside the chair. So close she could pick out the individual strands of his hair, dark, wavy, brushed back from his forehead. Ayla took a shuddering breath. He smelt clean, of the countryside, fresh hay, nice shampoo.

'I'm not going to hurt you.' He took her hand, his voice filled with amusement at her fear. 'You're safe.'

His fingers were cool against her skin as he brushed the redness with a light touch. 'I told you that last night.'

Ayla nodded. She moved to ease her hand away. The pressure from his fingers increased, preventing her from moving.

She remembered scrambling to get to her feet, hampered by the heavy rucksack, blinking against the harshness of the vehicle headlights. Surrounded by the fog, there had seemed to be only them present, the rest of the world blotted out by the swirling grey mist. He'd helped her to her feet, his fingers tight on her arm.

'Are you okay?' he'd said, concern etched on his face.

'I'm fine. Thank you. I'm sorry I scared you – being in the middle of the road like that.' Ayla had been reassured by his kindness. Her hand and knees stung where they'd made contact with the tarmac. One leg of her jeans had been ripped where the fabric had torn.

'You're not, I can see that. Let me help you. Sit down over here.'

She'd let him guide her to a low wall, the boundary of a garden and eased herself down, aware of how much her knees were stinging. She'd glanced down, seeing her legs jerking as they trembled, the shock of her fall and the near miss with his vehicle beginning to take over.

He'd sat on the wall beside her. In the pale light Ayla could see he was older than she was, but not as old as her parents, somewhere in between. 'I didn't see you until you were right in front of me. It's not the kind of night to be wandering around. This fog is horrible.' A slight smile had played on his lips showing just the tips of a row of even teeth. His gentle concern reassured her.

'I couldn't find the place I was staying, so I was going back to the city. Hopefully I can find somewhere to stay.'

'Were you booked into one of the bed and breakfasts up here?'

'Not really. I rang one when I got off the train, but I'd say she's given up on me arriving now. I wasn't even that sure of the address.'

'You just rolled up here without any plans?'

'I'm going to walk some of the coast path.' The idea had sounded crazy when she'd told him. She'd thrown clothes into her rucksack and set off on a whim. It had been madness not to have made proper arrangements. She should have found a place to stay, booked a taxi, something, anything.

'You shouldn't be out and about with nowhere to stay at this time of night. It's not safe.' He'd run a hand over his jawline.

'No choice,' Ayla had told him, getting to her feet. 'I need to find somewhere to stay. Thank you for helping me. Sorry if I scared you.'

She'd drawn her rucksack straps over her shoulders. He had remained sitting on the wall, watching her.

'Good night. Thank you again.'

She'd been halfway down the hill before she heard the noise of his engine.

'Wait,' he'd let down the pick-up window, slowing the vehicle to her pace. 'I've had an idea.' He'd pulled a tentative face, his voice filled with eagerness.

Despite her stinging knees and aching shoulders Ayla had smiled, his presence had made the foggy darkness seem a little less intimidating.

'I'm really worried about you being out on your own. It's not safe. Girl like you…'

She'd pulled a wry face. 'I'll be fine. The city is just there. There'll be a hotel…'

As she'd looked at him a movement behind his seat had caught her eye. A pretty toddler was strapped into a child seat. Noticing Ayla's eyes on her, the little girl had grinned and waved the teddy she was holding.

'That's Mia, my daughter.' He'd smiled proudly, looking in the driver's mirror at the child. His voice had been filled with love. 'She's been asleep for hours. We've been up country visiting friends. I left late so we'd miss the traffic.'

'She's so pretty,' Ayla hadn't been sure if she was more amused by the child's antics or by his Cornish phrase.

'I've got an idea,' he'd said, focusing his eyes once more on Ayla. 'There's a bed and breakfast place near where I live. It's a lot closer to the coast path than here. I could take you there. I know it's getting late, but the owner is a friend. I'll ring, get her out of bed if necessary.'

Seeing Ayla hesitate he'd laughed. 'It's okay. I'm not a mad axe murderer.'

Despite her trepidation, she'd smiled back.

'She is though.' He'd half turned to look at his daughter.

'I can see that.'

The little girl, sensing their amusement had begun to giggle, her round cheeks crinkling into dimples at either side of her rosebud mouth.

'It's up to you.' He'd pushed the gear stick forwards, changing the note of the engine. 'I'm sorry. Shouldn't have suggested it.'

Ayla had hesitated for a moment, then darted in front of the pick-up, hauled open the passenger door and got in. 'Yes please, that would be lovely. You're very kind.'

She'd breathed a sigh of relief. It was warm inside the pick-up. She hadn't been aware of how panicked she'd been until he'd been about to drive away.

'Let's get you somewhere safe,' he'd smiled, driving slowly towards the lights of the city.

'Thank you,' the thought of a warm bed had been very enticing. She'd turned to smile at the little girl who was resting her head on the edge of her booster seat, her eyes already heavy with sleep. 'She's beautiful.'

They'd skirted the city, driving around the outskirts, the fog making it impossible to see any landmarks.

'You're frozen,' he'd said, as he stopped the pick-up at a set of traffic lights.

Ayla had shuddered, she hadn't been aware of how cold she'd been until she was inside the warmth of the pick-up, a combination of the shock of her fall, and the panic at being lost.

'Here,' he'd reached behind her seat and pulled out a flask. 'There's tea in there. I brought it with me to keep me awake while I was driving.'

'Nice, thank you,' balancing the flask against the movement of the pick-up Ayla unscrewed the top and poured some of the liquid into it.

'There's sugar in it.'

Ayla had sipped at the liquid. It was tepid and didn't taste of much other than a cloying sweetness, but it warmed her slightly.

She was aware of draining the cup and him easing it from her hand.

'We've a way to go. Why don't you close your eyes?'

Ayla had tried to nod, unable to fight the overwhelming tiredness that had suddenly enveloped her.

Chapter Nine

'You're safe. I'm going to look after you.' There was an intensity behind his eyes she found hard to look at.

Wide awake now, Ayla pushed herself upright. Last night he had promised to take her to a bed and breakfast. She remembered nothing after being in the warmth of his pick-up, struggling to keep her eyes open against the overwhelming exhaustion.

'How did I get here?' Ayla could hear the panic in her voice.

'You fell to sleep. I didn't want to wake you.'

'But…' There was a gaping hole in her memory. How had she arrived at this house, in this chair?

'It's okay,' he stood up. 'I'm not going to hurt you.'

'Why didn't you take me to the bed and breakfast?' A band of tension tightened around her forehead. How had she got from the pick-up to the chair? Had he carried her?

'Please stop this,' his voice dropped, became little more than a whisper. He was smiling at her, but there was no disguising the threat. 'I'm not going to hurt you,' he repeated.

'I need to go,' Ayla scrambled to her feet.

'No,' he shook his head. His hand pushed against her shoulder, propelling her gently back into the chair.

'My walk… My parents are expecting me…'

'You're going to stay here. I'm going to take care of you.'

Ayla shook her head violently, as if she could rid herself of the ridiculousness of the situation. Last night he'd been kind, she'd trusted him, he'd made her feel safe, the little girl in the back seat had reassured her. Where was she? Ayla glanced around the kitchen, unwilling to look at him. Where was the child? Had she imagined her?

He had told Ayla he was going to look after her. She fought the urge to giggle hysterically. This was a joke, surely. In a moment he would tell her how dangerous it was to accept lifts from strangers, to go into situations without telling anyone where you were going, or when you'd be back. This could not be happening. The hysterical laughter that bubbled in her throat was replaced by an urgent need to vomit. These things happened to other people, girls on the news, in films. Not to her.

'I'm going to be sick,' Ayla got unsteadily to her feet, the slate floor seemed uneven beneath her, as if it were the slats of a roller coaster. He made no move to stop her. She seized the back of the chair to steady herself, the wood felt sticky beneath her fingers. She had barely reached the sink before she vomited a stream of acid bile.

'Another one of your filthy bitches.'

Ayla slowly straightened up and turned to face the older woman who had spoken. The pleasantness of her face at odds with the icy loathing in her eyes and the jutting bulldog set of her jaw. The young girl from the car was in her arms, her legs wrapped around either side of an ample hip, neat bottom resting on the curve of the woman's protruding belly.

He had retreated to the far side of the table, away from her. Ayla's eyes slid from one to the other. The family likeness was obvious. They must, she realised, be mother and son... Where did the child fit in? The woman was too old to be her mother.

The woman shifted the child to her hip before flinging open a cupboard. 'Here,' she tossed a bottle of bleach in Ayla's direction. 'You can clean up your mess.'

The bottle felt slippery in Ayla's fingers.

'I should go.' Ayla glanced at the man who was staring intently at the floor.

The woman gazed coldly across the room, her face half hidden in the child's hair. 'Clean it up.'

She turned towards her son. 'Eddie, you've no more fucking sense than those cattle,' she jerked her head towards the fields Ayla could see beyond the dusty window. 'What did you bring that bitch in here for?'

'I had to put Mia to bed, I couldn't leave her on her own while I dealt with ...'

There seemed to be no power in her fingers, Ayla struggled to open the bottle beneath the woman's malevolent gaze. Finally, she succeeded and poured bleach into the sink, the gelatinous liquid parting the yellow bile.

Ayla glanced out of the window, painfully aware of the hostile silence in the room behind her. Beyond the dusty glass she could see a cluster of old stone farm buildings, a cobbled yard, yellowed grass growing up between the stones. Beyond the buildings she could see fields, cattle grazing. Somewhere out there was a drive, and a road, freedom.

'I should go,' Ayla repeated, turning to hold the used bleach bottle in the direction of the woman, whose lips retreated further into the wrinkled recess of her jawline.

'Nan...' It was the first time he had spoken since the woman had come into the room.

'Eddie...' Nan mocked his wheedling tone. She eased the child into a high-chair and busied herself with pouring a bowl of cereal. 'You're nothing better than an animal. A pathetic creature.'

'Milk! Milk!' The little girl took the plastic spoon Nan offered her and banged on the table of the highchair. Her small legs beat a tattoo against its wooden legs. A broad smile split her chubby face, revealing a row of tiny teeth.

'Wait, Mia, it's coming.'

'Where's her mum?' Ayla's question went unanswered.

'Get rid of her,' Nan's tone was conversational as she pulled a bottle of milk from the fridge.

'I'll go. I'll walk from here. I won't say anything.'

Nan's head swivelled slowly to look at Ayla. She gave a snort of derision. 'Cat got your tongue. Eddie?' She crossed the room her bulk moving at an alarming speed. 'She said she won't say anything.'

Eddie hunched his shoulders, lowering his head. 'She was lost. She came to me.' The words tumbled from his mouth.

'You fool. You stupid animal. What have I bred? How did I get something as useless as you?'

Ayla watched horrified as the tall man seemed to crumble beneath the force of her verbal onslaught.

Immune to Nan's fury, Mia spooned cereal into her mouth, her chubby legs moving slowly, kicking at the wooden supports of her chair.

Unsure her quivering legs would hold her, Ayla took an uncertain stride away from the sink, her eyes watering from the stench of the bleach. Beside the sink there was a wooden door, coats hung on the back of it. A filthy looking raincoat, a cleaner looking short coat, and incongruously between the two, a small yellow plastic raincoat.

'Filth. You're filth. I should have aborted you when I had the chance.'

Behind her Ayla was aware of the tirade of abuse Nan was unleashing on Eddie, vile, cruel words spewing from her mouth.

Ayla shot an uncertain smile in the direction of Mia who was watching her solemnly, the plastic spoon halfway to her mouth.

She'd no idea where her jacket was. She had no recollection of taking it off the previous night. Her rucksack lay against a cupboard near the fridge. Her money, her clothes, credit cards, all neatly packed away in its pockets. It was pointless to even try to get to it. She had to run. Escape. She'd come back with the police. Later.

Taking a deep breath, she made a dash for the front door, the latch springing open beneath her trembling fingers. She hauled at the heavy wood, hearing the screech of protest as the damp fibres were dragged over the stone flagged doorstep.

The fresh air hit her, cool, sweet smelling, the tang of the sea overlaid with fresh grass, clean after the oppressive air that had permeated the kitchen.

She ran, the cobbles slippery beneath her feet. Behind her Eddie gave an angry bellow, a noise that struck terror into her heart.

Buildings surrounded the courtyard, sagging roofs, chipped paintwork, the smell of animals. From somewhere close by a dog barked hysterically, a pig squealed, the noises echoing off the dilapidated buildings.

Ayla turned, desperately looking for a way out, aware of the door banging against its frame as Eddie hauled it open.

Between two of the stone buildings, she spotted the darkness of a drive, almost hidden by the layout of the yard.

He was halfway across the space, shoes sliding on the cobbles, his face contorted with rage. He was closer to the drive, but she was faster. The air moved around her as Eddie made a grab for her arm and missed. The effort sent him sprawling onto the cobblestones.

Glancing over her shoulder to see him scrambling to his feet, Ayla ran headlong into a wooden gatepost. Staggering to keep her feet she forced air into her lungs and ran, the muscles of her ribcage screaming in protest.

Ahead of her, the drive snaked through forestry, beyond which stretched a ribbon of green. In the distance she glimpsed the hazy line where the land met the sea, the coast path she had come to walk. She made for the green, the drive had to meet a road. Cars. People. Safety.

Without so much as checking her stride, Ayla plunged into the safety of the forestry, arms flailing at the branches that whipped at her face, her leg muscles burning with the effort. She stumbled over tree roots, as she forced her way through the undergrowth, brambles clawing at her.

'Don't run. There's nowhere to go.' His voice echoed around the forestry, persuasive, insidious.

Lungs on fire with the effort, Ayla plunged into thick undergrowth, watching with a strange distraction as thick strands of sharp brambles raked through the flesh of her hands.

She crouched as low to the ground as she could. From close by she could hear his footfalls, padding on the leaf mould. 'I promise. I won't hurt you. I want you to be safe.'

He must, she was sure, be able to hear the thunder of her heartbeat and the breaths she tried hard to silence.

The footsteps came to a stop, he was close. Ayla closed her eyes, praying he couldn't see her. She daren't move, yet every fibre of her body told her to run, that he could see her and was about to haul her from her hiding place.

The air was filled with the sound of his breathing, and his softly whispered curses.

Terror took over, Ayla scrambled to her feet, plunging onwards through the undergrowth, the air filled with the sound of the thorns tearing the fabric of her jeans.

Without turning she could feel he was close by. Each breath was agony, sheer adrenaline mixed with panic the only things keeping her moving.

The light changed as Ayla emerged from the trees. She stopped. Trapped. She was on a rocky ledge. To one side a sheer drop, to the other a high cliff down which surged a wide ribbon of water. It cascaded into a pool far below her before plunging onwards, down another rock face. The water churned, brown, grey, topped with creamy foam as it boiled and finally merged into the river.

Eddie crashed his way out of the trees skidding to an abrupt halt. 'I'm not going to hurt you.' He held out a hand towards her. Ayla met his eyes, cold, above the burning red of his cheeks.

She shook her head. 'Get away from me!' The effort of screaming tore at her throat.

He took a stride forward, his arm extended, clawing the air.

Without hesitating Ayla turned away, letting her momentum carry her forwards. Feet scrabbling at the slippery rock, she half fell, half lurched, the air ice cold, water droplets hitting her face until she plunged into the dark depths below.

There seemed to be no end to the darkness. She cartwheeled, bouncing off the rocks at the bottom of the river, the pressure of the water keeping her down. She fought against it, desperate for air, frantic to reach the surface.

She emerged from the depths, choking as the water hit her throat, flailing weakly to keep herself afloat, surprised to find she was still alive.

Ayla let the current carry her away from the waterfall. It moved fast, spinning her downstream. Too exhausted to do anything other than float, Ayla clutched weakly at the grass bank, trying to grasp a handhold. Her feet touched the bottom, pebbles sliding as she scrabbled for a purchase.

'Let me help you.' Ayla felt herself lifted roughly by the back of her sweater, as she was hauled roughly out of the water, her feet slipping on the muddy bank.

'Why did you have to run? I didn't want to have to hurt you.' Eddie shook her, pulling the wet fabric around her shoulders, dragging Ayla to her feet. She met his eyes, seeing the triumphant rage in his face a moment before he punched her.

Chapter Ten

'You shouldn't have made me hurt you. That was your fault.'

Ayla blinked, slowly becoming aware of her surroundings. She moved, trying to ease the pain which consumed every part of her body. There was no escape, each muscle felt as if it screamed in torment.

He was sitting beside her, a vague silhouette. She couldn't see his face, but the malice was clear in the quiet tone of his voice.

Ayla blinked again, there was a harsh light overhead, it swayed lazily, the shadows it cast flickering over the walls.

'Where am I?' She was wide awake now. Fear prickling over her body in an uneasy wave. How long had she been unconscious?

'You don't need to know that.'

She forced her eyes to focus on his face. The threat in his voice was clear, and utterly at odds with the gentle, handsome face beside her. There was something, a blur just above her eyelid. She moved her hand to wipe it way. A chain bit into her wrist preventing her from moving.

'What are you doing? Let me go!' She thrashed in panic, body convulsing as she fought against the metal.

Exhausted, she stopped, jerking her wrists compulsively in fear and frustration. Tilting her head Ayla could see, in the harsh overhead light, thick, rusting loops of metal which circled both wrists, tying her to either side of an old-fashioned bedstead.

'I'm going to take care of you now.'

Ayla met his eyes. His focused on hers with a look of total devotion.

'I'm going to be sick. Let me go.' She pleaded her voice filled with panic.

'You're just hurting yourself.'

A trickle of blood dripped slowly down her forearm. Ayla watched it meander, gathering pace before it disappeared around the side of her limb. She didn't recognise the howl of sheer anguish that tore itself from the depths of her stomach.

'Stop it.' Eddie's voice was filled with scorn. 'Stop crying.'

Ayla jerked her head, trying to move away from him. Eddie was so close she could smell the coffee on his breath. She focused on his row of white, even teeth, not daring to meet the coldness of his eyes.

The tears wouldn't stop falling. He slapped her then, the noise of his hand on her skin seemed to echo in her head.

'I said. Stop crying.'

Ayla choked, fighting back the tears.

'It makes you look ugly.' His tone was almost conversational.

'What are you going to do to me?'

He smiled then. His chair creaked as he sat back away from her. He leant his head against the back of the chair, sighing contentedly. 'Anything I like.'

Ayla met his eyes and saw the pure pleasure his words gave him.

She whimpered, an involuntary sound which darkened his eyes. She tore her eyes away from him. Craning her neck, she glimpsed a flash of filmy red fabric. He must have taken her clothes off, replaced them with what looked like a nightdress out of a fantasy catalogue.

'Your clothes were wet,' he said softly.

Knowing he was watching her, Ayla slowly let her eyes rove around her surroundings. It was difficult from her prone position, but she could see rough stone walls, covered in places by chipped, stained plaster. There was furniture, a wooden wardrobe, a battered looking chest of drawers. To one side, behind where he sat, a faded shower curtain hung limply, a toilet just visible behind it.

Another whimper.

'I'm going to leave you now.' Eddie got slowly to his feet, regret in his voice.

'But...' Whatever terrors he held, the thought of being alone, chained, seemed even worse.

'I'll come back,' Eddie's fingers trailed softly over Ayla's face, moving a strand of hair from her forehead with infinite tenderness. 'I'm so glad you found me.'

'Found you?' Anger made her feel stronger. 'I didn't find you. I thought you were helping me. You deceived me.'

'Noooooooo.' He drew out the sound, releasing the final note as a snort of amusement. His fingers moved slowly downwards, tracing a circle around her neck. 'You came with me. You trusted me, and now, you're going to stay with me. I'm going to take care of you.'

'Someone will find me here. You'll be fucked then. You'll rot in jail, forever. Let me go.' Ayla wrenched hard on the chains, succeeding only in drawing more blood to her wrists.

He shook his head. 'No one knows you're here.' A smile tilted his lips upwards, crinkling the corners of his eyes.

Ayla opened her mouth to protest, but she knew it was true. She'd come to Cornwall on a whim. She hadn't told anyone, even her parents who were expecting her to visit in a few weeks' time. They thought she was still at university. No one would even know she was missing.

'Let me go, you bastard!' Ayla screamed, frustration mingling with sheer terror.

He straightened up, moving away from her, his face shadowed by the harshness of the single lightbulb. 'Don't make me angry,' his voice was soft, but the threat in it was clear. 'You don't want to do that.'

Ayla stared upwards, blinking against the light, trying to see his face, to look for any sign of compassion in him. He stood unwavering until, after what seemed an eternity, he stretched down towards her. 'I'm going to untie you.' His voice was conversational, as if he were asking her if she wanted a cup of tea. 'I'll come back later with something for you to eat.'

He fiddled with the chains around her wrists. Undoing first one, then reaching across her to do the other one. She gulped a tangy masculine aftershave as he leant over her. 'Scream all you want. No one will hear you. No one will come.'

Gingerly Ayla let her arms drop to the bed, muscles screaming in protest, a tsunami of pins and needles shooting through her fingers. She watched him back away across the room. 'I like screaming.'

Ayla scrambled to a sitting position as he left the room, tightening her hands across her mouth to stifle the sob of pure terror A moment later came the noise of a key being turned in the lock. She was trapped. Alone.

Silence, thick and impenetrable, descended. Listening, alert for any sounds of him returning. Ayla got slowly to her feet, the bed springs groaned. It was an immense effort to move, every muscle in agony.

Now she was standing Ayla could properly see her surroundings. The single bulb illuminated the room and its battered furniture. She could also see the repulsive nightdress that barely covered her body. The fabric, a garish red, was cheap, tarty looking, her bruised, scraped body visible beneath it. She hauled one of the blankets from the bed and wrapped it around her shoulders, wrinkling her nose at the musty smell of the wool.

Her shoes were neatly positioned beside the bed. They were damp as she slid her feet into them. The insoles sloshed with water from the river as she stood and took an uncertain stride forwards.

She circled the room, a small narrow bed, the chains that had held her wrists now dangling beside the metal struts. There were chains at the bottom of the bed too. Ayla brought her hand to her mouth, gagging.

The floor was filthy, old slate slabs, thick with grime. She gingerly pulled open the wardrobe door. Inside hung clothes, sweaters, pairs of jeans, a couple of shirts. She ran her hand over them, feeling the damp fabric beneath her fingers, filled with a growing sense of horror at knowing the clothes had belonged to someone else. Another person who had been trapped in this room at the mercy of Eddie. Fighting back a scream of despair she moved to the chest of drawers. The dampness of the wood made it hard to open the drawers. Determined, she forced them open, feeling the surfaces protest before they finally gave way.

Inside were more clothes. Underwear, socks, a pair of stockings. In one corner was a hairbrush. Ayla pulled it out. There was hair tangled into the brush. Ayla, fighting nausea, picked at the strands with trembling fingers. They were long, a deep red colour, and when she held one towards the light it kinked, the waves clearly visible.

Ayla threw it back into the drawer, unable to rid her fingers of the sensation of holding it. Who had it belonged too? Where was she now? The thought filled her with dread.

How could she have been so stupid as to get into the pick-up with Eddie? Stranger danger. She knew the adverts. And yet, he had seemed so nice, kind, gentle, good looking, well spoken. And there had been the child, smiling in the back seat. She had trusted him. Felt safe. The people to avoid were ugly, they had an air of danger about them. He hadn't.

She turned back towards the bed. There, beside it, in the stained plaster were scratches, short, thin marks, clustered together. It took Ayla a moment to understand what she was looking at, her mind slow with the horror of all she was enduring. Someone had marked off the days of captivity using that wall. So many scratches.

The nausea she had fought to contain welled in her throat. Ayla darted across the room, flung back the shower curtain and vomited into the toilet bowl. There was nothing in her stomach to come up, but still she retched, fingers clutching the sticky clamminess of the porcelain.

Beside the toilet, as she got shakily to her feet, Ayla noticed a small tangle of cloths and a bottle of cleaning fluid. The previous occupant of the room had tried her best to keep it clean.

To one side of the toilet was a shower, the tray cracked and stained. A dried-out bar of soap had been left on the shelf.

She froze at the sound of the key being turned in the lock. She wheeled round as the door opened, clutching the blanket around her shoulders with trembling fingers.

'I've brought you a sandwich.' He held out a plate on which was a neatly cut sandwich and an apple. 'I hope you like coffee.' He put his head on one side, looking at her, as if contemplating.

'Thank you.' She took the plate and the mug, the heat from it burnt her fingers.

'A shower might be a good idea. You look a mess.'

Before she could reply he had gone. The key was turned and a moment later the room plunged into darkness. 'Wait. Don't...The light...' Ayla could hear her heart beating, thundering in her chest, in the silence that filled the room.

She crept uncertainly towards the bed, scalding liquid sloshing against her legs as it spilled. She got gingerly onto the bed, curled beneath the blankets, listening to the sounds of the building creaking and settling around her. From somewhere close came a scratching noise. A mouse? Or a rat? She shuddered.

Despite her fears, Ayla ate the sandwich. She was starving, having had no idea when she had last eaten, let alone when he would feed her again. Then finally she lay down, shivering with cold and fear and watched the darkness which surrounded her.

The sound of a child chattering brought her to wakefulness. For a moment, Ayla had no idea where she was, stretching her limbs out, the cold bringing her rapidly to the realisation that she was still trapped, a captive.

It was light, sunshine streaming into the room through a tiny semi-circular window high up the wall. Through the window she could see plants, grasses waving gently in the breeze.

The chattering continued. The noise fading and then getting closer. Help?

Ayla scrambled from the bed. Dragging a pair of jeans and a sweater from the drawers she slipped them on. The fabric smelt musty. The jeans were enormous, with a wide elastic panel at the front. Maternity jeans? Had they belonged to the child's mother? Desperate to attract the attention of whoever was outside, Ayla scrambled onto the single chair and stepped onto the chest of drawers beneath the window. Her face now close to the glass. It was pitted, thick with dust, but she could see through it. Outside there was a garden. A little girl was skipping across the grass. It was the child from the kitchen, the one who had been in the vehicle the night she had been abducted. Mia. Eddie's daughter. Ayla banged on the glass. 'Help me!'

Attracted by the noise Mia turned. Her face curious. As Ayla watched the woman, Nan, hurried towards Mia and took the child's hand, turning to glare at the half moon of glass. Ayla stumbled back in fright at her malicious expression, the table and chair upending as she landed with a tooth-jarring thud on the filthy floor.

Chapter Eleven

'What does the doggy say?' Nan lay on her side on the floor, resting her weight on one elbow while she jiggled a small plastic dog in front of Mia.

'Oufff.' A wide smile spilt Mia's face, dimpling her cheeks.

'That's it. Woof.'

'Oufff.' Mia repeated solemnly.

Nan reached across the brightly coloured rug, rummaged in an old biscuit box, and selected another of the plastic animals.

'This one?' She air walked a cow past Mia's face.

The toddler, having been focused intently on the plastic dog, brought her eyes to the cow. The dog instantly forgotten; she waved a chubby hand in the direction of the new toy.

'Moooo.' Her brown eyes met those of her grandmother, she blinked once, long eyelashes flickering, before giggling in delight at the approval she saw there.

'Mia loves her animals, don't you? Clever girl.' Nan scrambled to her feet, smoothing down her tweed skirt. She scooped Mia into her arms, resting her on the curve of her belly, wrapping the child's legs around her hips.

'Nan.' Mia said gently, snuggling her face beneath her grandmother's chin. Her breath, warm against Nan's skin smelt of the fruit drink she'd gulped earlier.

Slowly Nan paced the room, Mia wrapped tightly around her body, one hand smoothing her dark mop of hair. She bent to straighten the small duvet that covered Mia's tiny bed.

'Nearly time for bed, Miss.' Nan rocked Mia. In her arms Mia stirred, pointing upwards. Nan followed her gaze; the child was fascinated by the florescent stars she had recently stuck on the ceiling. When Mia was in bed, they would be lit by the lamp beside her, shining brightly to illuminate the darkness. She'd bought them when Mia moved into her own small bedroom, graduating from the cot which Nan had kept beside her bed. She was too big for that now. It was time for her to grow up, take her first steps towards independence. Mia hadn't fussed about being put in her own room. The cot had been moved first, but now she was in her own tiny pine bed with an elegantly carved headboard.

Nan gently lowered Mia to the ground, smiling as she scampered across the floor to grab another of the animals from the biscuit tin.

'Ah, you know every trick. No Mia. It's bedtime. Where are your pyjamas?'

Mia faced her grandmother, a toy horse clutched in her chubby hand. Grinning she made a clicking noise and bounced up and down, mimicking the action of riding a horse.

'You're not getting around me like that.' Smiling, Nan dashed across the room, crouching her arms raised above her head. 'Monster's going to get you!'

Mia shrieked in delight, abandoning the horse and running across the room where she hid her face in the folds of her duvet, peeping out at Nan, her face filled with mischief.

In one easy movement Nan lifted Mia into her arms. Cushioning the child, she rolled onto the bed, the two squealing with laughter.

'Come on you. Madam.' Nan eased herself upright, pushing herself and Mia's weight off the bed. 'No more messing. It's bedtime. Pyjamas on, then you can have some cereal downstairs.'

As she stood at the pine chest of drawers that held Mia's clothes, a movement in the yard outside caught her eye. Nan froze, watching Eddie's loping gait as he walked towards the ruined cottage across the yard. Moving mechanically, her eyes fixed on Eddie, Nan pulled a neatly folded pair of pyjamas out of the drawer, her jaw clamped tightly shut with tension. A moment later he disappeared into the shadows of the old building.

'Hide,' Mia giggled. Nan turned slowly to see Mia burrowing into the folds of the duvet, her head and shoulders covered by the fabric, just her small bottom and legs visible.

'Stop it!' Nan crossed the room, seized Mia by the arm and wrenched her from the bed. 'Don't start that.' Nan snapped as Mia began to sob. 'Tears won't help.'

Nan, still holding Mia's arm, lowered herself onto the bed and began to haul Mia's clothes off, wrenching them over her head. The fabric, tangling into Mia's mop of hair, jerked at her scalp, increasing the volume of her wails. 'Look at your face. Ugly. Crying makes you look ugly.' Nan deftly pulled Mia's pyjamas on, lifted the child onto her hip and headed downstairs.

Mia, subdued by Nan's abrupt change of mood, sat quietly in her highchair, her fingers playing distractedly with the plastic animals Nan had shoved onto the table in front of her. Mia's dark eyes followed her grandmother around the room.

'Eat.' Nan filled a bowl with cereal and milk and put it in front of Mia.

The front door opening filled the kitchen with a breeze that sent the newspapers and letters skittering across the table.

'How's my girl?' Eddie crossed the room, shedding his coat and woollen hat. He ran a gentle hand over Mia's head, trailing his fingers tenderly down her cheek.

'Daddy.' Mia pronounced proudly.

'Been busy have you?' Nan's voice was barely more than a whisper. The skin on her hands stretched tightly over her knuckles as she ladled stew into a bowl. Adding a heap of mashed potato, she put it silently on the table.

Eddie glanced at his mother as he carefully eased a chair out from beneath the table and sat down, his eyes fixed on the bowl in front of him.

'I know where you've been,' Nan hissed, between clenched teeth.

Silently Eddie slid the bowl towards himself and began to eat.

'You're an animal.' Nan crossed the room to stand beside Eddie.

'Doggy!' Mia shouted, picking up on the familiar word. She kicked her legs against the frame of the highchair, brandishing her spoon in delight.

Eddie glanced at Mia and shot her a broad grin. 'Yes. Good girl.'

Nan poked a rough finger into Eddie's back. He winced, hunching his shoulders against her vehemence. 'You can't leave them, can you?' She punctuated each word with a prod. 'What if someone saw you? Why can't you be a normal man?'

'No one saw me.' Eddie spooned food into his mouth, his voice little more than a whisper.

'You'll have the police down on us.' Nan pushed roughly against Eddie's shoulders.

At the opposite side of the table Mia, watching silently, her eyes never leaving her father, slowly ate her cereal.

Nan hauled a chair out beside Mia and began to eat her own meal, her eyes narrowed to slits as she glared at Eddie.

'She was lost. She needed me.' A small droplet of the stew fell from Eddie's spoon. It landed on his face, balancing there, until it began its slow journey down the curve of his chin.

'She didn't need you.' Nan stopped eating, her spoon upright in her clenched fist. 'None of them need you. Get rid of her.'

Eddie stopped eating, wiping at the droplet of stew with the back of his hand. The moisture remained trapped in the hairs, glistening in the harsh glow from the overhead light.

'I don't know what you are.' Nan's jaws worked on a piece of gristle in the stew before she spat it viciously to the side of her bowl. 'I don't know what I did to deserve something like you.'

Eddie, head lowered, glanced at his mother from beneath his brows. Her eyes met his, glaring until his slid away.

'If I'd have known what a pathetic animal I had inside me I'd have ripped you out with a coat hanger.' She spooned food rapidly into her mouth, spitting out the words.

Eddie pushed his bowl across the table, his gaze fixed onto the wooden surface of the table.

'I could have had a proper son. One who wasn't a useless, filthy piece of shit like you. Disgusting animal.'

'Moooo!' Mia grinned, kicking her legs against her highchair. 'Oufff!' Oufff!' She banged her spoon against the plastic surface of her table, the empty cereal bowl clattered to the floor.

Eddie watched silently as it rolled, spinning, before finally coming to rest. A trail of milk-soaked cereal splattered across the tiles in its wake.

'More mess.' Nan's voice had a resigned note as she got to her feet, gathering a handful of kitchen roll she wiped the floor.

She hauled Mia out of her highchair before turning to address Eddie, her voice full of hatred. 'I imagine you'll be back with your bitch now you're fed.

As she left the room with Mia, Eddie released the breath he had been holding. Slowly he got to his feet, pushing the chair away with infinite care so as not to make any noise. He crossed the kitchen, pacing, raking a hand through his hair.

From upstairs came the sound of Nan moving across the wooden floorboards, her measured tread punctuated by the noise of Mia's scampering feet.

Eddie leant against the range, gazing through the window towards the ruined cottage, the heat from the metal warm against his back. Upstairs, Mia giggled, the noise loud in the silence of the kitchen. As he thought of the girl in the cellar, a small smile tilted the corners of his mouth. Eddie shoved himself away from the range, grabbing a knife he cut a hunk of bread, found some cheese in the fridge and wrapped the two solicitously in kitchen roll. He made a mug of tea, then listening for a moment to the noises from upstairs, he left the kitchen. He shut the front door silently behind him and padded across the yard to where he knew she was waiting for him.

* * * * *

Nan was in the kitchen when he returned. Eddie glanced in her direction, feeling her eyes on him. The rungs of the rocking chair creaked on the tiled floor as Nan moved it rhythmically.

He washed the mug, running hot water over it, rubbing at the surface.

'She can't stay. She's going to be trouble. Look what happened today.'

Eddie let the water cascade over his fingers, before gurgling down the sink. A chunk of carrot was stuck in the plug hole. He pushed at it, forcing the orange mush down the drain.

'Did you hear what I said?' Nan snapped. The rocking noise became faster, the rungs clattering forcefully against the tiles.

He turned, meeting her eyes. 'I'm going to take care of her.' He said, his voice emotionless. 'No one knows she's here. I want to keep her.'

Nan's fingers spread out slowly, gripping the arms of the rocking chair. The pace of her movement slowed, the creaking slackened, until finally it stopped.

'You have to get rid of her. What if she gets away again? She'll bring the police here. What then? What happens to Mia? To me?' She sighed, resting her head on the back of the chair, regarding him impassively.

Sullenly, Eddie pulled out a chair and sank into it slowly, putting his hands on the table at either side of him. His fingers curled into fists. He stared at them, his mouth clamped tightly shut.

'You're pathetic. A. Pathetic. Animal.' The rocking began again.

Eddie shook his head, his Adam's apple sliding painfully down his neck as he swallowed.

'I wish I'd drowned you when you were born.' Nan got to her feet. She crossed the room. 'If I'd have known what you were going to become, I would have.' Her fingers touched his hair. 'I'd have put you in a bucket, like an unwanted mongrel. Held you under the water.'

Eddie twisted his hands together, his fingers cold against his palms.

'Well...' Nan sighed, her hand sliding away from his hair. She turned, opening a drawer in the Welsh Dresser behind him. Eddie turned, watching as her fingers sifted leisurely through the contents, before she pulled out a rope dog lead. He let his hands drop onto his lap as Nan curled the dog lead around her hand, his eyes never leaving her as she crossed the room. 'If you won't get rid of her, I will.'

Chapter Twelve

'I brought you something.' Eddie pushed the cellar door shut behind him. The swollen, damp wood catching on the vast slab beneath it, groaned in protest.

She was staring at a point somewhere just over his left shoulder, her gaze filled with a mixture of resentment and terror. He sighed. He'd been gone too long. The narrow roads had been busy with tourists. 'I told you not to make trouble.' He shook his head, releasing a long breath.

He shook his head regretfully. 'I hope…' He eased his way into the half light of the cellar. Shadows cast by the foliage behind the small window high in the wall danced across the room. 'I hope you'll like it.' Eddie eased a small, red box out of his jeans pocket. 'I chose it for you.' With trembling fingers, he lifted the lid. A delicate silver bracelet, strands twisted together to form a thin rope, glistening in the light. Moving closer, he unhooked the bracelet from its anchor in the box and held it up. He let the strands of silver twist in his fingers as he held it gently, his fingers clumsy, too big to hold such a delicate object. 'I picked it especially for you. In Exeter.'

There had been so many bracelets to choose from, but he had known exactly which one he had wanted. The shop assistant had been different from the last time. Just in case though, he'd made a show of looking at other bracelets, all the time his fingers itching to pick up the one he knew he'd select.

'That's beautiful. I'd love that.' The girl in the shop had smiled at his choice, as she flicked back a strand of thick blonde hair, her eyes filled with seduction. Her raw sexuality had repulsed him. He'd left the shop knowing she'd have her regret filled eyes on him.

The girl in the cellar was the only one who would wear the bracelet. Gently, he sat on the bed beside her. 'Shall I put it on for you?'

Her wrist lay on the bed, palm upwards, her delicate fingers curled inwards. The nails were short, small half-moons showing above her fingertips.

He met her eyes. She stared back at him.

Gently he lifted her hand and slid the bracelet around her wrist, fastening the clasp with awkward fingers. 'Do you like it?' He eased her hand towards the window allowing the light to reflect onto the silver strands. Multicoloured stars danced on the wall beside her. Eddie moved her wrist, watching them.

He let her wrist drop onto his lap. In the dim light her skin had a blue tinge, small circles of a darker shade spanning its circumference. 'I hope you do.' Eddie eased himself off the bed and crouched beside her, running his fingers gently over her hair. She'd been alive when he had taken her a mug of tea and some toast that morning. She had pleaded with him to let her go, her begging turning to fury when he had told her he couldn't do that. He'd hoped Nan would have forgotten her threat and that the girl would remain in the cellar.

She was half turned towards him. Her eyes, when he looked into them, had spiders of red streaking across them. The sweater she had been wearing when he had first found her lay abandoned on the chair beside the bed. Eddie picked it up and wiped gently at the bubble of blood coloured foam at the side of her mouth.

Tenderly he stroked the icy planes of her face, letting his fingers move from the smooth skin of her cheeks, down her jaw line to the red wheal that circled her neck. 'I wanted to keep her,' his voice was little more than a whisper. 'Nan… Why did you take her away from me?' He rested his head against her chest, body juddering as he sobbed.

The sun had been at its zenith before he moved. The girl's body was cold. Slowly Eddie got to his feet, easing her stiff corpse away from him. She was ugly now, with mottled skin and a glazed expression.

One of her blankets was at the bottom of the bed, rumpled from her feet, churning in desperation to get away from Nan. Eddie eased it out from beneath her and tossed it over her still form, blocking out the spangles that danced on the wall.

A single thick strand of her auburn hair poked out from beneath the fabric. With gentle fingers he tucked it out of sight.

The girl's rucksack was still propped in the corridor outside, beside the door to the room. He'd left it there when he had carried her into the cellar. Eddie lifted it back into the room and tossed it onto the bed beside her. Pushing her stiff legs out of the way, he unclipped the top of the rucksack and began to unpack it.

There were clothes, neatly folded. A pair of jeans, two sweaters, tee-shirts, socks rolled inside one another, a pair of pyjamas, pink, decorated with unicorns. He eased open one of the drawers, lifting out a pale coloured shirt, its fabric, flimsy, light beneath his fingers. Remembering, Eddie brought the shirt to his face, burying his head in the fabric. He inhaled damp, sour fabric. Nothing of Glanna remained.

He sighed, pushing the shirt back into the drawer and covering it with the clothes from the rucksack.

He rummaged into the depths of the dead girl's bag. At the bottom was a flowered washbag. The zip stuck momentarily as he pushed it open. Inside was lip gloss, a brightly coloured stick of mascara, a tube of face cream. Eddie ran his fingers over the girl's toiletries before pulling up the zip and pushing it into the drawer. He returned his attention to the rucksack. Beneath everything was a small leather bag, his sweating fingers stained it as he tipped the contents onto the blanket. There was a purse, inside which he found her student card, its photograph showing the girl grinning at the camera, her eyes filled with laughter.

Gently, Eddie ran his thumb over the image, remembering. When he looked again there was a small notebook, filled with neat handwriting, a map of her journey, and a pair of sunglasses. He tucked the contents of her bag beneath his shirt and with a last look of regret at the shape beneath the blanket let himself out of the room and hurried up the steps.

Raising his face to the sunshine, he walked across the yard, humming softly to himself. The tractor shed smelt of hay and engine oil. Dust danced in the shafts of light that found their way in through gaps in the door. Still humming, Eddie eased himself past the tractor to the workbench at the back of the building. He crouched, feeling around beneath the workbench until his fingers touched cool metal. He grasped the toolbox and hauled it out into the light.

He lifted out the top section and laid it on the bench gently fingering the contents, a paper driving licence, hair slides, necklaces, purses, smiling at the memories they evoked he placed Ayla's possessions inside.

'There you are.' Nan's voice startled him. Her lip curled in distaste. 'Put that away, you need to start the digger.'

* * * * *

'Are you going to help me today, Mia?' Eddie took Mia's small hand in his as they walked across the yard.

She nodded solemnly; her face full of the importance of the job she had been given.

'We've got to dig a hole. With the machine.'

'Digger!' Mia let go of her father's hand and skipped ahead of him, her dark curls bouncing.

She reached the vast machine. As Eddie watched she disappeared. 'Mia?' The farmyard was full of places a small child could get hurt. He didn't like her to be out of sight for long.

'Digger. Digger.' Mia's stepped out of the machine bucket where she had been hiding. He released a breath of tension, drawing air that had the tang of the sea overlaid with newly mown hay into his lungs.

'Can you get in the cab?' Eddie ran across the yard, lifting and then flinging Mia over his shoulder. She squealed in delight, kicking her legs as he held her securely. In one easy movement, he swung her around so the small child was standing on one of the vast caterpillar treads. 'Climb up there.' Eddie reached upwards and opened the machine door, watching solicitously as Mia clambered up the rungs and into the cab. 'Squish over,' he said, pulling himself into the seat. With Mia balanced on his knee, Eddie started the machine, its powerful engine roaring into life.

'Hold tight,' Eddie slid an arm around Mia to support her as the vast digger began to move, its treads rattling over the yard. Mia, staring out of the window, wide eyed with delight.

He steered the machine out of the yard, inching it carefully through a narrow gateway into the orchard behind the stone farmyard buildings.

'Me. Me do it.' Mia put a warm, sticky hand over his.

'You are a good driver.' Eddie ruffled Mia's hair. 'Show me how you can count now.' He turned off the engine and stepped onto the tread, holding Mia to his chest as he jumped down. 'Can you count to ten?' He let Mia drop gently to the grassy surface.

'Onetwothreefourfivesixseveneightnineten,' Mia announced proudly, her eyes fixed on her father's face.

'Do it with me now. Slowly.' Eddie lifted a rock from the ground and laid it down in front of the digger, holding Mia's hand. 'Big steps.'

'One,' Mia leapt beside her father, keeping pace with his strides. 'Two.'

As they reached 'ten' Eddie rolled another rock into place.

'Now four,' he positioned the two of them in front of the digger, stepping out four strides, marking out the distance with two more rocks.

'Do you want to dig?' Eddie lifted Mia back into the cab and turned on the engine, positioning her onto his knee once again. 'You're good at this.' He eased her small hand backwards and forwards over the controls.

Below them, the machine's bucket dug into the red earth, its vast claw ripping through the soil, uprooting plants and rocks. Mia, perched on Eddie's knee, watched, the tip of her tongue poking through her teeth in concentration as the bucket swung backwards and forwards depositing the earth to one side of the hole.

'There. Finished.' Eddie, standing in the cab to look at their handiwork, nodded in satisfaction. 'You did a great job Mia. Do you want to drive it again later?'

'Digger!' Mia jumped up and down in the cab in her eagerness to continue their adventure.

He turned off the machine and helped Mia down.

Crouching so his eyes were on the same level as hers Eddie tilted Mia's chin towards him. 'I've got other jobs to do now. I'm going to take you back to Nan.'

Mia's face fell, her bottom lip protruding in a look of abject misery. 'Come on,' Eddie tugged at one of her curls, something which normally brought squeals of laugher from Mia. Pulling herself out of his grip, Mia ran across the yard towards the house, short legs moving easily across the rough ground. Eddie got to his feet, watching her go. She slipped inside the open kitchen door and then turned, gazing back at him.

'Won't be long. Nan needs you to help her feed the chickens.'

Pacified Mia nodded, watching as he walked across the yard.

The bundle was cumbersome, stiff and unwieldy. The wheelbarrow swayed, dangerously close to tipping over, as he steered it across the yard from the ruined cottage.

It seemed to have taken forever to haul it from the cellar, up the slippery stone steps, out of the semi-darkness, and into the daylight. Eddie hunched his shoulders to ease out the tension. It had been even harder to grapple the stiff bundle off the bed and into the wheelbarrow. He'd had three goes, the wheelbarrow having tumbled sideways, depositing its load with a thud once more onto the cellar floor.

Finally, his shirt damp with sweat, he succeeded in bringing it out into the bright sunlight and wheeling it across the yard, to the hard baked ground in the orchard where at the edge of the hole, he let it roll sideways. The bundle slid into the chasm, bumping against the edge, before coming to rest in an untidy heap far below. A tangle of red hair cascaded from the folds of the blanket.

Hastily he scraped the earth back over the hole with the machine, before driving it back into the yard.

'Take her, I'm tired.' Nan's eyes flickered impassively over the churned earth before she released Mia's hand.

'Daddy.' Mia stepped uncertainly towards him as Nan turned and walked towards the house.

'You couldn't help with that job; it was too dangerous.'

Mia took a long juddering breath, gulping back tears. 'Digger.'

'Come and help me now.' He took her hand and led her back to the orchard. 'We've got to stamp down the soil.'

'Show me how high you can go.' Eddie watched grinning with delight as Mia jumped up and down on the rectangle of raw earth.

Chapter Thirteen

'**P**lease ask. Please.' Katia made a whimpering noise like a lost puppy.

Grace rolled her eyes. 'Oh seriously, Katia. Rob's not here.' Grace looked over Katia's shoulder towards the bar, ignoring her friend's imploring gestures and pleading expression. The solitary barman was occupied by changing an empty whiskey bottle, sliding it from the optic above the bar and inserting a replacement. There was a self-conscious air to his movements, as if he could feel their eyes on him. 'You go.'

'He said he was going to be working here.' Katia gulped at her cider. 'Last time I saw him, a few weeks after the exams finished.' She sat back against the wooden seat, folding her arms with a resigned air. 'Perhaps he'll be here in a minute.'

Grace shook her head. 'Exams finished six weeks ago. We've been here for two hours already. Rob's not coming. Go and ask the barman when he will be working. Maybe he doesn't work her anymore.'

She took a swig of her cider. 'We'll be pissed if we don't do something.' Grace rotated her wrist, watching as the cloudy liquid swirled around the glass. The local brew tasted of nothing but slightly sweet apples, as if the maker had done nothing but pick the fruit, throw them into a bucket and trample on them to release the juice, as the advertising images portrayed. Its gentle taste was deceptive; the cider had a deadly kick to it that often caught the tourists out.

'I'm pissed now. You ask him, please.' Katia replied, lifting her glass to the light, contemplating it ruefully. In the time they had been in the pub the liquid they'd consumed seemed to have gone down at an alarming rate.

The pub door opened, spilling a group of lads into the dark interior. For a moment a shaft of bright August sunlight lit the slate floor and the battered wood bar stools. There was a blast of noise from outside, before it swung shut, enclosing them once more in the smoke and beer-tinged atmosphere. The lads glanced in the direction of the girls, giving them appreciative looks, which were met with cold stares.

'Emmetts,' hissed Katia, using the derogatory term the locals used to describe the tourists who descended on the county every year. Despite bringing essential trade to the area, and even being the lifeblood of Katia's parent's business, the outsiders were still despised for the noise and chaos they brought with them, clogging up the roads and beaches during the summer months.

The girls watched coolly as the group was served, the lads pint glasses of the heady cider to the pool table that occupied one end of the pub.

'Please. I daren't.' Katia put a cool hand on Grace's bare forearm.

'Alright.' Grace drained the last of her cider. 'We'll go if he's not working.'

Katia nodded, her focus somewhere slightly off Grace's left shoulder. Her eyes were glassy, the cider clearly having its effect.

Grace walked with great care to the bar. 'Excuse me,' She leant against it, trying and failing to raise one foot onto the brass rail that skirted the bottom.

'Yes love?'

'Rob Dunmore? Is he working today?'

'He's up country with his girlfriend.' The barman's voice was thick with the Cornish burr.

'Oh,' Grace winced. Her heart sank. A girlfriend. The whole trip from Truro had been a waste of time. They'd caught the train down to Penzance and come to the pub especially so Katia would have the chance to see him. She'd be devastated when Grace broke the news. She glanced across the room, seeing from Katia's stricken expression that she had heard the whole exchange.

'Let's go,' Katia came across the pub, her gait measured.

'Shall I tell him who was asking?' The barman grinned.

'No!' Katia cannoned into a bar stool as she headed for the door.

'We need coffee.' Grace slipped her arm into Katia's to steady her as the pub doors swung shut behind them.

'Definitely,' Katia squinted in the brightness of the sunlight after the dimness of the pub.

'We can get some at the café at Morrab Garden's,' Grace steered Katia out of the pub yard, up the short stretch of hill towards the edge of the town.

'A fucking girlfriend.' Katia's legs tangled and she stumbled.

'Prick,' Grace hauled Katia to her feet. 'I thought…'

'He must have been seeing her when we met him and Paul in Discord.'

Grace was silent, the memory of that night sitting uncomfortably on her shoulders.

'Good job I didn't fancy him that much.' Katia, sighed, shaking her head, regretfully. 'I wonder if Damien Cooper will have got a place at uni? He's very good looking.'

'Yep,' Grace shook her head, marvelling at her friend's ability to switch from one all-encompassing passion to another while barely seeming to pause for breath.

'I love it in here.' Katia buried her face in the depths of a fragrant plant as the girls strolled along one of the paths that criss-crossed the sub-tropical paradise on the edge of the town. Away from the bustle of tourists and locals that thronged the streets, it was silent in the gardens, as if the beauty of the plants hushed everyone's chatter.

'It is beautiful.' Grace's voice automatically descended to a whisper, their footsteps soundless on paths bathed in the dappled light from the ferns and palm trees.

The silliness of the last few hours seemed dampened by the reverence of the beauty of the park.

The small café in one of the old buildings that was their destination was thronged with locals and tourists. Katia queued for coffee while Grace secured a place for them to sit on one of the low walls surrounding the patio which was crowded with occupied tables.

'I'm sorry, I've wasted your day.' Katia sat on the wall beside Grace and handed her a mug of coffee.

'You haven't.' Grace smiled. While Katia hadn't got to see to Rob, the day had been filled with fun. The train from Truro had been packed with holiday makers, suitcases crammed into the carriageway, making it virtually impossible to move once they'd found seats. Penzance, as always had been beautiful, tourists and locals cramming the narrow streets, giving it a heady, fun-filled atmosphere.

'If we get the train back at five, we can get a lift home with my dad.'

'Oh, good plan, we can hang around here until it's time for the train,' Grace agreed. A lift would mean avoiding the long walk from one end of Truro to the other.

Coffee finished, they wandered through the park, emerging from the shadows of the pathways into one of the wide grassy areas where they found a bench to sit on close to the children's play area.

'I'm sorry Rob's got a girlfriend,' Grace ventured.

'Yeah,' Katia poked at the grass beneath their feet with the heel of her shoe. 'He's still going to uni though so perhaps our paths will cross there…'

'Imagine,' Grace grinned, 'We'll be off to Exeter soon, university, the next step to being proper adults, with degrees and jobs.'

'And boyfriends and parties.' Katia squeezed Grace's arm, her voice filled with excitement.

'Yes, but lots of work. I want to get a good degree.' Grace said, adding shyly, 'And Paul will be there.'

'And I'll be studying Law…' Katia said the word as if it were a foreign language, she hadn't quite got the grasp of. 'Sounds so grown up. Imagine… Horses are going to be my hobby. Not my job. I'm going to be a solicitor…'

Lost in their thoughts the girls watched a middle-aged woman and a little girl make their way to a bench across the other side of the grassy expanse.

'What a cutie,' Katia grinned, watching the child intently. 'I can't wait to have kids.' She found any excuse to talk about her love of children. 'A big family…teaching them to ride. Just need to find the right man!'

'It's probably not as much fun in a big family as we think it is.' Grace watched as the little girl ran across the grass, chasing after a butterfly that flitted just out of her reach. 'Karen Trevlyn, she's got four sisters, and she hates them all.'

'Well, I think it would be lovely.'

Grace leant against the back of the wooden bench, raising her face to the sunshine, watching the little girl and the woman she was with.

'She's very pretty.' Katia mused.

'Mmmm,' the warm sunshine and the two pints of cider were making Grace sleepy. Across the other side of the grass the woman had sat down on one of the benches. As Grace watched, she pulled a band from grey streaked hair and shook it free. She smoothed the wiry strands with a hand before she pushed it back behind her ears, her eyes never leaving the little girl. 'Don't go too far, Mia.' She warned, earning herself a look of mischief from the little girl.

In the centre of the grass stood the ancient bandstand, where at weekends the local brass band played to entertain the tourists. 'Mia! Nan will get cross.' The woman warned again as the little girl made her way up the steps to the deserted bandstand and began to weave her way around the carved wooden poles that supported the roof. As she reached each pole Mia leant out, grinning at Nan, dimples darkening beneath the curve of her cheeks.

'I mean it,' Nan's tone changed, the earlier hint of amusement replaced by irritation. 'You know what happens to wilful little girls.'

'Ohh, she's in trouble now.' Katia whispered, smiling as Mia waved shyly at her.

As they watched Nan got to her feet, smoothing down the cotton sundress she wore. Her sandals, Grace noticed, were flat, old fashioned, with thick leather straps across her feet.

Mia walked slowly down the steps, her eyes fixed on Grace and Katia, dancing with mischief. She dropped to her knees, picking daisy heads, ferociously intent on her task. As Nan sat back down Mia scrambled to her feet and darted towards the two girls, her short legs pumping beneath her flowered dress.

In a flash Nan covered the distance and seized Mia by her wrist, bringing her flight to a sudden end.

'Sorry,' she smiled tightly in the direction of Grace and Katia.

'She wasn't bothering us,' Katia smiled regretfully at Mia. 'We don't mind if she chats to us.'

Without replying Nan hauled Mia back to the bench.

'Cow.' Hissed Katia. 'The kid just wanted to talk to us.'

Mia obediently settled herself at Nan's feet.

'She's a right bitch,' Katia whispered, turning to flash a smile in the direction of the handsome man who crossed the grass in front of them.

'Daddy!' Mia wretched her wrist out of Nan's grip and flung herself at her father.

'Where've you been till now, Eddie?' Nan snapped curtly.

'Sorry,' his voice was contrite as he lowered himself onto the bench beside her.

Grace, curious at the family tableau playing out in the park watched the three. The man, seeing her eyes on them, stared openly back at her. Something about the naked challenge of his gaze made her drop her eyes hastily to the ground. When she glanced up a moment later, he was still looking at her.

'Katia. Can we go?' Something about him made her skin crawl.

'Sure,' Katia tore her eyes reluctantly from Mia.

As if aware of the effect his presence was having on Grace, Eddie smiled in her direction, running the tip of his tongue across his top lip.

'What's the rush?' Katia jogged to keep up with Grace.

'That man.' Grace couldn't frame the words to explain to Katia. 'He gave me the creeps. Pervert.'

'What's wrong with him? He looked nice. Maybe he fancied you.'

'Ughhh,' Grace shuddered. Katia obviously hadn't noticed the way he had leered at her. Grace was glad when the two of them left the park and were back amongst the crowds on Market Jew Street.

'We'd better head to the station,' Katia glanced at the clock, set high above the columns of the Market House building at the top of the street. 'It's nearly time, anyway.'

'We've still got time to go into the King's Head, we could get another pint.' It felt good to be talking about normal things.

'Ha. Ha.' Katia dug her elbow into Grace's side.

They reached the end of Albert Street and stood, waiting to cross the busy road to the train station. As the cars filtered past onto the traffic island, some instinct made Grace turn to look at the line of vehicles. Driving a pick-up was the man from the park, his eyes fixed on Grace. Transfixed she stared back, watching as the vehicle inched past them onto the island and was gone.

'Come on. There's a gap in the traffic we can get across if we dash.' Katia tugged at Grace's arm. 'What's the matter?'

'That man…'

Chapter Fourteen

'That man was seriously strange.' Grace leant her head against the carriage window, watching the landscape slide by as the train gathered speed after leaving the outskirts of Penzance.

'I told you. He fancied you,' Katia mused, her attention focused on the discarded newspaper she'd picked up from the seat opposite.

'It didn't feel like that,' Grace shuddered. 'He felt really creepy.'

'His little girl was really sweet.'

'Do you think he was like the man in the pick-up that went past us when we walked home that night…?'

Katia folded the newspaper, straightening out the horoscopes page as she considered Grace's question. 'Don't be silly we couldn't even see the driver in the dark.'

'Same sort of pick-up.'

'That battered old thing that just passed us?' Katia stretched out her legs, resting her heels on the seat opposite. 'That couldn't make it to Truro!'

Grace sighed. 'I guess so. But…'

'Oh Grace, stop it. What difference does it make? So, the man gave you the creeps. Our chemistry teacher did the same to me.'

'Ughh, yeah you're right,' Grace shuddered, picturing the small, balding man who had the reputation of positioning himself in the classroom so he could peer surreptitiously down the girl's blouses.

'Some blokes are just jerks.'

Grace nodded. 'True.'

Katia, under the ferocious glare of an elderly woman who sat on the opposite side of the carriageway, slid her feet off the seat and focused intently on the newspaper.

Grace closed her eyes, the effects of the cider replaced by the beginning of a headache, a tight band seemed to have settled around her forehead.

Katia was right, there were creeps everywhere, men who just saw women as sex objects. Boys at school who, when they spoke to you, focused their eyeline on your breasts. Grotty, spotty faced jerks who liked nothing more than standing in groups at the bottom of the steps at school, giggling together as they looked upwards to try to catch a glimpse of the underwear of some unsuspecting female. That attention had been almost good humoured, nothing like the intense focus of the man in the park. Whatever Katia said, Grace was sure it was the man who had passed them when they had walked home in the fog. The vehicle had been the same, she was sure, as had the shape of his body, broad shoulders, the same neat head.

'We should report him to the police,' Grace said as the girls left the station building and began to walk to the building where Katia's father worked.

'What on earth for?' There was an exasperated note in Katia's voice.

'I don't know…' Grace mumbled as she tried and failed to frame the myriad of thoughts that bounced in her imagination. What had the man done that night? Nothing. And yet he had felt frightening. What if one of them had been alone? Would he have been more of a threat?

'Please Mr Policeman, months ago we climbed out of our bedroom windows to go to a nightclub. We were underage and a man stared at us.' Katia mocked gently.

'Yes. Okay. I get it.' Grace's words were almost drowned out by the bells of the Cathedral in the city, chiming out the hour.

'Here's my dad,' Katia said as the familiar silver estate car came into view. 'Grace. Please stop going on about that man.'

Thirty minutes later, Katia's father pulled his car into the kerb beside Grace's home.

Katia and her father had spent the journey across the city discussing a horse show she was taking her pony, Blackbird to. Grace had been glad to be left out of their conversation. It gave her time to think. Time to mull over all that had happened. The more she thought about it, the more uncomfortable she felt about the man in the park and the way he had leered at her.

As Grace got out of the car Katia wound down the passenger side window. 'See you tomorrow.'

'Okay.'

Grace walked up the driveway to her home. The house was deserted, no cars were parked outside. Behind her, the noise of traffic was muted by the tall trees and thick bushes that surrounded the garden. The only sound was that of Grace's footsteps crunching on the gravel. She glanced behind herself, feeling as if eyes were watching her from every corner. It was broad daylight, and yet here she was, acting like a skittery deer. Fighting the instinct to run, annoyed at her reaction to the memory of the man in the pick-up, Grace forced herself to walk to the front door. She fumbled for her key, shoving it forcibly into the lock, turning it and scrambling into the house.

'Stop it,' she whispered, leaning against the door, her heart pounding.

The house felt oppressively silent, vulnerable. There were so many places someone could hide. Flicking on the radio, Grace made tea, glad of the background chatter. Usually, she enjoyed having the house to herself, the peace of being alone, but now she just felt scared, aware of how little stood between her and danger. Taking her tea, Grace curled in a corner of the sofa, facing the driveway, watching for her parents to return.

The way the man had looked at her had been different from the boys at school and that of the disgusting chemistry teacher. Those were looks of interest, appreciation maybe. The man in the park, had been possessive, intrusive, full of a threat she dare not identify. What if it had been him the night she and Katia had been walking home? But what if it had? He hadn't done anything, other than look at them. If there had been a report of someone being attacked in the area she would have wondered if it had been him. But there was nothing. Whoever that man had been, he hadn't done anything to them. He had, as Katia suggested, probably just been lost, perhaps looking for someone... Her mind was working overtime. Yet still, something about him made her skin crawl. Maybe he had been waiting for an opportunity.

Grace squeezed her eyes shut to block out the vision her thoughts created. She should tell someone about the man. Not her parents. They were jittery enough about her leaving home to go to university. The Police. Would they laugh at her? Accuse her of making wild, unfounded allegations? Be angry at her for wasting their time? Whatever the reaction, they were the right ones to tell. At least then they would be aware of the man.

* * * * *

She spent a sleepless night mulling over what to do. Telling the police would mean going against Katia's wishes and yet there had been something sinister about the man. The police needed to know, so they could keep an eye out for him. Katia didn't have to know. Grace could tell the police her feelings, her impression of the strange man. Then she would have done the right thing. Finally, her decision made, Grace curled into a ball and gave way to the leaden exhaustion she had been fighting all night.

'Take a seat please. I'll get someone to take a statement from you in a moment.'

Grace instantly regretted coming into the police station. Just going up the steps into the building had made her feel guilty. It had been bad enough lying to Katia about where she was going, but now Grace really wished she hadn't come.

The reception area had been quiet when she had arrived. She had slipped quietly in off the street, hoping no one would see where she was going. Grace had felt as if she were going into the headmaster's office, filled with the same sense of dread and fear of being found out.

She'd told Katia she was going to the library. The very mention of books had been enough to put Katia off wanting to come.

'Can I help you?' The female officer behind the desk had asked, sliding back the glass window to smile at Grace.

'I just want to report something.' Grace had felt her resolve falter as she spoke. The whole idea of telling the police seemed ridiculous. What on earth could they do?

'What is it?' Her tone was gentle, her eyes moving slowly over Grace.

Grace shook her head, meeting the woman's eyes. She was barely older than Grace, yet her smart uniform and neatly arranged hair gave her an air of authority. 'It's stupid.' She murmured. 'I shouldn't have come.'

'If it bothered you enough to walk in here, you had a good enough reason to come.'

'There's this man, I've seen him a few times. Acting oddly…' Colour flooded Grace's cheeks.

'Okay, you definitely should have come in. I'm manning reception for my shift, so I'm going to get another officer to talk to you. Please can you take a seat.'

Grace made her way to the uncomfortable looking wooden benches that lined the waiting area and sank down, her legs trembling.

The glass window slid back, leaving Grace alone. Perhaps she should just leave. Run out now, before the officer found someone to talk to her. The whole idea had been ridiculous.

As Grace slid to the edge of the bench the outside door banged open and a dishevelled woman hurried in. She glanced in Grace's direction, drawing a hasty hand over the trail of blood that trickled down her jaw beneath her swollen lip. Grace smiled in sympathy, wincing involuntarily at the livid bruise blooming on one cheek.

'I need to talk to someone.' She leant on the desk, her voice breathless, as if she had been running. 'About my husband.'

Grace watched; her horror tinged with fascination. She was little older than Grace, yet her cheap looking dress and high shoes gave the impression of someone much older.

'Sarah,' The policewoman smiled gently in recognition, sliding the glass panel to one side. 'How can I help?'

Sarah lifted her hands to her face, indicating the bruises.

'Did Mark do that?'

'Well, I didn't do it to myself.'

'Let me take some details, and then I'll get someone to have a chat with you.'

The words were barely out of her mouth when the station door swung open again.

'What the fuck are you doing, Sarah?' The man, Mark, Grace assumed, seemed barely able to control himself, his face puce with temper, as he spat the words. He was a lot older than Sarah, balding, with a face like an angry Bulldog.

Grace felt herself shrink involuntarily into the corner of the seat.

Mark crossed the waiting area, extending a muscled tattoo covered arm and grabbing Sarah by the wrist. 'Sorry she's bothered you. She's not quite right.' He tapped his temple.

'I think we need to chat to Sarah ourselves.' The policewoman's voice was filled with steel.

'The fuck you do.' Spittle sprayed from his mouth as he manoeuvred Sarah across the room.

The office door banged open, the policewoman crossed the room in two strides, facing the man. 'Mark Gascoyne, I'm arresting you…'

Grace watched fascinated. The top of the policewoman's head barely reached the level of his chest and yet her control of the situation, was evident.

'I'll talk to you when you come home.' He dropped Sarah's arm as if it were burning hot, before allowing the policewoman to lead him away.

'Grace Tallis?' As she had been engrossed in the scene Grace hadn't noticed a side door opening. A smartly dressed middle-aged man stood in the doorway. If he had witnessed the scene, he made no comment. 'DI Steve Cooper.' He shook her hand briefly, his fingers light against hers.

Grace followed him down a long, dimly lit corridor into a room, bare, except for a table and four chairs.

'What can I do for you?' Steve Cooper indicated that Grace should sit down.

Steve lowered himself into the chair opposite, looking at her expectantly.

'There's this man…' Grace fought the urge to put her fingers to her burning cheeks, horribly aware of the red flush that must be colouring them.

'Man…?' There was an impatient note in Cooper's voice.

'Yes, he…' This was stupid. Grace wished she had never come. Why hadn't she listened to Katia and forgotten all about the man and his leering expression. 'He was really staring at me in the park and a while ago… I'm sure he drove past me and my friend late one night like he was going to…'

'Looking at me… Drove past…' Cooper wrote laboriously on a notepad, the sarcasm clear in his voice.

When she was silent, Cooper laid down his pen. 'Look love, you're an attractive girl, you're going to have to get used to men looking at you.'

Anger bubbled to the surface. 'I'm trying to tell you, there's something not right about this man. I was worried he was going to attack …kidnap us.'

Cooper snorted in amusement, a noise he quickly turned into a cough.

'This has been a waste of time,' Grace shoved the chair back and got to her feet. Hot tears of frustration prickled at the back of her eyes.

'Waste of mine,' Cooper muttered, levering himself to his feet and crumpling up the paper he'd written on.

Grace turned to leave. It had been crazy to come to the police with a half-baked notion of someone scaring them. She had expected him to pay attention to her concerns, to be interested in what she had to say. His disinterest had thrown her. Whatever she had thought the police would say, it hadn't been this off-handedness.

'I came to you for help!' Grace snapped. 'And all you've done is laugh at me. I'm so sorry I bothered you. Ignorant twat.'

Chapter Fifteen

Bloody women. Always whining about one thing or another.
   'Boss?'
   'Gov, can I just…'
Steve ignored the clamour for attention from the detectives as he weaved his way rapidly through the crowded office. Papers on the notice board, crammed with information about the latest cases, fluttered in protest as he slammed his office door shut. He allowed himself a wry snort of amusement that it had, for once, actually closed properly.

Steve threw himself into his chair, spinning the leather seat to face the window. Throwing his head back he puffed out his cheeks, finally releasing the long breath of tension he'd been holding.

What had the girl called him? Ignorant twat? Nice. What a little bitch.

'Er, sorry, Gov. Can I…?' Steve's door swung open, filling the room with the hum of noise, from the telephones and office chatter. The odour of tension, unwashed bodies, the sickly smell of food, reheated in the microwave, drifted into Steve's office.

'Can it wait, Pete? I just need a minute.'

'Oh, sure.' Pete's eyes raked over his boss.

The door shut, Pete lifting it slightly on its sagging hinges, so it clicked into place.

As silence once more filled his office, Steve got to his feet and stood by the window, looking out over the city. A train moved slowly towards the station, about to spew out yet another load of tourists. More careless fools for him to take care of. For him to clean up their messes when they lost their possessions, got themselves into fights, or became light fingered in the shops after one too many pints of cider.

Once he'd had a vision of solving real crimes. Making a difference. The reality was this, nannying and hand slapping.

He stretched, trying to ease the painful kink in his back. He was normally immune to those stupid jibes. He received far worse on a daily basis, malicious, revolting threats from those who seemed to think they could take what they liked or hurt whoever they wanted. He shouldn't have let the girl get to him. She'd picked a day when he had really felt the futility of his role. Chasing the same criminals over and over again. He had really thought he'd gone into the police force to make a difference. When he wasn't watching the same thugs being got off their crimes by fat cat barristers it had become his job to listen to ridiculous complaints. Old women whose neighbour's hedges had grown over onto their side of the garden, families who had left their doors open when they went out and were then surprised when their possessions were missing when they returned. And girls, like the pretty redhead, with wild assumptions of major crime.

'Fuck's sake.' Steve ran a hand through his hair, feeling yet again the thinness of the strands towards the crown of his head. Something else for his wife, Mandy, to tease him about.

Taking a deep breath, he manoeuvred the door open. 'Any chance of some coffee, Pete?'

'Sure, Gov.' With a look of relief at being freed from the boring task of going through paperwork, Pete threw down the file he was looking at and made his way to the coffee machine.

Steve winced. Was coffee really the best idea? At this time of day, the brew would be rancid. Having been made first thing in the morning by one of the secretaries and festering all day on the burnt hotplate, it would have the look and taste of tar. Regardless, it would be a distraction. Leaving the door jammed into its familiar grove in the lino tiles, Steve lowered himself into his chair and hauled the heap of files towards himself.

'What did you want me for?' Steve rotated the mug, so the chipped edge didn't cut his lip. He took a sip of the bitter brew Pete put in front of him, rapidly masking his wince of resigned disgust with a look of feigned interest.

'Ohhhh,' Pete sighed, the chair creaking in protest as he slumped into it. He eased a finger around his collar in a gesture Steve had come to recognise as one of frustration. 'Couple came in earlier. Down from Scotland. Their daughter went missing from Exeter about six weeks ago. She was at uni there.' He shrugged. 'No evidence she's come here. They're just desperate to find her...'

'Right,' Steve pulled his notepad across the desk, searching beneath the scattered papers for a pen. 'So... they want us to do what, precisely?' Steve found a spare section of the pad which wasn't littered with notes written in his spidery hand and looked at Pete, expectantly.

Pete rolled his eyes. 'Fucked if I know. They are staying in one of the bed and breakfast places on Stanhope Road. They're coming back tomorrow. They want to talk to someone in charge.' Pete spat out the last few words.

'Cheers, mate,' Steve sighed, like he didn't have enough to do without fielding this kind of enquiry.

'Sorry boss.' Pete pulled a contrite face. 'They're very upset. The girl was studying in Exeter someone they spoke to mentioned her wanting to walk the coast path.'

'Who?'

'Another student, I guess. The girl is called Ayla McDonald. Her parents have just moved back to Scotland, somewhere called Nethy

Bridge. The girl is studying geology in Exeter. Apparently, she was due to visit them and didn't arrive. They've had no contact from her since.'

'They've not heard from her in those six weeks?

Pete nodded.

'Poor buggers.' Steve scribbled the girl's name on his pad, shaking the pen as the ink faded on the final 'd'. Kids. They were nothing but trouble and heartache. He'd dealt with enough missing persons enquiries to see the pain caused by someone disappearing from their life. Wives whose husbands had walked out, leaving them to deal with a mountain of dept; elderly people with dementia who wandered off; kids who'd not come home when they were supposed to. Most were found and returned home, but some never made it, corpses dragged out of the river, or cut down from trees. Some, those who didn't want to be found, vanished off the face of the earth, walking away from their lives and responsibilities to start again, far from home.

'Ayla,' Steve rechecked his pad, pressing hard on the final letter with his pen which had finally decided to cooperate. 'McDonald. Are there any signs at all that she actually did come to Truro? Has anyone checked with her lecturers in Exeter? Was she doing well? Was she sick of the course, rowed with her parents?'

'Her parents say she was happy, had made friends, was enjoying the course. But there is something else…' Pete levered himself to his feet, tucking his shirt tail into the back of his trousers. 'Ron!' he called across the room.

'More?' Steve tried and failed to keep the exasperation out of his voice. His team were brilliant. Far better than the bunch he'd worked with in Newcastle. At least these guys actually wanted to catch criminals, rather than trying to line their own pockets… but they were unruly, prone to going off on tangents, attracted by each new crime that came in rather than digging down and focusing on the ones that could be solved.

'Ron,' Steve nodded at the detective. 'Take a seat.'

In one fluid movement Ron hauled a chair from the side of the room and sat down, flicking his mop of hair out of his eyes.

'So…?' Steve faced Ron. He ought to take the young DS to task about his hair. Had the memo that the New Romantic hair styles had long gone out of fashion not reached the west country?

'Pete's been telling you about the girl from Exeter that's gone missing…'

'Uh huh,' Steve waited, the errant pen poised over his notepad.

'Well, I had a chat with a woman last week about her daughter.'

'Glanna Pendrick. From near Penzance. Nineteen. Went missing on her way back to university. She was reported missing in 1987, her mother's still chasing every police station from here to Exeter to see what's being done to find her.' Pete interjected.

'There's no evidence anything has happened to her,' Ron fumbled in his jacket pocket, unearthing a battered pack of cigarettes which he looked at mournfully. 'Got a light?'

Pete tossed him a box of matches. 'Just with this couple coming in to say their daughter was missing. I thought….' His words faded to nothing as he looked at Steve.

'Jesus,' Steve growled. 'Give me one of those.' He reached across and took one from the packet, looking ruefully at its battered shape. 'Two missing girls. Years apart. Now we've got another Yorkshire Ripper?'

Pete blew an expert smoke ring towards the ceiling.

'Apparently this Glanna girl was going to a party somewhere near Truro on her way back to university,' Ron stretched his legs out in front of himself, shifting his bulk to ease the pressure of on his waistband. 'She never turned up in Exeter.'

Pete grabbed his battered box of matches from the desk where Ron had tossed them and shoved them into the depths of his jacket pocket. 'Her family had reported her missing in Exeter and Penzance, but nothing's been heard of her. Poor woman is desperate. She's hounding the police to make sure we don't forget.'

Steve shook his head, stubbing out the cigarette, grinding the red ash to nothing. 'Come on lads, a nineteen-year-old student goes missing. There's no sign that anything happened to her. She'll turn up eventually, pregnant, living in some flat in London.'

'Tell me again. Why did the McDonald's come here?' Steve drew deeply on the cigarette, before remembering he'd told himself he would give up.

'One of Ayla's flatmates said she'd mentioned the coast path to her. She'd spoken about walking some of it.'

'Knowing she came here and following up on some off the cuff comment are very different things.' Stars danced in his peripheral vision. Steve closed his eyes as the nicotine hit his bloodstream.

'I just thought…' Ron stared intently at a dark, unidentifiable stain on the lino beneath his feet. He let his hair flop forwards to hide the red flush that had spread over his cheeks.

'Course you did.' Steve pushed his chair back. 'Out, the pair of you.'

He shook his head, watching as the two detectives made their way across the crowded office back to their desks. They meant well, he knew, but two girls who may or may not be missing meant nothing. There was nothing to suggest that either of them had come to any harm. There wasn't an endless budget to throw at every maybe that crossed his desk.

Walking back into the office a few hours later, after lunch, Steve made his way to the front of the room. The afternoon sun shone directly in through the windows, stupefying the detectives in the office. The hum of chatter was low, everyone focused on dealing with the mountain of paperwork their job demanded.

He felt calmer now, the frustration he'd felt at Ron and Pete now dissipated. Of course, it had been necessary for them to bring up the missing girls. It was their job to keep him informed of what was going on. His was to steer them in the right direction, to help them wade through the tidal wave of crime that swamped even this tiny far-flung backwater.

'Right lads,' Steve rapped on one of the desks to get their attention. 'And lady,' he grinned in deference towards Rachel, the sole female DS. She shot him a tight smile.

'There seems to be the opinion that we've got our own Yorkshire Ripper. Girls are going missing. Apparently.'

There was a general murmur of dissent. Pete drummed his fingers on his desk, while Ron, at the far end of the room, was engrossed in the form he was filling out. He lifted his head briefly, catching no one's eye.

'I appreciate how keen you all are.' Steve beamed one of his rare smiles around the room. 'But we can't follow up on scraps of evidence. The word of some kid's parents. There's no evidence the girl from…,' he tried and failed to recall the information Pete had given him.

'Exeter university,' Pete's voice was taut with barely disguised irritation.

'That this girl even came here.' Steve rested one leg on a chair back, leaning forwards to look at the expectant faces. 'What have we got to go on?'

He watched the shrugs and head shakes.

'Nothing.' Steve pushed himself upright and turned to the board behind him. 'These are our crimes.' He tapped the board, making the papers flutter. 'I can't waste time and money on vague ideas. We have to solve crimes that we have at least half a chance of getting somewhere with.' He stopped, watching the agreement settle into the faces. 'So, where are we with the White House Farm burglary? Did anyone chase up the missing trailer to see if it had turned up at any of the farm sales?'

Chapter Sixteen

'Pete, you look into this. Don't go wasting any time over it, though. Just make sure we've dotted all the 'I's' and crossed the 'T's.'

'I will boss,' Pete nodded in agreement, glad to be given rein to look into the cases of the missing girls. His eldest daughter had just turned eighteen, and he was sure his hair had turned grey overnight now she was stretching her wings. Steve was probably right, the two missing girls were just a drop in the ocean compared to the hundreds who went missing every year, but as a parent, he would hate to ignore something that might be important. As soon as he had time he'd go to Exeter and chat to Ayla's friends at university and see if he could find anyone who had been there at the same time as Glanna.

'Go on. Get out of here. Have you no homes to go to?' Steve Cooper flapped his hands as if shooing the detectives out of the office.

'Cheers Gov.' The recently arrived night shift watched regretfully as pens and papers were shoved into desk drawers and tension stiffened arms slid into jackets.

Rachel rummaged in her handbag, unearthing some lipstick from its depths, which she slicked around her full mouth, earning herself a whooping chorus of approval from the older men. 'Got a date, eh?' Ron asked.

'Maybe,' Rachel pulled on her suit jacket, easing her blonde ponytail out over the collar. With that she cocked one eyebrow in his direction and sashayed out of the office.

'Some lucky bugger,' commented another in the office, sighing as Rachel disappeared into the darkness around the corner of the building.

'Get out of it,' Pete chimed in, jostling him with a rough elbow, glad, as the new boy to be able to be part of the office banter.

'You coming to the pub, boss?' Ron asked, watching Steve walk back to his office.

'Not tonight. Going straight home.' Steve lied. He couldn't face the office gossip and noisy chatter.

Steve followed the line of detectives as they left the building, laughing and joking amongst themselves. The smell of cigarette smoke drifted back towards him. He found himself inhaling it involuntarily. Perhaps he should buy another pack. He'd already caved in once today. Another pack wouldn't do any harm. He'd cut down, make sure he didn't escalate to the twenty a day habit he'd had before he'd vowed to give up.

As his team disappeared from the station yard, their voices lingering in the air, Steve got into his car, sighing with relief at the silence as he slammed the door shut.

As he pulled out of the car park, at the end of the road the detectives were filing into the local pub. Their presence kept most of the trade, other than extremely respectable locals and unwitting tourists away. Steve steered his car in the opposite direction.

At the first junction, Rachel dashed across the road in front of him. She'd changed into high heels, her blonde ponytail swinging in time with her long stride. He slowed, watching her smooth down her skirt before she walked into the new Italian restaurant which had opened only recently. It's prices, apparently, were eye-wateringly expensive.

The traffic leaving the town was light and, as always, Steve relaxed, enjoying the easy commute home. The volume of traffic, no matter how much the locals complained was nothing compared to that around Newcastle. He'd spent what often felt like years of his life sitting in traffic queues on the A617. His current commute home was a doddle.

'Fuck it,' twenty minutes later Steve turned on the car indicator, pulling off the main road onto a narrow country lane. He'd meant to go home, but the thought of exchanging one noisy environment for another did not appeal to him.

Mandy would never think to wonder if he hadn't come straight home. She was used to life as the wife of a policeman, the long, uncertain hours. He tried and failed to ignore the sense of guilt. He should have taken the chance of an early finish to go home, help her with their boys and put them to bed. He just couldn't face the noise and chaos they created. No matter how much he loved them and Mandy, the thought of walking into the mess of toys and clothes, while the everyday drama of his work was still present in his mind, was something he could not face. He'd done it when the boys had been younger, when Neil had been a baby and Joel just a toddler. He'd tried to help Mandy, but she, slick with the routine of constantly looking after the boys, did the job easily. Why on earth she wanted another baby was beyond him.

Feeling guilty, he drove into the pub car park. The low-slung thatched building was brightly lit up and yet he knew it would still be relatively empty at this time. The pub was well off the tourist trail, and most of the locals would still be at home eating their dinner and relaxing after work. He'd have plenty of time to unwind in peace and quiet before he headed home.

He longed to go home as it had been before the kids been born. To the silence, to Mandy, still elegant in her office dress, cooking dinner. To sipping wine together by the firelight, before taking her hand and leading her upstairs. Those times had been replaced by two boisterous boys, their mother exhausted looking, clad in whatever clothes she'd dragged on.

Just one pint and then he'd go home. Hopefully, the boys would be in bed. With any luck, Mandy would tell him she'd decided against trying for just one more baby. Maybe, for once, they'd be able to spend a whole night asleep.

A few cars littered the area in front of the pub. Commuters, car sharing from jobs in Truro and Exeter often used it, leaving their cars during the day.

Steve found a spot and turned off the car, revelling in the quiet. At the far side of the car park, almost hidden in the shadows cast from the building, a woman crouched on her hands and knees beside the front wheel of a car.

Steve got out of his car and walked towards the woman. 'Are you okay?'

'Thanks. Yes. Someone's giving me a hand.' The auburn-haired young woman gave him a grateful smile. 'Bloody puncture,' she nodded her head in the direction of the front wheel. The tyre splayed out, flat.

'Oh, bad luck,' Steve hovered uncertainly, the thought of a pint foremost in his mind, tempting, and yet it seemed rude to leave the woman.

'My tyre wrench doesn't fit.' She got to her feet, smoothing down her dress. 'A man's helping. He's getting the wrench out of his car; he thinks it will fit.'

She waved the tyre wrench, pulling a face of mock despair.

'It looks like it should fit. Do you want me to have a go?' Steve held out his hand.

'Umm,' she hesitated, her voice uncertain, fingers gripping the wrench.

'Sorry, you're right.' Steve grinned, wryly. He'd spent the best part of the afternoon talking about weirdos and missing women, and here he was, putting her in an uncomfortable position. 'You shouldn't let strange men...'

'It's okay,' she handed him the brace. 'I've got two chivalrous gentlemen helping now.'

Steve bent beside the wheel, and as the wrench slid easily onto the first nut, he eased it slightly.

'Here he is,' the woman smiled in the direction of a man who was walking towards them, clutching a wrench.

'I've got…' he stopped, looking warily at Steve.

'This is the right wrench. You must have used the wrong end.' Steve undid the second nut.

'Oh.'

Steve felt the man's discomfiture as he shuffled his feet beside the car. 'Easy mistake,' he said, gently. There was nothing worse than trying to be a gallant hero to a damsel in distress, only to find your good intentions crushed by inadequacy. The poor bloke must have been cringing in embarrassment. Steve fought to keep himself from grinning in amusement as he eased the remaining nuts.

'Perhaps you'd get the jack under', Steve got to his feet, unwilling to dirty his suit grubbing around on the ground, no matter how much he wanted to help. The younger man was far more casually dressed. Good looking too. A few bits of dirt wouldn't make much difference to his jeans and sweatshirt.

'Sure.' The tall man lay on his back and eased the jack under the car.

'Thank you,' The young woman smiled at the tall man as he got to his feet.

'I'll do the nuts, shall I?' Steve enjoyed the feeling of supremacy over the younger man.

'Oh, yes please.'

Steve crouched, undoing the remaining nuts, painfully aware of the thinning spot in his hair which would be visible to both of them.

'I'm so glad you came along. Both of you.' She smiled as the wheel was replaced and the car lowered to the ground. Her words included the two of them, but her eyes were only for younger man.

'No problem,' Steve and the man said at the same time.

'Thank you so much.' The woman smiled as she got into her car.

'Good deed for the day,' Steve said wryly as the woman drove out of the car park, waving cheerily.

'Looks like it,' the man swung his tyre wrench softly against his thigh.

'She'd have been stuck without help.'

'Yes.'

'Good job you were here.'

'And you. I couldn't even get the tyre wrench to work.'

Steve grinned. 'Oh, you'd have managed, I'm sure.'

The man grunted in agreement.

'It must be tough for young women like that,' Steve's mind drifted back to the office. 'They're so vulnerable.'

'Yes. Easy prey.' The tall man nodded. He met Steve's eye and smiled, one corner of his mouth curving upwards.

'She was lucky you were there to help. Someone nice. Not dangerous.' Steve watched a line of cars pass the entrance to the pub car park. Somewhere out there the young woman was continuing with her journey, safely.

'She was wary enough to start with,' the tall man shuffled his feet, his eyes still locked onto Steve's.

'Wise. You never know.' Steve stuffed his hands into his pockets, longing for the comfort of the pub, and to lose himself in a pint of the cider he'd come to love.

The man shrugged. 'I'm sure she could tell I'm not a serial killer.' He laughed, a short burst of sound.

'Whatever one of those looks like.' Steve took a stride away. Behind them, the pub door opened, and a couple emerged. For a moment the car park was flooded with a shaft of light from the open door. The sound of chatter drifted over the parked cars.

'Well, thanks for helping.' The tall man turned and strode away across the car park, the wrench swinging as he walked.

Released from the conversation, Steve headed thankfully into the sanctuary of the pub.

'Old Bessie?' The barman had a pint pot under the cider tap before Steve could reply. He should change pubs. It didn't do to be too well known.

'Cheers. And give me a pack of Bensons.'

'Back on the fags eh?' The barman chortled, sliding a pack across the bar.

Steve grunted in agreement, watching through the pub window as a farm pick-up moved into the light cast from the pub. As the driver looked towards the building Steve raised his glass to the man whose act of chivalry he had thwarted.

Chapter Seventeen

1995

'A re you glad you joined the police?' Katia, sitting at her dressing table, met Grace's eyes in the mirror.

'Yes,' Grace sat on Katia's bed, leaning down to fasten the straps on the high heels she had chosen for the night. They belonged to Katia, slightly too small for Grace who had wider feet, but they were so pretty. Not something Grace would choose for herself. She knew later in the night, when the straps were cutting into her feet, she would regret the decision to borrow them. Grace was aware of the uncertainty in her voice, something Katia immediately picked up on.

'Sure?' She spun around on the low stool to face Grace. 'It's not too late to back out you know.' Katia raised her eyebrows, her eyes roving over Grace's face.

'Absolutely.' The two years of training had been tough. Harder than she had anticipated, hours of study combined with physically demanding training, learning self-defence and how to handle yourself whatever situation you found yourself in. There had been long hours of shadowing other officers, walking around city streets, feeling the hostility from some of the people she had encountered. All the training rushing forwards to culminate in this, her first real job.

The placement had coincided with Katia going to London on a short internship from her university course, shadowing a top criminal lawyer in the city. The two of them had decided to celebrate with a night out in their home city.

Grace looked around Katia's room, bookshelves, crammed with the silver cups she had won with her pony Blackbird, the pretty pink flowered wallpaper all seemed to belong to a life they'd outgrown. They had spent hours here, sprawled on the bed. Katia reading yet another of the pony books she loved while Grace had devoured ancient children's detective stories, *The Famous Five* and as she got older, the Sherlock Holmes books.

Katia's parents had promised to redecorate her room, but somehow, they never seemed to have gotten around to the task. Blackbird had been replaced with a bigger, more exciting horse, Tanny. He was now on loan to a riding school near the coast. Katia rode whenever she could.

Katia turned back to the mirror and rummaged in an overflowing makeup bag eventually unearthing a lipstick of the right shade.

'Are your parents okay about you joining the police now?'

Grace puffed out her cheeks, shrugging her shoulders. 'I don't think they ever will be.'

Her parent's disappointment had been the hardest to bear. The announcement that Grace hated her course and was going to apply to join the police had been met with a stony silence.

'Grace, what on earth are you talking about?' Her father had said finally.

'Darling, that's no career for a young woman. Please, stick with your course. You've only been on it a few weeks. Finish it, at least.' Her mother had been tight lipped with temper.

Grace had shaken her head. No matter how much it hurt them, and horrified everyone else, she'd made her mind up.

She'd hated the business degree. At the end of the first term, she'd known it was not for her. The modules were easy, accounting, typing, business law, French. And always the insidious assumption that, as a woman, you'd become someone's assistant. The university parties were great fun. Katia, when she wasn't chasing after Rob, was great at producing a steady stream of prospective boyfriends for both of them, but the course was pointless. And Grace hated it.

'But darling, why on earth the police?' Her mother's voice had held a note of hysteria, as if Grace had suggested she was going to join a cult.

'Because...' Grace had stumbled over her answer. How could she explain why? She wasn't even sure herself. She'd admired the young desk officer who had stood up to the threats of the violent man in the station, but that hadn't been the full reason for her decision. She wanted a place in the world where she could make a difference, where she'd be more than a cog in someone else's wheel.

'What about doing law like Katia? Or medicine?' There was a resigned desperation about her father's expression. 'What a waste of time, one year into your degree...you haven't given it chance. The money we've spent already.'

'Please. Daddy...' Grace rolled her eyes. 'I'm sorry I've wasted your money. I thought I'd get to like the course. But I hate it. I want to do something that's real. Worthwhile.'

'Leave her Richard,' Grace had watched her mother place a hand gently on his arm.

For a long moment he had glared at Grace before finally leaning back in his chair, raising his hands in a gesture of surrender. 'Grace,' he had said finally, his voice filled with the disappointed resignation she hated. 'Do what you like. It's your life.'

'I'm not sure they will ever be happy about it.' Grace got to her feet, if they didn't leave soon the whole evening would be wasted. 'Come on Katia.'

It was easier not to talk about it. Her parent's disapproval of her career weighted heavily on Grace. They'd attended her passing out parade, taken her out to lunch afterwards, made the right comments, but still, she had been painfully aware of the pained look her father tried and so often failed to hide.

People's fascination at her career was something Grace had become used too. Some wanted to know about the life, others seemed to have an inbred hatred of anything to do with law enforcement, while they undoubtedly would be the first to call the police if there was a problem.

An hour later, sitting in the bar of the small pub where they had arranged to meet the two men Katia had lined up for them, she was already regretting mentioning her new role. 'The police?' Keith chewed on the word as if it were a piece of gristle.

'Yes, I've completed my training and start a placement tomorrow in Penzance.'

Grace met his eyes across the table and saw the raw hostility in his eyes.

Beside him, Andrew the man who Katia had thought might be a date for her was staring fixedly at the table.

'Shall I order more drinks?' Katia's voice had risen an octave. Grace glanced at her friend. Two bright spots of colour stained her cheeks.

Grace shifted uncomfortably in her seat, what should have been a night out with two men Katia knew from the gym, two prospective dates, had turned into something alarmingly different. As soon as she had mentioned her job, the atmosphere had changed.

Keith lurched to his feet, his face drained of colour. 'My brother died last year in police custardy. They put him in a cell, he had epilepsy. He had a fit...No one helped him.'

Across the table Andrew looked from Katia to Grace, then to his stricken friend.

'I can't be around you.' Keith snapped, his hands balling into fists. 'I've got to go. I'll see you at work, Andrew.'

Andrew made a move to follow his friend, upending his glass, it skittered across the table, the dregs spilling onto the dark wood. 'I'll come with you.'

'That went well,' Katia commented wryly, watching the two men weave their way out of the crowded bar. 'Shit, I'm really sorry. I didn't know any of that.' She turned to smile wryly at Grace. 'Damn it. I really fancied Keith.'

Disappointment settled like a cloak over Grace's shoulders. The evening had held such promise

'It doesn't matter,' Katia stared at the contents of her wine glass, as if there was something of immense interest in the bottom of it. 'I should stick to horses. They are far easier to get on with.'

'I'll take your word on that.' Grace rolled her eyes in mock boredom at her friend's obsession with horses.

'I'm going to miss Tanny.' Katia sighed, there was no mistaking the catch in her voice as she thought about the horse she wouldn't see for weeks.

'I'll get us another drink,' Grace got to her feet, easing her way to the bar before Katia could refuse. This was their last night out, there was no way to know when they'd ever be together again.

Standing at the bar, Grace looked back at Katia. She'd lit another cigarette, and was staring into space, her thoughts a thousand miles away. It felt like the end of an era.

And just like that, the evening was over. The girls stood at the end of Katia's driveway. The hours had flown by as they had chatted and laughed. They'd had more fun on their own in the end, the encounter with Keith and Andrew quickly forgotten.

'Stay in touch,' Katia opened her arms to enfold Grace in a hug. Her breath smelt of wine, cigarettes and the chips they'd shared walking back up the hill, as they had so many times before.

'I will.' Katia felt fragile in Grace's arms, the bones of her shoulders prominent. She had lost weight while she'd been at university, away from her mother's legendary cooking, and at the mercy of convenience foods.

'I'll call you. Let me know when you're back. Good luck in London,' Grace released Katia, stepping away from her.

'Good luck to you too,' Katia began to walk away as was their habit. The conversation continuing as they went their separate ways. 'Hope you catch loads of burglars and axe murderers.'

'Hope you don't get to defend too many of them…'

Katia's reply was lost in the silence of the night. Grace stood, listening to the branches of the trees that surrounded the garden, creaking and moaning in the wind. A few moments later, through the bushes, she saw Katia's bedroom light go on and watched as her friend drew the curtains and was finally gone.

Chapter Eighteen

'The name is Rhonda. PC White. I'm going to be your babysitter.' Grace shook the woman's offered hand. Rhonda was a little older than Grace. Tall and well-muscled with blonde hair scraped off her face into a neat French pleat. When she arrived at the station Grace had changed out of her jeans and sweatshirt into the uniform she'd been given. 'Get changed in the station,' she'd been told. Of course, that made sense, with the 'love' everyone she encountered had for the police. Now, in uniform, she felt different. The previous day she had driven west from Truro and moved her belongings into the small cottage she had rented on the outskirts of Penzance. Now she was PC Tallis. Grace no more.

'Come this way… You're going to be shadowing me for a while.'

Rhonda smiled, her green eyes never leaving Grace.

Grace followed Rhonda into a vast open plan office. The room smelt of cigarette smoke overlaid with the odour of takeaway food and, more faintly, masculine sweat.

The policemen sitting at some of the desks watched them, their faces showing naked admiration for the pretty young officers. One, seeing Grace's eyes on him, dropped his gaze, focusing intently on the report he was writing, tapping furiously with two fingers on a keyboard.

Grace stared about herself, knowing that while everything felt strange and awkward now, soon she would fit in, know what to do, who to talk to. She'd have a desk of her own, reports to file, a difference to make to the people of the area.

'Take a seat, I'll be back in a moment.' Rhonda pulled out a battered looking swivel chair from beneath an equally decrepit desk. Grace sat. As Rhonda walked away Grace glanced around the room, taking in the notices that littered the walls, the overflowing filing cabinets and the piles of paperwork crammed onto every available surface.

Grace turned her attention to the desk where Rhonda had left her. A heap of files lay discarded in front of her, photographs and notes spilling out. Her fingers, itching with curiosity, eased one of the files towards her, reading the neatly written notes on a burglary. A suspect Jem Trevayne had been given an alibi by his wife.

The next detailed the murder of a man who had been having an affair, his wife had denied killing him.

She opened next one in the pile, letting the pages spill out over the table in front of her. There was a report on a missing woman, Glanna Pendrick, a local woman, she had been reported missing four years previously. The photograph in the file showed a tall, stunning looking woman. The image had been taken on a windswept beach. Glanna was grinning at the camera, her hands positioned as if she were trying to hold back the mane of red hair that billowed around her face in the gale.

The next file below held a similar story, another missing student, Ayla McDonald. Amongst the papers lay the photograph of a pretty young woman, blue eyes, a waterfall of glossy red hair. Grace read through the report, made by her parents. She had been a student at Exeter, as Grace had.

'You can't look at those,' Rhonda appeared at Grace's side.

'I just...' Grace couldn't draw her eyes from the file she was looking at. 'Has she been abducted?'

'Maybe.' Rhonda closed the files. 'Or more likely she could have just walked away from her life.'

'What the fuck are you doing?' An angry male voice startled Grace. She dropped her eyes, focusing on the clumsy, unflattering shoes she wore. Another pair of shoes came into her sightline, brown suede, scuffed at the toes.

'I er... just wanted to look.' Grace dropped the files as if they were burning hot.

'Well, don't.'

Grace turned to face the man who had spoken feeling colour flood into her cheeks as she recognised him.

'Our new recruit?' his lips curled into a sneer of distaste as his eyes raked over her.

'Yes.' Grace nodded slowly. She met the man's eyes seeing sheer dislike flash through his familiar expression. 'PC Tallis. Sir.'

He made to move away and then paused, his dark eyes raking over her. 'Tallis?' His eyes flickered over the open files on the desk, the photographs of the young women spilling out of them. 'Still obsessed with women being... what was it... kidnapped are you?'

'Yes. No,' Grace repeated, forcing the word through tinder dry lips. 'Sir,' she added hastily.

'DI Cooper. Detective Inspector to you.' His voice when he continued was little more than a whisper, his breath cool against her cheek. 'Or would you like to call me ignorant twat?'

'We'll go, shall we?' Rhonda's voice cut across the tension that crackled between Grace and the man who she had just discovered was her boss.

'Yes,' Grace was painfully aware of the high note her voice seemed to have acquired.

'What was that all about?' Rhonda asked as they crossed the car park.

'We've met before, at the station in Truro,' Grace took a gulp of the cool fresh air which held the tang of the sea, blown in from the nearby coast. 'It didn't go well.'

'Oh?' Rhonda's voice was filled with curiosity.

'I reported a man who was acting…weirdly…He…' Grace's voice faded to nothingness. 'DI Cooper took the piss out of me.'

'Ah.' Rhonda said, her voice expressionless. 'That must have been a good few years ago. He transferred down here about eighteen months ago.'

'He hates me already,' Grace sighed.

'He's a good detective. Long memory!' Rhonda laughed, prodding Grace's ribs with a sharp elbow. 'Forget it, just get on with your job.'

'Thanks,' Grace smiled weakly at Rhonda as she got into the patrol car.

'Straight in the deep end.' Thirty minutes later Rhonda drew the patrol car into the side of the road and turned off the engine. 'This is one of the roughest estates on our patch. You'll really see what a big part of our job is today.'

Grace looked out of the car window at the grimy row of houses. A young woman, little older than she was, walked past the car pushing a baby in a stroller in front of her, hauling a second, sobbing child by the hand. She looked tired and harassed. Grace caught her eye and gave her a sympathetic smile. The woman released the child's arm, gave her the middle finger gesture and walked on, the noise of the wailing child drifting back on the breeze.

'See what I mean. Not the best of areas. Most of the people on this estate have been moved from the inner city, apparently relocating them to a rural town is supposed to help. It doesn't. They're bored. Jobless. No money. They resort to petty theft, shop lifting. Most of the people we see here will have dealt with the police and the courts many times. We aren't too popular around here.' Rhonda commented wryly, watching the young woman's hunched shoulders as she made her way down the street.

Grace shook her head, surprised at the hatred in the gesture, directed, not at her, she assumed, but at the organisation she represented. The woman turned a corner at the end of the street and was gone.

'This is probably a long way from what you are used too.' Rhonda's voice was emotionless.

'Yes, I've never…'

'It's a whole different world on some of these estates. You'll learn.' Rhonda smiled gently.

Grace gazed out of the car window at the scruffy, junk piled front gardens in front of the grim looking rows of identical houses. The one they had parked outside had a boarded-up window upstairs and the one in the cheap looking front door was cracked.

'Let's go.' Rhonda nodded her head in greeting at the passengers of the car which had driven up and parked in front of them. 'Grim job I'm afraid. The social services are taking a baby into care, for his own safety. Both parents are addicts. Zac is their second baby. He's got a brother Zane who's been in care since he was about eighteen months old. One of the neighbours found him wandering in the street. We're just here in case there's any trouble. You don't need to say or do anything, just watch for now.'

Rhonda introduced Grace to the two social workers, 'Michael. Cathy, this is PC Tallis. We're going to assist you.'

'Ready?' Michael squared his shoulders, before releasing a long breath. He led the way up the short, rubbish strewn path to the house. The front door was opened, by a man who looked barely twenty years old, his eyes fixed on the group were filled with resentment.

'Thank you, Phil,' Michael's voice though polite, had a steely edge. Grace followed, stepping into the dimness of the house. She breathed in the staleness of the air, fried food, nappies, dirt and damp, the smell of despair.

Rhonda walked beside her, across a lino floor, sticky with dirt, silent, watchful as Michael and Cathy chattered, their voices merging into a blur of noise. Michael led the way into a room off the cluttered hallway. Phil threw himself onto a battered sofa beside a plump sour faced looking girl whose blonde hair had a good two inches of greasy dark roots showing. The couple sat, half submerged, in the depths of a stained, sagging sofa.

'Alison, Phil, do you know why we're here?' Cathy's voice was steely.

Phil glared aggressively at the group, his fingers clenching and unclenching in a slow rhythm. His movement had the barely controlled menace of a caged animal. Beside him Alison rocked compulsively from side to side, her gaze never wavering from the torn lino at her feet.

Beside them on the sofa rested a small, grubby-looking Moses basket.

'We need to take Zak,' Michael's voice was filled with determination.

'Do what you fucking like.' Phil shot to his feet, crossing the room to stare out of the window. Anger followed him like a wave as he moved. Grace instinctively stepped out of his way, hurriedly moving forwards again, joining the unwavering Rhonda.

Cathy lifted a small baby from the Moses basket. 'He's beautiful, Alison,' she said softly, cradling him in her arms. 'He's going to be fine.'

'And when you're both better…' Michael directed his words at Phil's rigid back.

'Can I see him soon?' It was the first time Alison had spoken, lifting her gaze to the small bundle in Cathy's arms.

'Of course you can, he's going to be in foster care with Zane, so you'll be able to see Zak too,' Cathy said gently, easing her way quietly out of the room.

'Incentive for you to both get clean.' Michael turned his attention to Alison. 'Get both of your boys back with you.' His voice had a defeated air as if he knew how unlikely the pair were to wean themselves off the drugs that controlled their lives.

The air in the patrol car felt cleaner after the grime of the house. 'That was horrible,' Grace, clenched her fists, determined not to cry in front of Rhonda.

'Poor things…' Rhonda looked back at the house. Phil had gone from the window. 'Drugs.' She sniffed, releasing a slow breath before turning on the car and steering out of the estate.

'Next call.' Rhonda drove across the town. As they stopped at a junction, Grace glanced at the woman who was with her, seeing the determination in Rhonda's eyes. She needed to put a veil of protection around her emotions, like Rhonda managed too, she couldn't let what she witnessed affect her, or she would spend every day in tears.

'Bobby Duncannon.' Rhonda parked the car on the driveway of an elegant looking bungalow. 'He's been broken into.'

Grace let herself out of the car, breathing in the heady scent of the roses that filled the flower beds beside the driveway. She followed Rhonda up the path.

A middle-aged woman stood in the open doorway. 'Marie,' she introduced herself. 'Dad's very upset.' She led the way down an airy hallway into a kitchen at the back of the building.

'Dad?'

'Mr Duncannon. How are you?'

Grace felt her eyes widen in surprise as the elderly man turned to face them. One cheek was hugely swollen, with a livid, purple bruise beneath his eye. She tore her eyes away, not wanting to stare, looking instead at the tiled floor at her feet. Droplets of blood marred its pristine surface.

'You should see the other fella.' Bobby twisted his face into the semblance of a smile.

'Nothing was taken, I understand?' Rhonda said gently.

'He fought them off.' Marie shook her head, looking at her father.

'Young thugs.' Bobby shook his head, 'I answered the door thinking it was my neighbour. Two of them came running in.'

Horrified at the ordeal he'd been through, Grace watched Bobby become animated as he recounted the previous evening.

'They wanted money. Broke my walking stick over one of their backs.'

'And got a black eye in the process.' Marie pulled out one of the kitchen chairs and sat down heavily as if her legs would not support her. 'Oh, Dad. When I think what could have happened.'

'They didn't take anything?'

Bobby snorted. 'I think they were surprised I put up a fight. Cowards, they fled like whipped pups.'

'He could have been killed,' Marie met Grace's eyes.

Grace smiled with what she hoped was a mixture of sympathy and understanding.

'Can you remember anything about them? Ages? What were they wearing?'

He shook his head, leaning back against the kitchen work surface. His shoulders sagged. 'Young, one had dark hair… jeans… trainers…' His voice faltered. 'Sorry. It's just a blur.'

'Well, it's not going to happen again,' Marie slapped her outstretched fingers onto the table. 'Dad's going to come and live with me. It's not safe for you to be on your own, is it?'

As Marie turned to face her father, Grace watched him glance around the home he so clearly loved.

'I'm not being put out of my home by the likes of them.' He snapped, his expression bleak.

'Dad…' Marie glanced at the officers, twisting her mouth into a wry expression.

'We'll leave you to it.' Rhonda backed away, smiling sympathetically at the two of them after they had filled in the necessary paperwork.

'Bastards,' spat Rhonda slamming the car into gear. 'That poor old man. He might have fought them off, but he's now fighting for his independence…'

'I wonder who will win?' Grace asked, glancing at Rhonda who shook her head in reply. 'We'll probably never know.' Rhonda steered the car out of the gentle silence of the neat estate and across the town back to the station.

'I'm ready for a coffee,' Rhonda turned off the car engine and slumped back in the driver's seat.

'Me too.' Grace rubbed her fingers across her forehead, in a vain attempt to ease the taut band of tension that gripped it. She looked across the car park, crowded with a jumble of police cars, and those of the staff, double parked and squeezed into every available gap. The station building, starkly modern in the 60's when it was built, soared above them. Somewhere in there was DI Cooper.

'We'll head out again this afternoon. We have to follow up on a couple of farms that have been broken into. The boss thinks it's our local bad boy, a guy called Jem Trevayne. We've not been able to prove it. Yet.' Rhonda led the way into the station building. 'That's how things go.' She sighed, before hastily changing the subject. 'What do you think of the day so far?'

'Yes, it's really interesting.'

She glanced at Rhonda aware of her snort of derision. 'Interesting? Seriously! This morning was about as exciting as it gets around here.'

Chapter Nineteen

'It's a dump. I hate it here.' Carrie threw her schoolbag onto the kitchen table, scattering the mess of bills and discarded newspapers. She glanced through the kitchen window to where the pale morning light was just beginning to brighten the small back garden.

'I know you do, sweetheart. Just give it chance, you'll see.' Her mum's voice was irritatingly placating.

Carrie hauled out one of the kitchen stools and slumped down on it. The tiles below were uneven, tilting the stool slightly. 'This place. This house...' Carrie took the box of cereal her mum handed to her and shook a heaped pile into the bowl in front of her.

'Look love,' Jean Anderson sighed, 'you've only got another couple of years at school. Just till you've done your exams. I've got a good job here. We can move when we're more settled, after we get to know the area. Somewhere nicer. Out into the country, maybe...?' Jean's voice faced into nothingness as she faced her daughter, seeing the anger in her face.

'Why did we have to come here? To fucking Cornwall?' She glanced at Jean, expecting the usual reprimand for swearing. It didn't come. Instead, Jean turned her back, focusing on the sandwiches she was preparing.

'I hate it,' Carrie, stirred her spoon listlessly through the bowl of cereal, lifting milk and cornflakes halfway to her mouth before tilting it and letting the mixture drop. She rested her elbows on the table, resting her chin in her hands, watching Jean's mechanical movements as she buttered the bread. Only the taut set of her shoulders gave any indication of the hurt Carrie had inflicted.

'Carrie,' Jean threw down the knife and spun around to face her daughter. 'We... I just couldn't stay in Manchester. Here, we have a new start. It's a good job for me. With a future.' The words, 'away from your dad,' went unspoken.

'Why couldn't you get a new job nearer Manchester?' Carrie snapped sullenly.

'Oh, for god's sake, Carrie,' Jean crossed the space between them. 'Will you look at what you have here? The beach. Beautiful countryside. A fabulous school.'

'What good is the beach?' As Carrie met Jean's eyes, she could see the hurt she had inflicted reflected in their blue depths. 'I miss my mates. The shops.'

As Jean turned away in exasperation, Carrie lowered her gaze to the bowl of cereal, dashing away the tears that were making their way down the curve of her cheeks.

Jean had been so excited about the prospect of a new start that Carrie had said nothing, swept up in the chaos of packing, yet the whole process had filled her with dread. She'd hated Cornwall from the moment they'd arrived. Now, two months later, Carrie wondered why she hadn't protested. Why she hadn't told Jean she didn't want to leave. That she wanted to be near her dad. Just because Jean didn't want to be with him shouldn't mean Carrie couldn't see him either. The whole episode had been like a dream. Carrie felt at any moment she would wake up.

Jean had been so thrilled with the little house she'd rented on a side street, off the main road which ran through the village of Hilden. Shops, which catered mainly for the tourists, were scattered at intervals throughout the village. A posh boutique, an art gallery, the ubiquitous Cornish pasty shop, all mingled uncomfortably with those aimed at the locals; a cheap off licence and a small corner shop, smelling of Indian spices, which sold everything from plastic buckets and spades to toilet rolls. Hilden was a world away from the bustling streets of Manchester.

'I need to go,' Carrie placed her bowl on the counter beside the sink.

'Right, I'll see you later,' Jean's voice was taut with unshed tears of frustration and temper.

Fighting the urge to slam the front door, Carrie shouldered her schoolbag and set off towards her school. The walk led her past the ribbon of shops and houses. Behind the main road the river snaked, spilling into the sea at the opposite end of the village. She could see it, through gaps in the houses, a dull, malicious-looking grey that reflected the gunmetal colour of the sky. She sighed, breathing in the salty tang of the sea.

Ahead, pupils making their way to the school walked in groups, jostling and giggling. Carrie walked alone. At the Post Office, still festooned with beach inflatables which danced in the cutting autumn wind, Carrie dashed across the main road and into the small supermarket. It was already crowded with school children buying food for the day. The meaty smell of the Cornish pasties made Carrie long even more for Manchester where pies were proper ones, rich meat, and soft, flaky pastry, not the chunky offerings of gristle and vegetables the Cornish seemed to love.

Avoiding the crowds of children, Carrie ducked behind one of the aisles and feigned an interest in the goods displayed there, waiting until the shop emptied.

'Hi Carrie, what are you looking for?' One of the girls in her class stood at the end of the aisle, her head tilted to one side, brown eyes dancing with amusement.

'I was just…' Carrie stumbled away from the display, realising with horror that in her effort to hide, she had been gazing sightlessly at a display of sanitary products. Colour flooded her face.

'See you later,' the girl, Ann, Carrie thought her name was, re-joined her friends. They stared openly at Carrie, before turning away as a group of lads came towards the shop.

Carrie released the breath she'd been holding and made her way to the counter, grabbing crisps and chocolate to see her through the long, dull hours at school.

She trailed after the line of pupils into the school yard, feeling curious eyes watching her. A tinkle of laughter drifted across the expanse of tarmac. Someone laughing at her, no doubt.

Relieved at her timing, the school bell rang as Carrie followed the others into the starkly modern school building. Arriving just as the bell sounded meant she had avoided having to stand conspicuously alone in the yard.

Still finding her way around the school Carrie was late for her first class, wandering through corridors, looking for the right room. Every eye turned to stare at her as she slipped through the doorway and made her way to the only vacant desk, right at the front of the class.

'Morning Carrie. We're on page seventeen.'

Carrie clamped her mouth tightly shut to subdue the giggle that bubbled from the depths of her stomach at his broad, Cornish accent.

Aware of the clattering and banging she was making, as she pulled out a chair and found the right book, Carrie finally turned her attention to the lecture.

'How would you describe Heathcliffe's character?' Mr Middleton addressed the class, flicking through the pages of a battered Wuthering Heights.

Ugghhh, the Bronte's. She was sick of hearing about them. Carrie doodled on her notebook, her eyes drifting restlessly to the window. Behind the unruly tangle of stone and brick houses was the grey ribbon of the river. A short distance from the village it spilled out into the sea alongside which spanned a vast expanse of golden sand. Her mum walked there every morning. Carrie couldn't bear the wind that whipped in from the sea, the silence broken only by seabirds wheeling overhead. She'd been once. That had been enough.

Shifting in her seat slightly, Carrie let her gaze wander to the abandoned boatyard, a sad testament to a vastly depleted fishing industry. Boats lay half submerged in the water, alongside the skeletons of disused buildings.

'And your thoughts, Carrie?' Mr Middleton's voice brought her back to reality.

'I... Er...' she fought to remember anything about the book. They'd read it months ago at her last school. 'I'm not sure...' Carrie shrugged, her memory failing her.

'Well, I suggest you actually do the homework I set you before the next class.' Carrie met his eyes, seeing the delight at having exposed her failings in front of the whole room. He had wiry red hair, a strand of which had fallen forwards over his forehead and danced in time with his words.

Carrie nodded miserably, her face flooding with colour at the barely suppressed giggles from behind her.

The next class was no better. She hated maths. The teacher at her last school had been good at explaining the intricate workings of algebra, but here, Mrs Tew, a dumpy middle-aged woman in a dog shit brown skirt which sagged around her ample torso, rambled through the lessons, expecting everyone to understand.

Carrie put down her pen. What was the point? She'd get all the answers wrong anyway. It was a waste of time even trying. The classroom, positioned at the back of the building, looked out over farmland. Caterpillars of tractors and trailers were snaking their way across the red-tinged earth, followed by lines of people, picking what she assumed were potatoes from the soil. Her last school had looked out over the city, the tangle of buildings had seemed to buzz with life, possess an air of excited expectancy. Here, it was as if the world stood still, like time had passed by and forgotten it.

At lunchtime, Carrie left the school. The yard was crowded, everyone in their cliques. She shouldered her bag, pushing open the gate. If anyone even noticed, she knew they wouldn't care.

The house was deserted when she got home. Jean wouldn't be home for hours yet. Carrie flung her bag into her room, came back downstairs, and turned on the tv, sinking into the depths of the sofa. She watched the flickering images, her mind wandering. They should go back to Manchester. This place, Cornwall, had been a huge mistake. She would never be happy here.

Carrie let hot tears trickle unchecked down her cheeks, feeling them roll over her chin and splatter onto her school shirt. Why couldn't her mum have stopped arguing with dad? What had made her row with him all the time, when she could have just said yes? Surely that would have been easier, instead of leaving him, getting a new job in a primary school, and hauling the two of them to the wilderness of Cornwall. If they hadn't left he would never have moved his new girlfriend and her three small children into their old home. Carrie would leave her mum and go back to Manchester if it wasn't for them.

Carrie was still curled on the sofa when Jean returned from work a few hours later.

'You're back early.' Jean's voice was filled with frustration. Normally she'd be back long before Carrie's classes ended.

'I'm not going there anymore.'

'Carrie,' Jean perched herself on the arm of the sofa, 'You need to get your A levels. There's only another two years and then you can leave anyway.'

Carrie shook her head. 'I hate it, everyone laughs at me. They're all in little groups.'

'I know,' Jean said softly, 'I feel the same at work, but it will get better. You need to make an effort. Perhaps a Saturday job would get you out of the house, help you make friends.'

'A Saturday job! Friends!' Carrie scrambled to her feet, mocking her mother's tone. 'Why did we have to come here? Why couldn't you stay with dad? Why do you have to be such a bitch?'

'Thanks, Carrie. Would you like me to tell you why we needed to come here?' Jean's voice had a cold edge to it. She got slowly to her feet, her expression smoothed of all emotion. 'I appreciate your support.'

Jean made her way into the kitchen, where she began to open the cupboard doors, taking out the ingredients for dinner. Wordlessly, she slid her shirt sleeve upwards, running cold fingers over the circular scars that marred her skin.

'I know why,' Carrie came to stand in the kitchen doorway, unable to let go of the argument. 'Because you always want your own way. Dad said…'

'Carrie,' Jean interjected, holding up her hands. 'Please love, I know you love your dad but he's not the saint you seem to think he is.'

'If you hadn't been such a cow to him…' Carrie whispered.

'Is that what you think?' Jean's voice had an exhausted edge.

Carrie put her head on one side, glaring at her mother. 'I know. Dad said.'

'Get out of my sight, before I say something I regret.' Jean clutched the kitchen work surface, her knuckles white with temper.

'I'm going out,' Carrie grabbed her jacket from its peg behind the kitchen door.

'Where are you going?' Jean glanced at her daughter.

'No idea.' Carrie snapped. 'Away from you. And I'm not coming back.'

Chapter Twenty

Carrie slammed the front door behind her and began to run, legs pumping. The more distance she could get between her and her mother, the better. Rain was falling hard, battering against the pavement, the light shining through curtains closed against the darkness, illuminating the tarmac.

Breathless, her lungs hurting with the effort, Carrie finally stopped, at the far end of the village and staggered into the shelter of a deserted bus stop. Legs trembling beneath her, she lowered herself slowly onto the wooden bench, leaning her head against the glass panel.

The road was busy, commuters hurrying past on their way home. Carrie watched them, cars full of people chattering, solo drivers, their fingers tapping to a tune on the radio, couples, everyone heading home.

Carrie scrunched her toes inside her sodden runners, shivering now the cold of the evening had crept its way through her sweatshirt. Her mum would be worried, expecting her to go back, to apologise for her behaviour.

She eased the sweatshirt away from her shoulders, feeling the dampness of the fabric chilling her skin. She pictured going home. Jean, triumphant, listening to Carrie's apology. She'd expect Carrie to promise to stay at school, to get a job, make friends, to accept Jean's decision to move to Cornwall. Carrie shook her head, trying to rid herself of the vision. She couldn't face going home. Not yet anyway.

Jean, she knew, would be making dinner, eating it from a plate balanced on her knee while she watched television. When she got home Jean would wordlessly fetch her the plate of food, she would undoubtedly be keeping warm in the oven. Neither would say anything, but Carrie would know that Jean had won the battle. Eventually she'd bring the conversation around to Carrie's outburst and wait for her apology.

A car, one in the line of traffic, slowed as it got level with the bus shelter. Carrie looked up, seeing the four lads inside gazing at her with naked curiosity, she glared back, daring them to stop, to say anything to her. The adrenaline coursing through Carrie's veins made her feel as if she could battle anything. Punch their lights out, just for letting their eyes stray in her direction.

An old lady, battling a huge umbrella against the wind that blew in from the coast, hurried into the bus shelter.

'Horrible night.' She let down the umbrella, shaking the water off it, a myriad of raindrops glittered in the streetlights.

'Yes.' She could feel the old lady's eyes on her. Carrie could only imagine what she thought, seeing her damp clothes, bedraggled hair and sodden runners.

'I thought I'd missed the forty-nine.'

'Did you?' Carrie's teeth were chattering so much it was hard to talk. She wished the old lady would leave her alone. The last thing she wanted was to make polite conversation.

'They come at funny times. Depends on the traffic, I imagine...'

'I suppose so.'

'Are you alright dear? You look soaked.'

Carrie's throat had constricted, making speech impossible. She nodded. 'Yes.' The word sounded like a strangled croak. How could she begin to explain she was the furthest thing from alright? That everything was very much not alright. She wanted to go home, to the familiarity of the Manchester streets, she wanted her dad. 'Thanks,' Carrie added, forcing her mouth into something she hoped resembled a smile.

'Here it is,' the old lady got to her feet as the bulk of a double decker bus came towards them. 'You go first,' she said, as the bus doors swished open, waving her hand to indicate that Carrie should get on.

'I'm not...' Carrie stared at the pavement, longing to be getting onto the bus, going somewhere familiar.

As the bus doors closed the aching cold drove her to move again. There was no way she was going home. Jean would have to wait, let her stew, begin to panic about where her daughter was.

Her runners felt leaden with the water they had soaked up from the pavement. She could hear them sloshing above the sound of the traffic which splashed through the puddles on the road. Her toes curled against the uncomfortable sensation.

Finally, she gave way to the tears that had fought their way to the surface. In Manchester when a row broke out, Carrie could go to a friend's home. Hole up there, warm and dry, waiting until the inevitable knock came when one of her parents came looking for her. There would be the usual recriminations, apologies, cuddles and laughter. Here there was no one. She didn't know a single person who wouldn't think it bizarre if she knocked on their door.

She didn't have anywhere to go. But, Carrie knew, there was no way she was going to turn tail and head home. She was determined to stay out, to make her mum wait, panic, worry about her. Perhaps then she'd realise what a mistake it was for her to have dragged the two of them away from Manchester. Maybe then she'd go back where they belonged, find a job up there. Carrie could go back to her old life, her friends, the streets she loved, see her dad sometimes.

Suddenly, she knew where she could go. Somewhere sheltered, where there would be other kids her age. Without pausing, Carrie launched herself into the line of slow-moving traffic, sticking two fingers up to the driver who honked his horn in protest.

Wandering the streets during the evenings when they had first arrived, Carrie had seen other youngsters, bored and listless, waiting out the long evenings in the shelter of the ruined boatyard. She was willing to brave their curiosity, the teasing and mocking. Anything had to be better than going home.

As she had expected, a group of teenagers, lads she recognised from school, were huddled beneath the darkness of one of the boat sheds.

'Hi,' Carrie said coolly, walking into the shelter.

'Hey,' the speaker, Alan, a gangly red-haired boy, who Carrie knew was in some of the same classes as she was, dragged deeply on a cigarette, the red end glowing in the darkness.

'Can I have one of those?' Carrie leant against the open doorway.

'I guess so.' A packet was offered in her direction. She took one and accepted a light.

'Shit night.' Carrie drew deeply on the cigarette.

'Where'd you go today? You didn't come back to school after lunch.'

Carrie shrugged. 'I was sick of it. That English teacher. He's a wanker.'

She faced the group of lads, meeting their eyes, enjoying their blatant curiosity. It was different here from school. Out on the streets, she knew how to act, what to say and do. It was at school she floundered, beneath their massed inquisitiveness and the easy familiarity from years of knowing one another.

'Is this all there is to do here?' Carrie shoved a broken brick with the toe of her runner, watching it skitter into the building, the noise echoing around the high, broken roof.

'Pretty much.' It was Tom who spoke. She'd seen him in class too. He was short, stocky with dark eyes that never quite met hers. 'It's better in the summer when the tourists are around. There's always something to do then.'

'Beach parties. Usually, we find someone to hang around with who's camping or renting one of the cottages.' Simon another of the other lads from school spoke. Carrie let her eyes flicker over him, taking in his carefully tousled blonde hair and the firm set of his jaw. He was the tallest of the group, already muscular, with the supreme confidence that came from being very good looking and knowing it.

'We have fires on the beach.' Tom moved out of the doorway to swing on a rusting metal strut. The shoulders of his sweatshirt were dark where the rain had soaked them.

'I collect driftwood all winter,' Alan said, his eyes roving appreciatively over Carrie.

'Nice,' Carrie was aware of the sarcastic edge in her voice.

'During the winter it's shit here, isn't it, Simon?' Alan shuffled his feet, kicking at an unidentifiable piece of rusting iron on the ground.

'Total and utter shit,' Simon puffed out his cheeks to release a long sigh, as he shoved his hands into the front pockets of his jeans.

'Sometimes we get a lift into town.' Alan moved closer to Carrie. His breath smelt of cigarette smoke. 'Or we just make our own amusement.'

'Right.' Carrie met Alan's eyes, staring at him until he dropped his gaze. She moved closer to Tom. Alan felt weird. She wasn't comfortable with him too close to her.

Jan, her friend from Manchester, would have made mincemeat of him. She loved nothing more than putting overly keen, testosterone-fuelled lads in their place.

'You got a boyfriend?' It was Simon who spoke.

'Of course.' Carrie lied, shrugging her shoulders nonchalantly.

'What are you doing out and about on your own then?'

Carrie met Tom's eyes. 'He's busy tonight. I was bored, thought I'd have a walk around.'

'On a wet night like this?' Alan snorted in amusement. 'I'd have stayed at home if my dad wasn't a complete tosser.'

In the half-light Carrie watched as Alan drew himself up to his full height, holding himself stiffly as he waggled a finger. 'You'll do what I say.' His voice took on a deep growling tone, mimicking that of his father. 'Prick.' Alan reverted to his own tone.

'I've come to get out of the way of my mum.' Carrie confessed, relaxing slightly in their company. 'She's being a right bitch.'

'It's what they do best,' Tom pulled a small bottle of vodka out of his jacket pocket, unscrewed the top and took a long swig. 'I can't wait to leave home. Get out of my parent's way.' He handed the bottle to Alan, who gulped the liquid, covering his mouth with his hand to stifle the coughing fit afterwards.

'Cheers.' Simon grabbed the bottle. 'Do you want some?' He held it in Carrie's direction.

'Sure,' she took the bottle, feeling the fiery liquid burn the back of her throat as she drank.

'Save some for me.' Simon pulled the bottle out of Carrie's hand. 'Here's to summer and beach parties in the sunshine!'

'Too true!' Tom grinned, reaching for the bottle.

A few hours later, warmed by the alcohol and the company, Carrie stopped shivering. Maybe it wasn't so bad here after all.

'It's getting late, I need to go.' Simon handed Carrie another cigarette and a battered box of matches. 'For the walk home. Give me the matches back tomorrow. If you come to school, that is.'

'Sure, thanks.' He was nice. Perhaps someone who would break up the monotony of school.

'Time to go.' The murmur of agreement swept around the lads.

'I'm going to stay a bit longer.' Carrie hoisted herself onto the bottom of an upturned, abandoned boat.

'Are you coming to school tomorrow?' Alan asked.

'I guess so,' Carrie shrugged. She should go home. It was getting late. Her mum, she knew, would be worried now. She'd wait a while longer. Carrie watched the boys go, their chatter fading into silence as they vanished into the gloom. It had stopped raining. High above the derelict buildings the moon had appeared, a tiny sliver, lying on its back.

Headlights appeared on the dockside. Carrie squinted as they swept past her. She watched the shape of the pick-up as it pulled up at the far end of the docks.

She moved back into the building, her footsteps crunching on broken glass and chips of concrete. Carrie moved her wrist so that her watch caught the pale glow from the one remining working arc lights. Eleven fifteen. One more cigarette, and she'd go home. Carrie pulled the matches from her jeans pocket, smiling. Simon. She'd finally made a friend. And someone good looking.

She put the cigarette to her lips, striking the match. As it flared, the light shot long shadows around the ruined building, dark, spooky shapes, the remnants of old sails hanging from the walls looked like ghosts, creepy, watchful figures. Shuddering, she dropped the match, drawing deeply on the cigarette. Time to go home.

She felt, rather than saw him. A rapid movement close to her. Her head jerked back as something heavy hit her. She saw the redness of the end of the cigarette tumble into the night before the darkness reached up to enfold her.

Chapter Twenty-One

'Carrie?' Jean woke with a start. Blearily, she rose from the sofa where she'd been asleep, easing her neck, which was stiff from the position she'd been in. The room was lit by the flickering light from the television. For a moment, she watched the images, a violent fist fight between two unrealistic looking monsters.

'Carrie?' The air in the hallway was frigid. Had Carrie just come in, the cold air from outside permeating the downstairs? Jean listened, her hand clutching the bannister at the bottom of the stairs. What had woken her? Carrie coming in, surely. Jean massaged her neck with chilled fingers.

She'd spent a miserable night after Carrie had stormed out,

alternating between anger at her daughter's tantrum, to fear, worrying about where she had gone, and anticipating the horrible row there would undoubtedly be when she returned. At least she was home now.

When there was no answer, Jean went back into the living room, giving the sofa cushions a cursory plumping as was her normal night-time routine. She tutted at the ridiculous programme on the television before pointing the remote at it and darkening the screen. Perhaps she should leave the confrontation until the following day, let Carrie stew, but Jean would be going over what she wanted to say knew she'd never sleep. At least if she had the inevitable row with Carrie now, they could make up. Jean knew she'd sleep better if that was done.

Carrie's bedroom door was firmly shut. Jean leant against the wall beside the door, her hand on the doorknob.

'Can I come in?' Jean liked Carrie to have her privacy. The days when she would have liked to see her mother coming into her bedroom were long gone. Somehow, they had transitioned from being a team, becoming strangers sharing the same space. Silence. Jean pictured her daughter curled in bed, the covers pulled resolutely around her head, in that cruel way she'd developed of blocking out her mother.

Jean balled her hands and tucked them into her eye sockets, determined not to cry. She'd cried so much recently, she was resolute Carrie's behaviour wasn't going to make it happen again. She was the adult. Carrie, whether she liked it or not, was going to have to toe the line. Accept she was stuck with Jean, at least until she was old enough to leave home.

No matter how much she read about parenting difficult teens, dealing with Carrie never got any easier. The girl seemed to resent her mother no matter how hard Jean tried. They weren't friends, not anymore. Pulling herself upright, Jean arranged her face into a stern expression and shoved open Carrie's bedroom door.

'I'm sorry that you...' She shouldn't start by apologising. It was Carrie who had started the row, her who had stormed out of the house and kept her mother on tender hooks all night waiting. The words died on Jean's lips. Carrie's bed was empty.

Fear flashed through Jean like a jolt of electricity, mingling uncomfortably with the feeling of anger that twisted in her stomach.

Whatever had woken her, it hadn't been Carrie coming home.

Jean glanced at her watch, eleven. Late, but not terribly so, especially if Carrie wanted, like she clearly did, to prove a point. Jean drifted slowly around Carrie's room, her fingers straying over her daughter's makeup, the garish pink lipstick she'd started to wear, the horrible black eyeshadow from when she'd been going through a goth phase. Carrie's school bag lay discarded in a heap beside her bed.

Knowing there was no way she'd settle, let alone sleep, until Carrie was safely home, Jean made her way back downstairs, shivering against the chill of the house. Ten past eleven. At half past, she'd really worry. Until then it was still a normal time for Carrie to come home, especially on the nights when they'd argued, and Carrie stormed out.

Pushing the curtains to one side, Jean positioned herself by the living room window, resting one hip on the low windowsill. From here, she had a good view of the street. Although it was dark, there were streetlights which illuminated and brightened the pavement area. When Carrie appeared, Jean knew she'd have time to duck back behind the curtain before she was seen. It wouldn't do for Carrie to know how worried her mother was. She'd never known. Jean had made sure of that. She'd protected her from the day she was born, ensuring Carrie never witnessed the horrific rows when Jean had discovered her dad with yet another of his girlfriends. Not knowing how bad things were meant that Carrie assumed her mother had moved on a whim, that she had been the abusive one in the relationship. Perhaps it was time to tell her some home truths about her father.

At the end of the road, a shadow crossed the rain slicked pavement. Relief surged through Jean. The feeling lasted moments as the shadow lengthened, growing closer, becoming a figure. Jean could see it was a man, shoulders hunched against the rain, hands tucked firmly into his pockets.

The feeling of panic grew, like a living thing, growing from a seed of tension at the pit of her stomach to cloak her whole body with a leaden terror. Eleven thirty. It was too late. Carrie had been gone too long. She'd proved her point. No matter how angry Jean was, now she just wanted Carrie home safely. It didn't matter how much they'd rowed, nor if Carrie understood why they'd moved. Nothing mattered, except getting her home safely.

She paced the living room, unable to settle. Moving from the window to the hall, watching the front door, hoping to see Carrie come in at every moment. Time seemed to have slowed, every second an eternity, waiting, watching, and yet the minute hand on her watch seemed to move at breakneck speed, sliding relentlessly towards midnight. She couldn't wait in the house any longer, doing nothing. She didn't care how foolish Carrie would think she was when she found her, Jean just wanted her home safely. They could talk about the problems they were having. If needs be, she'd go back to Manchester. Where Carrie wanted to be. Anything to make her happy.

Jean grabbed her car keys, pulled the front door shut behind her, and hurried out into the night. Her breath plumed into the damp darkness with each exhalation. Carrie would laugh if she saw her mother's frenzied anxiety.

Jean's breath caught as she glimpsed a shadow shift across the pavement.

'Hi, Jean. It's Lizzy. Sorry if I scared you. I'm just on my way home from work.'

Jean shook her head, in a distracted gesture, recognising the woman who lived in the house next door. Lizzy's daughter Stephanie was at the same school as Carrie. 'Lizzy…' Jean could barely speak with panic.

'Are you okay?' Lizzy's voice was filled with concern. She moved out of the shadow to stand beside Jean.

'Carrie's gone off… We had a row. I'm going to drive around looking for her. I don't know where she is.'

'Bloody kids,' Lizzy sighed. 'I'll come with you. Show you the local haunts.'

Jean fumbled with the ignition, eventually succeeding in getting the key in and turning it. For a moment, the interior was filled with the noise of the radio. Carrie had turned it up the last time they'd been in it together. A song had come on she'd liked.

She snapped off the radio, silencing the inane chatter, listening instead to the noise of the tyres on the rain-soaked road, and the monotonous sound of the windscreen wipers as they slicked backwards and forwards.

Someone had parked their car too close behind Jean's. It seemed to take forever for her to manoeuvre the vehicle out of its parking spot. Slowly, she drove through the village. Where would Carrie have gone? Did she have any friends whose houses she would go to? Perhaps, even now, she was walking into the house from a different direction.

'I'm sure she will turn up. There isn't much trouble kids can get into in Hildon.' Lizzy put a reassuring hand on Jean's arm. 'Try the school, sometimes kids hang out in the bike shelter.'

Jean focused on driving, steering along the roads lined with parked cars, the houses beside them in darkness. The whole village seemed to be deserted. Asleep.

She reached the school Carrie had just started attending. The gates were open as always. As Jean drove into the schoolyard, a movement in the shadows attracted her attention. Carrie? The car headlights raked over a group of teenagers, their faces resentful at having been disturbed turned away from the glare.

'I know these lads,' Lizzy said, peering through the windscreen into the darkness. Jean spun the car in a wide circle. Carrie wasn't with them.

Lizzy let down the window, rain splattering against her face as she called out to the group.

'Tom, Simon. Do any of you know Carrie? Carrie Anderson, she's just started school here.'

There was a uniform shrugging of shoulders, blank expressions gazing at her.

'She hasn't come home,' Jean's voice cracked, tears of frustration and fear close to the surface.

'She was over at the arches earlier.' One of the lads pointed towards the derelict boatyard.

'Thanks Simon.' Lizzy gave him a thumbs up sign.

Relief flooded through Jean. Carrie was undoubtedly still there, probably drinking with some other wild kids, their parents suffering as much as she was.

She turned the car and drove the short distance to the boatyard. 'Why do kids flock to places like this?' Jean mused, steering her car around the ruined shells of boats, past a pick-up abandoned in the middle of the yard.

'God only knows.'

The car headlights raked over the skeleton of the building, casting eerie shadows. Stopping the car, Jean narrowed her eyes, trying to see anything amongst the dark shapes of boats covered in tarpaulins, heaps of rusting metal, the detritus of an abandoned lifestyle. No one was there.

Jean put the car into gear. There was nothing to see. However long-ago Carrie had been here she wasn't now. Perhaps she was reaching home at this moment, cold and miserable.

'Maybe she's home now.' Lizzy suggested. 'Perhaps we missed seeing her.'

Jean steered out of the boatyard and back towards the village. She stopped once more beside the entrance to the school. The yard seemed deserted, the teenagers who'd been there were gone.

'See, she's back,' Lizzy's voice reflected the relief Jean felt. Carrie's bedroom light was on. Jean eased the car back into its tiny spot on the road outside the house. 'Thanks for coming with me.'

'No problem.' Lizzy hurried towards her own front door. Jean felt weak with relief. Carrie was home. Slamming the car door shut she dashed inside.

'Carrie?' Jean called, hurrying up the stairs. 'I've been out looking for you.' Carrie's bedroom door stood open, just as she had left it. The room was starkly empty. Jean must have left the light on.

On trembling legs, Jean made her way back downstairs. She turned on the gas fire, hauling the blanket from over the back of the sofa around her shoulders, the cold seemed to have seeped into her bones. Jean wondered bitterly if she would ever be warm again.

Shivering, she stood beside the window, gazing out at the silent, deserted road. Carrie must really be doing a job on her. This time, she'd clearly meant to hurt her mother. Undoubtedly, she'd stayed with some friend, having weaved them a tale of a horrible mother who was dreadfully unkind.

Eventually, exhausted, Jean curled in one corner of the sofa, legs tucked beneath herself, the blanket draped around her knees. She dozed, lulled by the warmth of the gas fire, only to wake with a start at the front door banging. Relief coursed through her. Throwing the blanket off, Jean struggled to her feet, stumbling as its folds tangled around her legs.

'Where the hell…?' the words died on her lips as Jean realised what the noise had been. Three brown envelopes lay scattered on the hall floor. The Postman, sliding them through the letterbox, had been what had jerked her awake.

The house was empty. Still no sign of Carrie.

An hour later Jean found herself walking into the Police Station in Penzance, the closest town to the village. Her eyes felt gritty from lack of sleep. She pushed the door open, glancing around the unfamiliar building. A man, vomit staining the front of his shirt, was sprawled on a wooden bench at one side of the room. He opened his eyes briefly as the door swung shut behind her.

Almost dreamlike, Jean saw herself walk to the desk. She leant against the wooden surface, clinging to it as if she were drowning. Looking into the kindly eyes of the chubby policeman behind the desk she heard herself speak. 'Can you help me please? My daughter is missing.'

Chapter Twenty-Two

'**M**rs Anderson,' Rhonda's voice was gentle as she crossed the station reception to take Jean gently by the arm. 'Let's get you a seat.'

Grace followed as Rhonda led the visibly trembling woman into one of the side rooms beside the reception area. The older woman's pink shirt was rumpled as if she had slept in it.

'Grace, please will you get Mrs Anderson a cup of tea.' Rhonda looked at Jean as she spoke, her raised eyebrows poising a question about the choice of drink.

Jean nodded gratefully, letting Rhonda steer her towards a chair. She pushed her tangle of dark hair off her face, tucking it behind her ears in a distracted gesture.

The kettle in the office behind the reception area was already warm, kept so by the near constant use by the officers. Grace made tea, found a tray, added sachets of sugar, tipped a few chocolate biscuits onto a plate and hurried back.

'Thank you,' Jean turned her tear ravaged face to smile weakly at Grace as she put the mug of tea in front of her.

Rhonda pulled out the chair beside her, indicating that Grace should sit down.

'So…your daughter…?' Rhonda spoke softly.

'Carrie,' Jean spoke her daughter's name with reverence. 'She's sixteen.'

'How long has she been missing?' Rhonda asked, pen poised over the regulation form.

'Last night. We had a row. She ran off. I thought she'd come back. I was out half the night with a neighbour, looking for her.' Jean's voice caught in her throat as tears of despair began to fall once again.

Beside her Grace was aware of Rhonda releasing a long breath. A runaway. She had a sudden vision of rows with her parents, the anger at what she saw as their stupid rules, slamming doors, raised voices. While as she had got older those parental instructions had usually been bypassed by climbing out of the bedroom window, she could not ever imagine being so upset to have run away.

'Hopefully, she's just cooling off somewhere and will come back when she's bored and fed up.' Rhonda sat back in her chair, smiling sympathetically at Jean.

'We looked everywhere, Lizzy, my neighbour has a daughter too, she knows where the kids congregate.' Jean tried and failed to bring the tea to her lips with a hand that trembled so much the liquid slopped from the mug. Bright, cheap looking rings glittered on most of her fingers.

'Friends?' Grace prompted.

'We've only just moved here.' Jean brought a hand to her mouth to stifle a sob. 'We came from Manchester. My marriage broke up. I wanted a fresh start. Carrie's been so angry at me. She wants her dad. She doesn't understand he's not interested. He's got a new family.'

Rhonda grabbed a dusty looking box of tissues off the windowsill and pushed them in Jean's direction.

'Could she try to get back to Manchester?' Grace asked. It seemed the most likely scenario.

Jean shook her head violently, turning wild eyes to look at Grace. 'She wouldn't do that.' She grabbed a fistful of tissues and dabbed ineffectively at her eyes, discarding the sodden balls of paper on the table. 'Some lads saw her around nine. Lizzy knew them. We spoke to them outside the school.'

'Maybe she went to one of their houses?' That was a logical explanation to where Carrie could have gone. She was probably safely snoozing on someone's sofa, unaware of the trauma she had created. Or, Grace mused, if she was a little cow, probably only too aware of it and revelling in the pain she had caused her mother. There were other, darker explanations, but she pushed those to the very back of her mind. This was Cornwall, a peaceful backwater where nothing happened except, what some other forces would consider, very petty crime.

'What does Carrie look like?' Rhonda's voice, while gentle, had a steely edge, designed to focus Jean.

'She's...' Jean tried and failed to bring her thoughts into order.

'How tall is she?' Rhonda began, prompting Jean.

Describing her daughter brought fresh, heart rendering sobs from Jean. The box of tissues exhausted, Grace fetched new ones and then sat beside Rhonda, listening as Carrie's description was slowly drawn from her mother.

'Five foot seven, long auburn hair, blue eyes, wearing jeans and a sweatshirt.' Rhonda read aloud.

Jean nodded, she'd stopped crying now, her eyes, red above ghostly white cheeks. 'What happens now?' Jean wrapped her arms around her body as if to warm herself.

'I'm going to get you taken home. I don't think you should drive. We'll make some enquiries. Hopefully Carrie will be at home waiting for you.'

Jean nodded bleakly, shooting a tight, hopeful smile at the two officers.

'Shit, I hope she's there waiting for her mum.' Rhonda released a long breath as Jean, left with the officers who had been given the job of getting her home. 'The alternative is that she's halfway to Manchester now.'

'Okay,' Steve Cooper puffed out his cheeks, as Rhonda handed him the information about Carrie. 'Missing teenager.'

He read the form, despatching an officer to the school to talk to any pupils who knew Carrie. 'Keep your eyes open for this missing kid.' He addressed the officers and detectives. 'I'll bet she's home by lunchtime.'

Grace sat beside Rhonda as they drove out of the station car park a few minutes later. Rhonda's eyes swept the pavements at either side of the road. 'She's probably already home. Spent the night with some friends.'

'Little Riverton,' Grace intoned, looking at the list of calls she and Rhonda were to make. 'Sheep on the road.'

'Siren on do you think?' Rhonda's voice had a wry edge as they left the town and headed out into the countryside.

Half an hour later, Rhonda was reversing the car into a gateway and accelerating back towards the station. 'Oh no.' She slammed her hand on the steering wheel, the first time she had spoken since the radio had crackled into life. 'A girl has been found at the old boatyard. Looks like she's been attacked. We're assuming it's our missing teenager.'

Rhonda steered the patrol car along the narrow lanes. On the dual carriageway she put on the siren, scattering traffic in their wake.

'A dog walker found her near the derelict buildings on the old boatyard,' Steve Cooper's voice came through the radio. 'Poor kid.'

Rhonda, her eyes never leaving the road, grimaced. 'Shit. Hope you're ready for this, Grace.'

A few moments later they left the dual carriageway, hurtling around the traffic island at breakneck speed. Their progress seemed painfully slow as they drove through Hildon.

'That's where she lives,' Rhonda, recognising the address from Jean's interview, pointed towards a small, old-fashioned row of stone terraced houses, just off the main street.

At the end of the village, they turned off the main road into the old boatyard. The ruined remnants of buildings, a rusting patchwork of steel girders and corrugated sheeting, stood incongruously beside the achingly beautiful blue ribbon of the sea estuary.

'There's the ambulance.' Grace craned forwards to look through the windscreen as Rhonda drove quickly across the abandoned boatyard, tyres bumping on the uneven ground. At the far end of the concrete apron, they could see the ambulance, a tangle of people standing around in the gaping doorway of one of the buildings.

As they reached the ambulance Steve Cooper's car, with one of the other detectives in the passenger seat, skidded to a halt beside them.

'Here goes,' Rhonda was out of the car and jogging towards the ambulance before Grace had undone her seatbelt. Fingers fumbling at the clasp, Grace hurried after her.

They plunged into the semi darkness of the building. Grace had an impression of corrugated sheets high above her, one swaying gently in the breeze. Around the building was a mess of steelwork, upturned boats, unidentifiable machinery and heaps of ropes.

'What have we got?' Steve asked, as he reached the ambulance attendants.

Grace just stopped in time to avoid cannoning into him.

'It's not looking good.' One of the ambulance attendants said shortly, kneeling over the blanket covered form. The figure on the stretcher looked tiny, frail, scraps of bone and skin held together by the tattered clothes she wore. Above the hospital blanket poked a bony shoulder, the skin scraped, raw looking. Beneath a tangle of red hair, what parts of the girl's face were unhidden by the oxygen mask, looked like raw meat, bruised, swollen, her closed eyes barely visible beneath the battered skin.

One arm sprawled sideways from beneath the incongruously coloured baby blue blanket. Grace could see bruising, livid purples and deep reds staining the pale skin.

'Leather bracelet, black nail varnish' Steve spoke as if to himself. 'This has to be Carrie.'

Grace glanced into the building where Carrie had lain. The scene of crime officers were photographing the scene. As she watched one laid a marker against a shoe print outlined in blood.

Grace turned away, fighting the nausea that bubbled in her throat.

'All right love? Tough one.' Steve glanced at Grace.

'Fine. Thank you.' Grace was determined not to show him how upset she was.

'Jesus, poor kid,' Rhonda voiced, echoing all their thoughts.

'Will she make it?' Steve's professional voice was business-like.

The ambulance attendant shrugged, still working on the girl.

'Was she…?'

'Jeans round her ankles, so yes, I'd assume so. We'll know more when we get her to hospital.' He stood, facing Steve for the first time, his bitter sounding voice, coming through lips twisted in anger.

'Who found her?'

'The man, there. With the dog. Brian Morris, he said his name was.' He pointed in the direction of one of the upturned boats, on which sat a man draped in a green hospital blanket, his face mirroring its colour.

'Take a statement, Rhonda, will you?'

Grace hurried after Rhonda, glad not to have to look at the broken figure of Carrie any longer.

'Sir. Mr Morris, you found her?' Rhonda gently touched the dog walker's arm. He jerked the limb away in surprise, looking at the two policewomen as if he had no idea where he was.

'Yes,' his eyes were drawn relentlessly towards the ambulance, and the still form on the stretcher.

'Can you tell me what happened please?' Rhonda's voice was gentle.

'Alfie found her.' The man rubbed at his dog's head. 'I always walk here before I go into work. I do an afternoon shift at the supermarket.'

There was a stain of what Grace took to be vomit on the lapel of his jacket. Whatever he did for a job, Grace knew he wouldn't be doing it today. She couldn't imagine the horror of stumbling upon someone so badly injured.

'Alfie started barking.' He covered his mouth with bloodless fingers. 'When I came to get him…' The man leant forwards as if he thought he would pass out, resting his elbows on his knees.

'We'll need a statement from you, but perhaps later when you feel…'

He nodded, waving a hand as if to bat irritating flies away.

'Could we take your address?' Rhonda said quietly. 'We'll visit later.'

Grace patiently waited as the man stumbled over the lines of his address. 'Sorry,' he shook his head. 'Brain not working.'

They helped the man to his feet, watching as he walked away, his face turned determinedly away from the scene around the ambulance.

'I don't know if she's going to make it to the hospital,' the ambulance driver slammed the ambulance door shut.

'Bastard. I'm going to catch whoever did this to her.' Steve turned, running a hand through his thinning hair, his face set in anger.

'Sir?' Grace couldn't contain the words that bubbled out of her.

Steve glanced in her direction; his eyebrows raised expectantly.

'Could this be connected to the other missing girls? Someone who…'

'Fuck's sake, Tallis. This girl has been attacked. We've got a serious crime on our hands. Let's solve this.' Steve shook his head impatiently. 'I know you're keen but for heaven's sake stop going on about missing girls.'

As if he had never spoken Steve turned his attention away from Grace. 'Rhonda. The two of you had better go and tell Jean Anderson we may have found her daughter.'

Chapter Twenty-Three

'Shit. Great. Door knocking with this kind of news is the worst job he could have given us. You need to learn to keep your mouth shut,' Rhonda glared at Grace before turning to stare out of the windscreen at the scene of crime. She flexed her fingers around the steering wheel. 'Steve Cooper is the boss. He's a good copper, but he won't stand for you butting in with your opinion like that.'

'I just…' Grace released the breath she'd been holding.

The two were silent, watching as the white suited officers picked their way intently around the area where the girl had lain.

'I know.' Rhonda spun around in the driver's seat, facing Grace. 'You just want to help, make a difference, but you have to leave Steve to it. I know you'd love to think there's some weirdo going around kidnapping girls, but there's no evidence.'

Grace bit her lip, determined not to give into the tears that prickled at the back of her eyes. 'The people from Scotland whose daughter, Ayla is missing. There's another, Glanna, from near Penzance, who was at university, she's vanished. Now Carrie.'

Rhonda shook her head. 'Grace, were you awake during your induction classes? You know how this works. There are hundreds of people who go missing every year. Most of them come back in a few days, some just don't want to be found.'

Beyond the car, the officers were packing up their equipment, heaving it into the back of their van, stripping off their white suits to reveal jeans and sweatshirts beneath.

Rhonda pointed in the direction of the officers. 'That, right there. Examining where she was attacked. Do you know how much that costs? Do you know how those officers spend their days? Trawling through things like this, costing the force a fortune, often for nothing.'

'I'm sorry. I won't say anything again.' Grace stared hard at her hands, twisting her fingers together in her lap.

'You've a lot to learn, Miss Marple,' Rhonda said kindly, shaking her head as she started the car.

It took only minutes to drive the short distance from the boatyard to where Jean and Carrie lived.

'Number sixty-three.' Rhonda manoeuvred the car slowly into a gap between the parked cars. There was a steady deliberateness to her driving. Grace wondered if she wanted to delay the awful moment when they had to go and tell Jean her daughter had been found.

'There's always the chance that her daughter is home and that the person we found is totally unconnected to this.' Rhonda mused. 'But I doubt it. She was wearing clothes that fitted the description her mother gave.'

'Poor woman,' Grace said, following Rhonda towards the house. Grace took in the neat pocket handkerchief front garden, terracotta pots overflowing with plants, the smell of lavender.

The front door opened before Rhonda had time to ring the doorbell. 'Have you found her?' Jean's words tumbled together. Her voice had an almost hysterical edge. It was hard to imagine anyone being told their daughter had been found, barely clinging to life.

'We've found a girl who fits the description of Carrie.' Rhonda said quietly, her eyes never leaving Jean's ashen face. 'Can we come in?'

Jean stumbled backwards, her hand clinging to the door frame, the only thing keeping her upright. She took a long, juddering breath, visibly squared her shoulders and led the way down the hallway.

Grace followed the two women into a brightly lit kitchen at the back of the house. Although it was mid-afternoon, the strip light burned, as if Jean had forgotten it was still on. 'Perhaps you should sit down.' Grace pulled one of the chairs out from beneath the kitchen table.

'Is she dead?' Jean's wild eyes moved from Grace to Rhonda.

'No. But she is badly injured.'

Jean covered her mouth with her hands, as if trying to contain her howl of pain.

'We'll take you to the hospital, you can see her there.'

Jean nodded, her eyes blank, uncomprehending.

'Is it okay for PC Tallis to get your coat and handbag?'

'Yes.' Jean seemed incapable of any movement. She sat hunched, dry-eyed, while Grace found a coat and her handbag hanging on a hook behind the front door, amongst a brightly coloured selection of hoodies, all of which must have belonged to Carrie.

Obedient as a small child, Jean allowed Grace to help her into the coat and took her bag, looking at it with sightless eyes.

Jean sat in silence in the back of the car, staring blankly out of the window as Rhonda drove to the hospital.

'What's happened to her?' Jean whispered, as Grace helped her from the car.

'We don't know yet, Mrs Anderson,' Rhonda led the way through the hospital. 'We'll know more once the doctors have looked at her.'

The walk to the emergency department seemed interminable, an endless meandering through a rabbit warren of long corridors.

'There's a family room just here.' Rhonda eased open a door, checking it was empty, before guiding Jean inside and helping her to sit down. Her knowledge of the hospital and its inner workings made Grace realise that this horror was nothing unusual to Rhonda.

'Stay with Jean. I'm going to find out what's going on.' Rhonda gently patted Grace's back as she eased herself past.

Grace sat beside Jean, watching as the woman began to shift through her handbag, her fingers moving listlessly. 'When can I see her?' Jean asked suddenly, abandoning her search.

'Rhonda… PC White will be back in a minute. She'll know more.'

'Was Carrie outside all night?' Jean pulled out her purse, looking at it as if she had no idea what it was. She opened it, removing the contents, before putting them back again.

'I'm not sure.' Grace felt helpless, afraid of Jean's pain. She looked up, relieved as Rhonda returned.

'Jean, I'm going to take you into Carrie's room.'

Jean got slowly to her feet her movements measured. 'Thank you.'

Steve Cooper was in the corridor, 'The doctor is in with Carrie,' he said gently, touching Jean's arm to get her attention.

Jean nodded mechanically, following Rhonda into Carrie's room.

'Poor woman,' Steve met Grace's eyes as Jean's cry of horror echoed through the half open door.

'I'm sorry, sir. About earlier.' Grace stammered as the silence between them lengthened.

Steve shook his head, one corner of his wide mouth tilting upwards in the semblance of a smile. 'You're new. You're keen. It's not a bad thing.' Grace met his eyes, seeing the amusement that danced there. 'You'll learn.'

'What did the doctor tell you about Carrie?' Grace ventured.

Steve's eyes flickered over Grace's, before sliding away to look intently at one of the many official notices posted on the institution green walls. Moments slipped by while Grace wondered if she had asked too much, gone too far, angered Steve again.

'She's not good,' he said finally. 'Some bastard did a right job on her. Her head's been half caved in. He did that before, or perhaps after he'd…' the words faded on Steve's lips.

'Poor girl.'

'It's a wonder she's alive.'

'She probably wouldn't have been if the dog walker hadn't found her.'

155

'Is she going to make it?'

Steve shrugged. 'I don't know. Look at her.' He turned to look through the glass into the intensive care unit. Grace followed his gaze, drawing her eyes unwillingly to Carrie's bed. Her still form was festooned with tubes, surrounded by machinery which bleeped and flashed. Jean sat beside Carrie, her hand entwined into her daughter's, her lips moving, whispering to her daughter, willing her to live.

Rhonda met Grace's eyes through the glass. She shrugged helplessly.

'I'm hoping she's going to come around. Tell me who did this.' Steve's mouth twisted in anger.

Grace saw the pain in his face. He was taking this personally. No matter how much of a bad start they had got off to, she could tell he was a good man, who took his work seriously. Grace knew he'd be determined to find out whoever had done this to Carrie.

What, she wondered, had she been doing while Carrie lay motionless, in the cold darkness. Presumably she had been warm and safe at home while some faceless monster had attacked Carrie. Who was he? What was he doing now? Or was there more than one attacker? Grace tore her mind away from the horrific images that danced in front of her eyes. How much had Carrie endured before she had mercifully passed out? How could anyone do that and then return to a normal life?

It seemed they had been in the hospital forever, the hours slipping by unnoticed. The end of their shift came and went. Neither wanted to leave despite Steve telling them they should go home, that he would get other officers to sit with Jean and Carrie. He had insisted he was staying. The doctors and nurses came and went, monitoring Carrie. Grace fetched innumerable cups of tea from the canteen. They went undrunk, but somehow there was comfort to be found in the routine of holding the warmth of the cup, abandoning it only once the liquid became cold. Steve left and returned with sandwiches. Grace nibbled on the edge of one, before sliding it back into its packet, leaving it uneaten in the centre of the table along with the others.

It was dark outside when Jean emerged from Carrie's room. 'I don't know how to help her.'

'Come and sit in the family room. I'll get you tea. Something to eat?'

Rhonda guided Jean back to the family room where she sank down into the depths of one of the armchairs.

'Nothing. I couldn't eat. Tea? Yes, maybe tea.' Jean stared blankly around the room as if seeing it for the first time, her eyes flickering over the television, silently broadcasting a chat show.

'I'll fetch something.' Steve looked relieved to have something to do, other than waiting.

'She wanted to hurt me.' Jean folded her hands into her lap, looking at them as if she wasn't quite sure what they were. 'After the row. She went off in a huff.'

Rhonda nodded, her lips moving as if she were searching for a reply which would make things better.

'You didn't know this would happen.'

Jean looked up, tears falling freely down her pale cheeks. 'I was so angry at her. She just wanted to go back to Manchester to her dad. I felt safe here. Away from him. Carrie didn't know...'

Grace's throat constricted, she forced herself to swallow, the noise loud in the silence of the room.

'You mustn't feel guilty.' Rhonda said gently. 'You didn't do this to her.'

'I drove around looking for her. All night. I kept thinking she'd be hiding somewhere. Wanting to make me suffer. I kept thinking she'd come home. That she'd just walk in.'

'At least she's safe now.' Grace forced herself to meet Jean's eyes, seeing the pain reflected in them. 'She's in the best place.' She gently laid her hand on Jean's arm, feeling the rigid muscle beneath her blouse.

'Safe?' Jean wrenched her arm from Grace's hand. 'She doesn't even know where she is.'

'But when she comes around...'

Jean made a strangled noise. 'She's never going to come around. Her head's so badly damaged, the doctors think she'll stay like this forever. She's a vegetable.'

'But they can...'

Jean shook her head vehemently. 'Carrie's never coming back to me. There's no sign of brain activity, other than whatever is keeping her heart pumping and her lungs functioning. She's gone. My Carrie may as well be dead.'

Chapter Twenty-Four

'Tallis,' Rhonda pulled out a chair and sat down opposite Grace. 'We're going to bring in the lads Jean said Carrie was with the night she was attacked.'

Grace pushed her tea away.

'Come on, I'll drive.' Rhonda made her way out of the building with Grace on her heels. 'Steve wants us to have a quiet chat about what happened that night.' Rhonda puffed out her cheeks. 'If one of them hurt that girl…' She accelerated the patrol car out of the line of cars onto the traffic island.

Grace nodded. Could the lads have done that to Carrie? It was hard to imagine anyone possessing that level of violence, let alone some kids. Perhaps, if spurred on by one another… drink… drugs, maybe?

The women were silent as they drove past the abandoned boatyard. All the recent police activity had disappeared from the deserted land, the clutter of machinery, upturned boats and derelict buildings once again lonely and isolated. Grace shuddered. Carrie had lain there all night, unconscious, the life slowly draining away from her. Who could have done that? Who thought so little about another human being they could be so callous?

'That poor kid,' Rhonda voiced Grace's thoughts.

Their route took them past the house road where Carrie and Jean lived. Grace's eyes were drawn restlessly to the small, semi-detached house. Carrie had gone out from there, never thinking she would come to any harm. Her thoughts had only been occupied with hurting her mother.

'Why are we picking the lads up at school?' Grace winced, as Rhonda drove into the school car park. Regardless of whether or not they had attacked Carrie, it seemed so blatantly accusatory to pick them up from school.

'Because Steve says so.' Intoned Rhonda. Pulling into an empty parking spot, she turned to face Grace. 'He doesn't want them talking to one another, getting their stories straight. He called ahead, and they've been brought out of class and into Mr Maplin, the headmaster's office. We'll quietly bring them away and off to the station.'

'That makes sense.' It was an horrific thought, imagining the lads, if they had indeed hurt Carrie, discussing the crime, being cynical enough to cover their tracks.

Rhonda led the way through the silent hallways of the school. Their visit had been timed so the pupils would all be in class. There would be no curious eyes watching the three lads leaving.

'Up here.' Rhonda gestured towards a sign on the wall, directing them to the headmaster's office, up a short flight of stairs. 'I was always in trouble at school.' She turned to grimace at Grace.

'Come in.' The headmaster's voice had a resigned note to it.

The three youths were sitting on plastic chairs, lined up against the wall of the office, their faces equally pale and set.

'Here they are. Tom, Simon and Alan.' The headmaster gestured towards each of the lads before he stuck out a hand towards the policewomen.

'Thanks for bringing them out of class.' Rhonda smiled sympathetically, briefly shaking his hand.

'Right lads.' Rhonda turned to face the terrified looking boys. Whatever bluster they possessed as young adults had vanished completely in the face of the seriousness of the situation. 'Mr. Maplin has explained to you what's happening. We just need to take you to the station for a few questions.'

Alan sniffed, all semblance of bravado gone. 'Will my parents be there?'

'Another officer will let them know what's happening, but since you are all adults, they don't need to be present.'

'Do we need solicitors?' Simon shuffled his feet, staring at the tiled floor. Were those the boots that had made the bloodstained footprints around Carrie, Grace wondered shuddering involuntarily at the thought. The lads looked so normal, so ordinary.

Rhonda shook her head, 'No,' her voice was gentle, recognising the fear in the youths. 'We aren't charging you with anything. We just want to chat about the night Carrie was attacked.'

'She was fine when we left her.' Tom, the shortest of the lads, crowned with a mop of wiry dark hair, said sullenly.

'We've a car outside.' Grace stood to one side indicating with a wave of her arm that the group should move.

One by one, the lads trooped through the corridors, the silence broken only by the squeak of their soles on the floor, and the occasional raised voice from behind the closed doors.

Back at the station, the three lads were put into separate rooms before they were interviewed.

'We can watch.' Rhonda said, opening the door into a room behind the interview suite.

Grace pulled out a chair, resting her chin on her elbows, watching Steve and Paddy another of the detectives asking what had happened on the evening Carrie had been attacked, where they had been, where they had gone afterwards. Each told the same story, in different rambling versions, the various parts of the night being related from their points of view, each remembering things slightly differently.

Rhonda stood up as the interviews finished. 'I don't think they had anything to do with what happened to her.'

'So, who did?'

After the lads had been released and driven home, Steve called a briefing. 'You two come on in.' He called Rhonda and Grace, holding open the door to let them into the briefing room.

'We've spoken to the three boys who were with Carrie Anderson on the night she was attacked. Their stories tally. My feelings are they aren't involved. One of them said they went off to smoke in the grounds of the school before they went home, and that Carrie stayed in the boatyard.'

A murmur of agreement went around the assembled officers.

'She stayed. Why?' Paddy asked running a hand over the stubble on his chin.

'We don't know.' Steve shrugged. 'I would imagine she just didn't want to go home. She wanted to frighten her mum, and so she decided to hang around the boatyard for a while longer.'

'Whoever attacked her... Did they mean to kill her? Do they think she's dead?' Paddy spoke again, fumbling in his pockets for, and eventually finding, a pack of cigarettes.

'Your guess is as good as mine, Paddy.'

'If they know she's still alive, maybe they're panicking? They could do something stupid. Someone around them might notice something's wrong?'

Steve turned to look at the pictures of Carrie on the whiteboard behind him, lingering on the stark contrast between her smiling face and her ruined body. 'I don't know.'

'None of the lads saw anything.' Paddy released a plume of cigarette smoke towards the ceiling.

Steve shook his head. 'So, they said. Alan, the red-headed lad, thought he saw some kind of farm pick-up on the site, which he assumed belonged to a courting couple. He didn't pay much attention to it.'

'Could be our man?' Paddy tapped the ash from his cigarette into the rubbish bin beside him.

'Could there be someone targeting young women?' The words were out of Grace's mouth before she could stop them. 'There've been reports of other girls missing...'

She met Steve's eyes, saw him grimace.

'If we tried to find a connection between every missing person, we'd

161

spend our lives chasing our tails. This is a random, if nasty, attack on a poor, daft kid. Grace, just focus on this attack.'

'Let's just find this bastard.' Paddy stubbed his cigarette out viciously against the side of the bin. 'I want to tear him limb from limb.'

A weekend off came as a much-needed break, made all the better by Katia being home. The sunshine drew them to the beach where they sat outside one of the beachside bars. The image of Carrie still played in Grace's imagination. 'That poor girl. I can't get her out of my mind, Katia.'

Katia took off the glasses she had recently begun to wear and began to polish them on a handkerchief she'd pulled from her jeans pocket before putting them back on. 'Your job is so tough Grace. I couldn't do it.'

Grace put down her coffee cup and met Katia's eyes. Behind the lenses, they were a brilliant blue. Usually, they danced with pent up laughter, but today, they were filled with concern.

'I mean, she'd just had a row with her mum and stormed out.'

'Oh, the number of times we did that.' Katia lifted her head, looking beyond Grace, out to sea. Below them, on the beach, families were soaking up the sun, sprawled out on the sand, relaxing. She watched a toddler run on unsteady legs into the shallows, screaming and stumbling as a small wave rolled over its feet. The little girl fell, with a scream, she was scooped up a moment later by a man who wrapped his arms around her, soothing her cries.

'I know...' Grace replied, cringing at the memories.

'Were we just lucky we got away with it?'

'These kind of attacks are very rare,' Grace circled a finger in the damp mark left by her coffee cup. It was hard to comprehend the dangers there were in the world, that a stroke of bad luck, a chance encounter could change everything.

'Well, we did.' Katia was silent for a moment, watching the shadows of emotion flit across Grace's face. 'Are you okay?' She laid a gentle hand on Grace's, stopping the distracted movement of her finger in the cold coffee.

'It's so hard,' Grace addressed her words to the battered wooden bench. 'I've come to learn that we make plans, but there's no way of knowing if they'll ever be kept. We think we'll be doing something as simple as going out for a coffee with our friends, but a fraction of a second can change all that. Being in the wrong place, at the wrong time. Two years in this job has shown me a lot.'

'Was joining the police a mistake?' Katia asked tentatively. 'I couldn't begin to imagine what you go through in your job.'

Grace turned, staring out to sea once again. Close to the blue horizon she could see a line of boats, their white sails gleaming in the sunlight. 'I love my job. I didn't make a mistake doing it. But sometimes, there are things which are hard to deal with.'

She turned back, meeting Katia's eyes, and saw the sympathy that glowed there. How could she ever explain the horrors she had seen in the time she'd been in the police? Car crashes, domestic violence.

'It can be pretty boring too,' Grace tilted her lips upwards, knowing her smile had not met her eyes. 'Hours pounding up and down the streets, giving people directions, taking drink off school kids, getting cars moved.'

'What happened to the girl that was found by the old docks?'

Grace watched a tall man, his wetsuit folded down around narrow hips, haul a surfboard from the roof of his car, making his way down the boat ramp to the beach, as she tried to frame her words.

'I'm not supposed to talk about it, but it will probably be in the newspapers anyway...'

She and Rhonda had spent time with Jean after the accident, hoping Carrie might be able to talk to them, that she might defy the doctor's diagnosis and regain the spirit that had sent her running out the night she'd been attacked.

'She's...' the words froze on Grace's lips. It was impossible to frame Carrie and Jean's situation into words. What the future meant for them. A rehab unit when she was well enough. It was hard to imagine how Jean's life would now be spent caring for her daughter, trying to find some remnant of her personality in the blank expression of what remained.

Speaking about them brought the whole horrible nightmare back to life. It was better left, tucked away at the dark recesses of her mind.

'Another coffee?' Grace got abruptly to her feet, needing to move to free herself from the images. She moved into the bar without waiting for a reply, blinking against the dimness of the interior after the bright sunlight outside.

'What can I get you?' The young barman met her eyes, his lips tilting into a smile. His muscles rippled beneath his shirt as he raked long fingers through his hair.

'Coffee. Two coffees. Black.' It wasn't until he turned away that Grace realised he'd been flirting with her. Where had her mind been that she hadn't noticed? He was gorgeous, too. She shook her head, annoyed at herself. 'Get a grip,' she muttered, managing a bright smile when he returned with the coffees.

'You need something to take your mind off your work.' Katia assumed a motherly expression as Grace returned with the coffees and eased herself into the seat.

'You're right,' Grace agreed. She had to find an escape from the darkness that swirled in her mind.

Chapter Twenty-Five

'This is guaranteed to do you good,' Katia grinned, a few days later, lowering a riding helmet onto Grace's head.

'I'll reserve judgment on that,' Grace replied as she pushed it further down, unused to the unfamiliar feel. 'The gossip at the station is that I'm going to turn up for work tomorrow walking like a cowboy.'

'You won't,' Katia handed Grace a pair of riding boots. 'These are my second-best pair. You're very honoured to be able to borrow them.'

'Second-best?' Grace undid the laces on her trainers and slid her feet into the long leather boots. 'How many pairs do you need?'

'Oh, how little you know!' Katia joked. 'Many, many pairs, boots and hats, jodhpurs and tops. And that's just for riding out. Wait until you start competing! It was a shame you didn't want to ride when we were kids. We could have had lots of fun together.'

Grace shrugged. Ponies had always been Katia's passion when they were growing up, somehow she had never seen the appeal. It was only that she desperately needed a distraction from the stress of work she had agreed to come to the riding stables at all.

Katia fastened her helmet and slapped Grace on the back. 'You'll be hooked. I'd stake my reputation on it.'

'Make sure you look after me,' Grace followed Katia out of the changing room. 'I have a vital role to play keeping down Cornwall's criminals.' The boots felt stiff, the leather tight against her calves. Feeling ridiculous in the tall boots and tight hat, Grace walked self-consciously across the stable yard in Katia's wake.

Grace was already regretting her decision to accompany Katia on a ride. There was plenty to do other than this which would distract her.

'This is Tanny.' Katia announced, opening one of the stable doors. 'I've owned him for about three years. I think Dad bought him to make sure I'd come home from uni regularly.'

'Lovely.' Grace was unsure of the right way to complement Katia on her choice of steed. The horse, in her eyes, looked enormous, a vast, clumsy looking beast, dressed in more leather than a fetishist.

'You can say hello. He won't bite you.'

'Good.' Did they bite? Grace gingerly stretched her hand out, touching the horse's suede-soft muzzle, before running her fingers down the length of his face.

'Here's yours.' Katia pointed across the yard to where a good-looking man was leading a fox-red horse towards them.

'That's Copper,' Katia grinned. 'His name is to do with his colour, not anything to do with your job.

'Ha ha.' Grace watched the horse and man come towards her.

'That's Kaden. He runs this place. Everyone fancies the pants off him.'

* * * * *

'This is your first time?' Kaden stopped Copper beside Grace. As the big horse tossed his head, Grace took and involuntary stride back out of his way.

'Yes.' Grace felt foolish for having leapt away so quickly.

'He's as gentle as a lamb. He'll take great care of you. Do you need some help getting on?' Kaden's brown eyes danced with gentle amusement.

Without waiting for her reply, Kaden led Copper towards a tall stone block beside the stables. 'Hop up there. Put your foot in the stirrup, and just fling your leg over.'

Grace did as she was told.

'Okay?' Kaden met Grace's eyes.

'Yes, thank you.' It was easy to see why Katia said everyone fancied him. Kaden was gorgeous.

'I'll just sort out your stirrups.'

Copper, eased forwards by Kaden, took a gigantic stride. Grace resisted the urge to cling to his neck, forcing herself to relax.

'Oh, you're a natural.' Kaden adjusted the stirrups, helping Grace to slide her feet into them. 'Hang on there, I'll just get my own horse.'

Grace watched as Kaden, accompanied by what seemed to be a swarm of teenage girls, disappeared into one of the stables, emerging with a tall, elegant grey horse.

One of the girls held the horse's bridle, while Kaden nimbly got on.

'Ready?' With the reins in one hand, he fastened his riding hat and rode out of the yard.

'Okay?' Katia steered Tanny alongside Copper as they walked steadily out onto the lane.

'Yes,' Grace, relaxed, adjusting her body to Copper's steady stride. 'Yes. I am.'

'You'll have to agree I have the best ideas.' Katia grinned, as Tanny began to trot past Copper, slotting into place behind Kaden's grey horse.

Grace forced a breath between dry lips, feeling her heart thundering against her rib cage in terror.

The lanes away from the stables were narrow, a line of grass growing up the centre. Tall hedges grew at either side, providing shelter from the wind. Occasionally, where there was a gap in the foliage, Grace glimpsed the sea, blue, blurring on the horizon where it met the sky.

Kaden led the girls along the lanes, the horses walking calmly together. Later they rode a short distance along the beach, their horses' footfalls deadened by the golden sand. Gradually Grace relaxed, focusing on the movement of the horse beneath her. Katia had been right. This had been the perfect way to take her mind off the turmoil of policework and yet gave her chance to mull over her work.

On the way back to the stables, Kaden took a different route, stopping his horse beside a field, where a dark horse, galloped towards them the green turf.

'My new boy,' Kaden turned in his saddle to speak. 'He's just arrived from Ireland.'

Grace watched. She had never seen anything so beautiful, so full of power and majesty.

Back at the stables, Grace slithered out of the saddle, watching as one of the teenage girls led Copper away.

'You were right,' she admitted to Katia. 'It was just what I needed.'

She followed Katia to her car, 'I'm really sorry you're going back tomorrow. I'm going to miss you.'

Katia started the car, casting a look of regret around the stable yard. 'I hate going. Once I'm qualified, I want to come home and never have to go away again.' She reversed out of the parking spot. 'I'm glad you enjoyed riding. It did you good to stop thinking about crime. What else could you do to keep your mind off your job?'

'You know,' Grace met Katia's eyes, nodding. 'I might just continue riding.'

Chapter Twenty-Six

'Six weeks.' Kaden exhaled, sitting back in his chair, and placing his feet on the battered office table, crossing his booted legs at the ankles. 'That's pretty impressive.'

'Thanks,' Grace watched him coolly, never sure if he were teasing. 'So, you'll sell me the Irish horse.'

Kaden's easy manner was part of his charm. It was clear to see why, whenever he walked across the stable yard or rode one of the horses in the sand arena, all the eyes of the horse-mad girls were on him.

'He's not cheap.' Kaden lit a cigarette, putting his head back to leisurely blow smoke rings towards the cobweb strewn ceiling.

'How much?' Grace struggled to pull herself upright in of one of the battered armchairs. The only other chair, in the riding school office,

169

the most comfortable, had been occupied by one of the elderly terriers who lived at the stables. He had growled when Grace had approached it, warning her not to move him from his prized position.

'Come on, let's go and have a look at the horse.' In one swift, graceful movement, Kaden got to his feet, crossing the room to offer Grace his hand to help her out of the armchair.

She took his hand, letting him pull her upright. Her head barely reached the top of his shoulders. Once standing Grace stepped back abruptly, not used to being so close to him.

'Err…' Grace looked down at their still entwined fingers, her heart thundering uncomfortably. Kaden released her hand. She followed him across the cobbled yard, her fingers still tingling from the touch of his against hers.

'He's done so well. He's very bright, and kind.' Kaden flung open the horse's stable door. Sunlight streamed in, the shaft of light illuminating the horse's dark coat. He took a stride forwards, nuzzling gently at Grace's pockets, looking for the treats he had come to expect. 'The girls have him spoilt. They're all in love with him.'

'Him and you,' Grace snorted in amusement, watching as Kaden's face twisted into a broad grin.

'Six weeks. You've learned to ride really quickly. You're a natural,' Kaden ignored her comment, busying himself with adjusting the horse's rug.

'You're a good teacher.' Grace eased her shoulders. She was still sore from one of the many falls she'd had as Kaden had pushed her to greater feats in one of the many riding lessons he'd given her. It had been a difficult time, trying to fit in as many lessons as she could alongside a tough shift pattern. She'd managed though, coming to the riding school, sometimes in the early morning after a long, boring nightshift driving around the Cornish lanes on traffic duty, or after a long day walking the streets when she ached with tiredness. Kaden had been relentless, quickly getting her used to the gentle pace of Copper, where she had ridden for hours without stirrups, circling in the dusty sand arena.

She'd quickly progressed onto more advanced horses, developing her skill and sense of balance astride their different shapes and sizes.

Alongside her own lessons she'd watched Kaden riding the handsome black Irish horse, now called Sisco.

Grace, aware of Kaden's frown of disapproval, pulled a packet of mints from her jeans pocket, and gave one to Sisco, his big lips gently taking the sweet from her outstretched palm. She met Kaden's eyes and grinned, wondering if half of her pleasure in keeping the horse at the yard would be that she got to spend time with Kaden.

A few moments later Sisco belonged to Grace. She shook Kaden's hand, sealing the deal, before driving home, her head spinning at the eyewatering amount she had paid for him.

But it would be worth it. The time where she could relax, take her mind off her job was beyond value.

She was still reeling when she walked into the station for the late shift, an hour later, hair still damp from the shower.

'Just slow down.' Rhonda, on duty at the reception desk, was holding up her hand to slow the torrent of noise coming from the couple standing beside the glass screen that separated her from the public.

'Slow down?' snapped the woman, bringing a hand to her neck, as if to cool the hot flush that stained her skin. 'How can I slow down? My daughter is out there, somewhere, and I don't know where she is.'

'I just need to…' Rhonda paused, her pen poised over the notepad.

'You need to get out there, start looking for her.' The woman leant against the desk, as if her legs wouldn't support her any longer.

Grace went to stand beside Rhonda, meeting the panic-stricken expression of the smartly dressed man who was with the near-hysterical woman.

'It's your daughter that's missing?' Grace addressed the man. The late afternoon sunlight streaming in through the dusty station windows highlighted the grey which streaked his hair. He wore a blue suit, which hung on him in elegant folds. the top buttons of his pale blue shirt were open, revealing a smattering of dark hairs. A tie, hauled out of its knot, hung limply, halfway down his chest.

'Yes, Julie. Julie Peterson. She's fifteen.'

'We came home from work and the house was empty. She should have been there. She always comes straight home from school. We've telephoned all her friends. Anyone we could think of.' The words rattled from her lips like machine gun fire, her eyes darting from Grace, to Rhonda, and back again.

Looking at the woman's smart dress and high heels, Grace imagined her walking into her home, expecting to see Julie there. What horrors had flitted through the couple's minds before they had come to the station, she wondered?

'I'm going to take some details. Then, you need to go home, I'll get an officer to come there straight away. Try to have something to eat, I'm sure Julie will come home safely.' Rhonda's voice was calm and measured.

'Safely?' snapped Julie's mother, 'How can you say that? After what happened to the Anderson girl. There could be a maniac out there.'

'I'm sure Julie is fine. Please, don't worry.' Grace backed up Rhonda with more reassurance than she felt.

As the Peterson's made their way out of the station, Grace slid the form from the desk. 'I'll tell Steve Cooper.'

'Grace. Don't ...' She heard, and ignored, the warning tone in Rhonda's voice.

Grace hurried along the narrow corridors making up the warren that were the inner workings of the station. Steve's office was at the back of the building, its window looking out over the town's rooftops, and down to the sea.

Tapping lightly on his door, Grace walked into his office. 'There's another girl gone missing....' She slid the paper across his desk.

'Tallis....Slow down.' Steve Cooper puffed out his cheeks.

'There's a girl missing from Penzance, Glanna Penrick. Ayla McDonald. Carrie Anderson. And now, another one. There could be a link.'

'Tallis. I'm getting tired of your attitude.' Steve's voice had a hard edge. 'I'm the detective here, you're just a novice plod. Maybe you should let me do my job.' Steve's chair creaked as he leant back. 'I've dealt with missing people before. If I had a pound every time I get a panicking parent through the station doors...'

'But Sir...'

'Back off Tallis.' Cooper's voice had a taut edge.

Grace retreated back to the reception office.

'Shit. I just got a dressing down from DI Cooper.' Grace blurted out, fighting the urge to vomit with nerves.

'Nice one.' Rhonda's eyes danced with good-natured amusement. 'I hope you have a good flak jacket.'

'He was furious at me.'

'I'll bet he was.' Rhonda shook her head, pulling a wry expression. 'Why didn't you listen to me?'

She was on tender hooks all night, waiting for the inevitable call from Steve, knowing just how furious he was with her. A team was dispatched to the Peterson's, while Rhonda and Grace were sent out into the town to pound the streets.

Early on in their shift came the call that Julie had returned home safely. The highlight of their night was arresting a man for drunk and disorderly conduct.

It was daylight, the streets just beginning to come alive again, when the two made their way back to the station. 'Oh no, he's going to kill me.' Grace saw the reception phone line light up, knowing Steve would undoubtedly summon her to his office.

'Yes, I think he is.' Rhonda said a moment later, wincing as she replaced the telephone receiver. 'Good luck.'

It seemed to take forever to walk to Steve's office, the knowledge of the dressing down she was going to receive filling Grace with dread.

'Ah, thank you for coming' Steve's voice dripped sarcasm as he opened his office door and waved a hand airily in the direction of the seat opposite his.

On shaking legs, Grace sat, blinking at the sunlight that streamed in through the window behind him, knowing his expression was hidden, while hers was in full view of Steve's.

'Don't ever do that again.' Steve's voice was cold.

'I'm sorry.' Grace wiped at the sweat that had broken out on the bridge of her nose, hoping he wouldn't think she was crying.

'Sorry?' he hissed. 'Fuck's sake Tallis, who do you think you are? Barging in like that, making demands.'

Grace forced herself to look in the direction of his face, glad she couldn't see the anger and disappointment she knew were there.

'Julie Peterson was home when her parents arrived. She'd stayed with some boy they knew nothing about. Fuck knows what was going on in her empty head, doing that to her poor parents.'

'Yes. PC Eastwood let us know. I'm so glad she's safe.'

Steve drummed his fingers on the desk, the silence between them lengthening. Through the window behind his head, Grace watched a seagull wheeling in the blue sky.

'Bloody idiot, you'd have had half the force out arresting any man with even half a testicle.'

Grace's shoulders slumped as she fought back bitter tears of disappointment. Steve was going to sack her. She'd messed up the one career she had really wanted to pursue.

'I hope I'm not going to regret this.' Steve leant forwards, his face moving away from the harsh light behind him. 'But I think you're wasted in uniform. I want you to train to be a detective.

Chapter Twenty-Seven

1997

'Higher!' Mia squealed with delight, kicking her legs into the air, twisting her body so she could haul on the rope swing, propelling the tyre higher into the air.

'Wait a minute,' Eddie made a grab for the nylon rope, catching it, bringing its motion to an abrupt halt. 'Get off a minute, let me put this under you so it's more comfortable.'

Mia wriggled out of the tyre, watching as Eddie pulled off his tattered work sweater, using it to pad the bottom of the tyre. 'There, try again.' He held the tyre steady while Mia slipped her slender body through it and perched her bottom on the sweater. It felt a lot more comfortable than the rough edges of the inside of the tyre, the fabric still retained some of the warmth of his body.

'Push me, please. You said I could go high when I was eight.' She pleaded, leaning her body away from the tyre as she clung to the rope, lifting her legs so the motion began to swing it further and further into the air. Mia lay back, watching the sunlight dance through the leaves of the tree, her long hair trailing on the ground.

'I can't. I have things to do. You can do it on your own, you're a big girl now, you don't need me pushing you.' Eddie gave Mia a final shove, the swing catapulting into the air, the rope coiling into nothingness as she went upwards before it snapped back down, her laughter ringing out at the giddy motion.

It wasn't as much fun without her father to play with. Mia swung idly, watching him work, chopping wood with the axe he swung so easily. Then, bored, she let the motion of the swing come slowly to a halt, before wriggling out of the tyre.

Mia drifted around the outside of the house, continuing to watch Eddie, then, bored, she wandered into the yard, picking a handful of grass to feed to the calves in one of the sheds. She found an abandoned bucket and stood on it to try and tempt the calves with the grass. They huddled at the back of their enclosure, puffing their breath out in fear. Annoyed, Mia threw the grass towards them, the strands scattering on their straw bed.

Humming a tune, Mia let her imagination run wild as she drifted into the machinery shed. She was a wizard, looking for potions to cast spells with. There were bottles and containers of assorted colours and sizes stacked high on a shelf. Perfect for a wizard's concoctions. The shelf was too high, though. Mia stood on her tiptoes, fingers outstretched, but try as she might, she just couldn't reach. She dragged an empty oil cannister over to the workbench to stand on, but that tilted abruptly, sending her tumbling to the ground.

Rubbing her elbow, Mia sat up. Something glittered beneath the workbench that attracted her attention. A toolbox. Perhaps she could stand on that to reach the shelf. She pulled it out, idly lifting the top, before selecting a screwdriver. She pointed it in the air, waving it like a wand. It was too small. The one in Harry Potter was far longer. She lifted off the tray of tools, searching for bigger ones beneath.

Instead of the tools she had expected, there were small plastic bags heaped inside. Curious, Mia crouched, pulling them out into her lap, unfastening one of the bags to investigate its contents. Inside was a purse. The leather felt damp, sticky beneath her fingers. She opened it, letting her fingers rifle through the plastic cards. One had a picture on it, a smiling young woman, who beamed back at her. She opened more of the bags, finding necklaces, and a silver bracelet. Mia held one of the necklaces between her fingers. It was heavy, large colourful beads held together on a thread. She slipped it over her head, lifting her hair so it fitted in the nape of her neck.

Engrossed, Mia slid bracelets over her narrow wrists and necklaces over her head. She strutted the length of the building imagining she were a princess, covered in jewels. The ginger yard cat, balancing on the window ledge outside the shed, caught her attention. 'Simba, where've you been all week?' Mia wrenched the bracelets and necklaces off, pushed them back into the toolbox and slid it beneath the work bench, before heading out into the sunshine to find the cat.

Simba lay in the sunshine beneath the tangle of bushes that grew up the wall of the ruined building at the far side of the yard. Nan had told her to stay away from there, but Nan wasn't around. Besides, Simba lay in the undergrowth close to the almost hidden tiny window that fascinated Mia. She'd peered in there once before, seen shapes in the darkness. That had been before Nan had grabbed her shoulder and hauled her away.

She was halfway across the yard when the sound of an engine alerted her to the approach of a car. Mia glanced around, seeing Eddie abandon his work and head into the centre of the yard to meet the car. She darted into the shadows of the house, hiding behind the half open door. 'Hide if anyone comes.' Nan's words were never forgotten. 'Don't ever talk to strangers.'

Curious, she watched the car pull into the yard. The driver let down his window. 'I'm sorry, we're lost.'

'Yes, I can see that.' Eddie slid his hands into his pockets. 'Where are you looking for?'

'Middleton Farm. I don't think we're far away. It's a guest house, owned by people called Pascoe... We're staying there tonight. I tried to call but couldn't get an answer.'

There was a child in the back of the car. A young boy, her age, Mia guessed. He was engrossed in a book. One she recognised. Harry Potter. She'd read it already. She watched, fascinated at the boy's blonde hair, his face intent on the pages.

As if he sensed her eyes upon him, the boy looked up, his eyes meeting Mia's. In the driver's seat, his father glanced at the same time. Mia, shocked, darted behind the door.

'What are you doing?' Nan hissed, seizing Mia roughly by the shoulder and hauling her inside. Mia scrambled to keep her feet. 'Stay out of the way.'

Hot tears of fright prickled behind Mia's eyes, as she fought to contain them.

'What have I told you about talking to strangers?' Nan's fingers gripped the shoulder of Mia's top, pulling the fabric tight around her arms and neck, her voice barely more than a whisper.

'Dad was there.' Mia struggled, trying to get out of her grandmother's grip.

'I don't care who was there. Anyone comes here, you come inside.'

'They wouldn't hurt me when Dad was there,' Mia willed herself to meet Nan's eyes. Nan stared out of the window, looking at the car in the yard. The man who had come looking for directions was showing no sign of driving away, but instead had rested one arm on the driver's door and was chatting to Eddie.

'How do you know that?' Nan's mouth turned down, her lips clamping into a tight line that made them disappear into the folds of her face. She punctuated her words by giving Mia a final shake, before releasing her abruptly.

Mia opened her mouth to reply but thought better of it.

'What's this?' Nan's fingers found a necklace Mia had forgotten to take off, twisting it hard, so the beads pressed painfully into Mia's skin.

'I found it.' Mia whispered.

'Where'd you find it?' Nan hauled the necklace over Mia's head, her clumsy fingers twining in the long hair. Mia yelped as the strands were tugged.

'Shut up. Be quiet,' Nan clasped Mia's top again, the beads in her hands digging into Mia's skin as she shook the child, jerking her roughly from side to side. 'Tell me. Where did you steal it from?'

'I didn't steal it.' Panic made Mia's voice high. 'I found it. In the shed. I was looking for a wand.'

'A wand?' Nan shook her head, incredulously. 'What else did you find?'

Mia stared at the floor. 'There was other stuff there. A purse, bracelets.'

'You don't go there again. Never touch that box. Ever. You're a wicked girl. Those things belong to me. And your dad. If I find you in there again, I'll cut your fingers off.'

Mia nodded silently, biting hard at the inside of her lip.

'Now, get upstairs, and stay there till I say you can come down.' Nan tugged at Mia's arm, propelling her towards the stairs. 'Go on. Up to your room. Out of my sight.'

Mia trudged slowly upstairs, looking back towards the kitchen, Nan was glaring through the kitchen window at the strangers. Mia rubbed her neck, fighting back tears, determined not to let Nan make her cry. The skin burned where Nan's fingers had gripped it.

Mia made her way to her bedroom at the front of the house, her stomach growling hungrily. She knew better than to risk going back downstairs while Nan was in a temper. Later, when her dad came inside, she'd risk it.

As she pushed open her bedroom door, Mia walked slowly to the window. From there, she could look out into the yard. The car was still there. Her dad stood in the centre of the yard, his arms folded across his chest, one foot tapping restlessly on the stone surface of the yard.

She stood beside the curtain, knowing that from here, she could not be seen, but could listen to the scraps of conversation that drifted in.

'It's good to get away,' the car driver was saying. 'Get out of London for some clean air.'

Eddie nodded.

'You're so lucky to live here. It's the most beautiful spot. Cornwall… I'd love to move down here.'

Mia saw Eddie nod once again, hearing his grunt of agreement.

179

'Be great to get Sean's nose out of a book for once. He's obsessed by this new one. Can't get a word out of him.'

'I should get on,' Eddie took a step backwards.

'This is a fabulous place for children. The moors, the beach, so much fresh air. My lad is cooped up indoors most of the time. We try to get down here as often as we can.' The car driver turned around in his seat to poke the boy behind him, trying to get his attention. He flashed Eddie a friendly grin, as if they were fellow conspirators, when the boy shouted in annoyance.

'See, always got to be reading.'

'Oh,' Eddie's voice had a taut note, which the man, garrulous in his delight at being in the countryside, seemed not notice.

'Is your little girl into this new wizard book, Harry Potter?'

Mia eased the curtain across the window a fraction more, afraid the man would glance up and see her. Whatever danger strangers posed she didn't want to risk it.

'There's no child here.' There was an aggressive edge to Eddie's voice.

'Oh, I thought I saw…' Mia jumped back, seeing the man gaze in astonishment at the house, at the doorway where she had hidden.

'You were mistaken.'

'Yes… I must have been.' There was a confused tone to the man's voice. 'Well, thank you for your help. We were further away than I thought.'

'You're welcome.' Eddie's voice was curt.

Eddie backed away across the yard, keeping his eyes firmly on the driver of the car. As Mia watched, hidden behind the thick curtains, the driver steered his car around the yard. He hit one of the uneven stone slabs, the car stopped abruptly. Grimacing awkwardly at Eddie he restarted the car, manoeuvred it around the yard, before finally managing to turn it and drive away. Eddie, arms folded in the centre of the yard, his eyes never leaving the car as it disappeared down the drive. Only when the engine noise had faded into silence, did he finally return to his work.

Chapter Twenty-Eight

'Surely, the best way to the camp site would be to go towards this village,' Lindy tapped her finger on the unruly mass of the roadmap she'd spread out over the car bonnet.

'That's miles out of the way,' JJ, her boyfriend, of a few weeks, grunted, pushing his floppy fringe out of his eyes. He pulled the map towards him. 'This road,' he traced a pale line on the paper with one long finger, 'is the best way. Trust me. I know how to read a map.'

Lindy straightened up, glancing at JJ as he grinned conspiratorially at Luke, the two men rolling their eyes in a gesture of agreement. 'Women drivers.' JJ smirked.

'Oh, let him decide,' Wendy smiled sympathetically at Lindy. 'They always think they know best.'

Lindy glanced at the two men, leaning over the bonnet, engrossed in deciding which way would be the best. There was a rip in JJ's jeans, a smattering of golden hairs just visible through the frayed fabric. Mid-morning, just before they'd set off from Weston-super-Mare, they'd relaxed on the side of the road outside her flat waiting for Wendy and Luke to arrive. She'd found the rip fascinating, sliding her fingers between the gap to touch the coolness of his skin. Now, the rip, and everything else about JJ, set her teeth on edge.

Ever since they'd left their hometown, JJ had seemingly been doing his best to make her feel like an idiot. It felt as if each time she opened her mouth he disagreed with her. When they had first met, he had seemed kind and gentle. But together with Luke, and the pint of cider they'd had for lunch on the journey, he'd become increasingly belligerent, seeming to delight in putting her down in front of their companions.

Lindy shrugged. What did it matter anyway? She knew the route they should be taking. She'd travelled it often enough to her aunt's home in Goldsithney, the festival site was a short distance further on, near Land's End.

The route JJ was insisting they took might look quicker on the map, but she knew those roads. They were tiny, narrow, and twisting, full of tourists exploring the county with their huge, ill-suited caravans.

A journey that should have taken just over three hours seemed to be taking forever. She could just sit in the back of the car with Wendy, admire the stunning views, and smile to herself when Luke and JJ, who were sharing the driving, inevitably found that she was right. But, somehow, it did matter. JJ was an asshole.

She turned away, hot tears of frustration prickling at the backs of her eyes. She focused on a group of wild ponies, grazing at the side of the road. They were close enough to be touched, yet, from their body language, she could tell that with a single step toward them, they'd flee.

'Another pint at Jamaica Inn?' Luke hauled open the car door and slid into the driver's seat.

'Excellent plan,' JJ meticulously folded the map. 'Come on girls, in you get.'

Dusk was falling by the time they reached the campsite. Lulled by the adventure and the heat of the sun, they'd spent longer sitting outside Jamaica Inn than they'd intended. Lindy prickled with irritation. The route JJ had chosen had indeed turned out to be the disaster she'd known it would be. An unwitting tourist, hauling a huge caravan, had driven down one of the narrow lanes and gotten stuck between the high, narrow banks. A line of cars waited patiently while the caravan was unhitched, and tractor from a nearby farm hauled it out of the way. The farmer's face seemed impassive as he accepted a wedge of bank notes from the grateful driver, yet his eyes danced with amusement at the familiar predicament.

Finally, the traffic jam had been sorted out, and they'd been able to continue their journey. The delay had added hours onto the trip. Lindy had told the camp site owner they'd arrive at six, yet it was almost nine when they finally pulled onto the gently sloping field.

'I hope he hasn't let someone else have our pitch.' Lindy sighed as she tried, and failed, to keep the irritation out of her voice.

'He won't have.' JJ's voice was decisive.

'We'll go and check. Will you come to the site office with me, Wendy?' Lindy almost wished their spot had been given to someone else, just to prove JJ wrong.

'You're very late,' the campsite owner folded his arms, in an impatient gesture. 'Another few minutes and I'd have given your pitch away. There's lots of demand this weekend.'

'Yes, I'm sorry, we got delayed. There was a caravan stuck, we should have rung.'

She'd asked Luke to stop the car at a telephone box, so they could call ahead, but JJ had talked over her, his voice filled with self-importance, insisting the owner wouldn't give their spot away.

'Well, it's still available,' the site owner's cheeks glowed red above his fleshy mouth. 'You're very lucky.'

'Thank you,' Lindy gave him an apologetic smile as he handed her their shower tokens.

'Are you going to tell JJ how lucky we were to still have a spot?' Wendy asked, as they walked back to where the men were waiting by the car.

'No,' Lindy shook her head. What was the point? They were still able to stay at the site; the man hadn't given their pitch away. In the mood JJ was in, he'd just talk over her and make her feel stupid. She'd been delighted when he had asked her to go to the festival. At college he had seemed so charming, interested in her. She wouldn't be seeing him again, once the weekend was over, that was for sure. The way he addressed her, hurt badly his rudeness left her reeling.

Things didn't improve. While the tents were being erected JJ, in full flow, took charge over the proceedings, organising everyone to assist him. 'Pass me the hammer,' he demanded, waving a hand in Lindy's direction when she was slow to jump to his commands.

'Yes, captain,' Lindy mocked.

'It's not level,' JJ announced, surveying their tent once it was erected, demanding she pulled up the pegs and reposition them. By the time they'd unpacked the car and got into their sleeping bags Lindy could barely control her temper.

'Breakfast first, then showers and then we'll walk down to the beach,' JJ was still in full commander mode as they emerged from their tent the following morning. Wendy caught Lindy's eye and offered a sympathetic smile. Even Luke rolled his eyes, before digging the gas cooker out of the back of the car and handing it to JJ, who was, of course, in charge of organising breakfast.

Once they'd eaten, had their showers, as JJ had decreed, they made their way to the beach, following a ragged line of other festival goers.

'You carry the beer,' JJ handed Luke a chiller bag filled with cans. 'I'll take the seats. Lindy, can you manage the rugs?'

'I'll try my best.' Lindy said, between gritted teeth, heaving the rucksack onto her back.

The route to the beach led through fields of golden corn, interspersed with single track lanes.

'It's a long way,' Wendy stopped, fifteen minutes later, putting down the bag she was carrying, stretching her fingers. Harsh red lines marred her palms. 'Why did we have to stay so far away?'

'Do stop whining.' JJ's voice held a patronising tone.

Lindy bit the inside of her lip to stop herself from snapping at JJ.

He'd been adamant the camp site was the closest to the festival and would be the one where "everyone was staying." Quite clearly, he had been wrong, as they made their way across yet another field and came out on a narrow lane, they had passed another camp site, crammed with brightly coloured tents, from which a long line of people were making their way towards the beach.

'Looks like that site is closer than ours.' The words slipped out of Lindy's mouth before she could check them.

'Ours is far less crowded,' JJ retorted immediately, but she could see from the set line of his shoulders that her words had cut deep.

'Ours is fine, though.' Wendy, always the peacemaker, commented gently.

The path down to the beach followed the side of a steep cliff, along a sandy path which wove diagonally down the slope. The amount of people going down to the beach made for slow going. Lindy eased her shoulders. It would be a nightmare, hauling the equipment back to the camp site after the festival.

The wide sandy beach above the high-water level was crowded. Everyone had brought beer to drink and blankets to lie on. Following JJ, Lindy breathed in the heady aroma of someone's joint.

'Where do you want to sit?' Luke turned slowly, looking at the crowded beach. 'How about here?' He pointed to a space amongst the crowds.

'Too close to the band,' JJ announced. 'This way, I think.'

'Why don't you pick where we sit?' Lindy snapped, irritably.

'Oh, just go along with him,' Wendy smiled sympathetically at Lindy. 'Anything for a quiet life.'

'Here?' Lindy threw down the blankets as JJ stopped, surveying the spot he'd snagged, the image of a king looking at his kingdom. 'Is here suitable for you?'

'Perfect,' JJ nodded, her sarcasm going completely over his head.

'Where do you want these?' Luke held up the bag containing the beer cans.

'Beer cans here.' JJ directed Luke, 'Blankets here, Lindy. Well done, thank you.'

'Can you move over a little? Your blanket is in our space.' JJ addressed the young couple who had just arranged their possessions beside them.

'Whatever,' the man grunted, glaring at JJ.

'You can't just…' Lindy hissed, staring at JJ in disbelief.

'What?' JJ's face was incredulous.

The afternoon only made matters worse. JJ, once he'd had a few drinks, became even more obnoxious. The couple who had been beside them moved away, clearly sick of listening to JJ holding court. He didn't let up, even when they had all the blankets arranged neatly, with the beers stacked at one side. Lindy felt sick with temper. She hated JJ more with every second. He was such a know-it-all, but even worse, he saw nothing wrong in constantly putting her down, disagreeing with everything she said.

Chapter Twenty-Nine

'You fool.' Nan' mouth curved down, giving her the look of an angry trout. 'It's one thing, bringing Mia to a park every once in a while. But I keep telling you not to drive around with her in the pick-up...' She glared at him coldly, her eyes hooded beneath her brows.

The silence between them lengthened. Eddie's eyes slid away first. Mia sat at the kitchen table, engrossed in the picture she was drawing. Crayons, pencils, and scraps of abandoned paper littered the pine surface. The tip of her tongue, poking through her teeth, was stained deep purple from the fruit drink beside her.

Mia looked up. 'I've drawn the flowers we planted in the orchard.' She held up the picture, eager for their approval.

'Beautiful.' Eddie nodded, recognising the Sweet Williams Mia had helped him plant after they had stamped the ground down. 'You did a good job.'

Silently, Mia went back to her drawing, rubbing absent-mindedly at the livid bruise that discoloured the pale skin at the back of her neck.

'I know why you want to go.' Nan hissed. 'Can't you leave them alone?'

Eddie grunted, his eyes sliding to stare at the slate floor tiles beneath his feet.

'You disgust me.' Nan took a stride forwards, the angry bulk of her body inches from his. 'What are you?' She jabbed a finger into his chest, the violence of the movement pushing him back. 'Worse than an animal.'

'I need food for the dogs, and Ursula.' He muttered, sullenly.

'Ursula,' Nan mocked, her tone matching the whispered croak of his voice. 'Shame you can't satisfy yourself with the pig. Save us a lot of trouble.'

Eddie turned away silently, pulling his jacket from the back of one of the chairs.

Mia glanced up from her colouring, relieved Nan's fury was not directed at her.

'No answer to that, have you?' Nan wrenched the jacket from his hands, balling it into a bundle, her knuckles white with anger. 'What did I do to deserve you?' She thrust the jacket in his direction.

'Everything.' Eddie wrapped the jacket over his arm, holding it between them like a shield. 'There's no love or kindness in you.'

'Oh!' Nan let out a breath, a cross between a snort and a sigh, 'So you can speak. How could anyone love you? Look at you.' She crossed the kitchen to stand beside the sink, her back to the window. 'No one could want you. You are…'

'I love you.' Mia came across the kitchen to stand beside her father.

Nan snorted, rolling her eyes. 'Go on. Get out of my sight.' She sighed, releasing a juddering breath. 'Come here Mia.' She crouched down, opening her arms, her tone suddenly gentle, 'Give me a hug. Have a good time.'

Mia paused, looking at Eddie, who flashed her a taut smile, before crossing the room into Nan's arms.

'Have a good time,' Nan ran a brusque hand over Mia's head. Releasing Mia, she got slowly to her feet. 'Make sure she doesn't talk to anyone.'

Silently, Eddie turned away, taking Mia's yellow raincoat from the peg behind the door.

'Can I go on the swings again?' Mia's chatter drifted back through the open door as she trotted beside her father.

'Maybe,' Eddie helped Mia into the back seat of the pick-up and pulled the seatbelt across her chest.

He steered the vehicle out of the farmyard and drove away, the noise of the barking dogs receding into the background.

'Are we going to Penzance?' Mia had to raise her voice to make herself heard over the noise of the engine.

'Yep. To the place where they sell food for the animals.'

'Can I come in with you? It's boring in the pick-up.'

'It's not safe in there.'

'Why?'

'Too many things that might hurt you. Only grown-ups are allowed in there.'

In the driver's mirror he watched Mia absorb the information, her small mouth twisting into a scowl.

As they drove through the town, she pulled forwards on her seatbelt to look out of the window, her face alive with curiosity.

'They can't see you,' Eddie turned to smile at Mia, seeing the disappointment on her face after she had waved to some children with their mother as they waited to cross the road at a set of traffic lights. They hadn't waved back. No one could see through the dark glass at the back of the pick-up.

'You need to stay here. Don't move.' Eddie parked the pick-up in a narrow laneway.

Mia nodded unwillingly.

As Eddie turned the corner at the end of the lane, heading towards the feed merchants' yard, she unclipped her seat belt, turning to kneel on the back seat, to look out of the back window.

He'd left the vehicle near the park. Mia, gazing out, recognised the street. They'd parked there the day they'd all come on a rare trip into the town and gone to the park. That seemed like a lifetime away. She'd disobeyed Nan and tried to talk to some girls near the swings. They hadn't come again.

As Eddie came back around the corner, two bags of animal feed slung easily over his shoulder, she spun around, fingers clumsy as she refastened her seatbelt.

The vehicle jolted as Eddie tossed the feed bags into the back.

'Good girl,' he said softly, easing his frame into the gap between the pick-up door and the wall. 'We've another place to go to. It's quite a long way. I'll get you something to eat in a while.'

* * * * *

'Nan will be missing us.' Mia squirmed, jerking her body against the confines of the seatbelt. They'd been driving for a long time. The pasty Eddie had brought her from a van in a layby on the dual carriageway had satisfied her hunger but done nothing to pacify the boredom she felt.

'Stop Mia.' There was an edge to his voice. 'We've already stopped so you could go to the toilet and to get some food. Give it a rest now, will you?'

'That wasn't a toilet,' she retorted sullenly. 'That was a climb over a gate to hide in a field.'

'Well, it did the job,' Eddie shot back, as he accelerated past a lorry, the slipstream bouncing against the pick-up.

Mia released a long sigh, staring out of the window as the countryside slid by.

After what seemed hours Eddie parked outside a shop and went inside, returning a while later with a long, shiny pipe. 'All this way for a tractor part,' he said throwing the pipe on the passenger seat. 'Come on we'll find a park, you can play for a while.'

'This is a long way to come for the swings.' Mia said, a short time later, clutching Eddie's hand as they crossed a busy road towards a small park adjacent to a housing estate.

Eddie made no reply, instead opening the gate to let Mia into the grassy area.

'Off you go.' His voice was distracted as he made his way to the benches, where he sat while Mia played.

She tried out the swings, then the roundabout. It was hard to make it go fast on her own though. Later she made her way to the slides, trying the smaller one first before plucking up the courage to go on the bigger one.

High on the top of the steep slide, Mia spotted a line of people beginning to make their way out of a stark concrete building. Clad mostly in jeans, shouldering large bags, they moved in pairs, some in groups, walking along the pavements surrounding the building. Perhaps some of them would come into the park and she'd be able to talk to them if Eddie wasn't looking. Mia giggled with delight as she whooshed down the slide.

'We need to go.' Eddie held his hand out to grasp Mia's as she reached the bottom. 'We've been here too long.'

'But I…'

'Now Mia.'

'Okay.'

'Hop in. I won't be a minute.' Eddie opened the pick-up door, holding Mia's arm to help her scramble up the tall step, and into the back of the vehicle. 'Stay there.' He clipped the seatbelt around Mia.

Through the half open front window Mia could hear him humming softly as he lifted the bonnet of the pick-up.

'It's overheating. Do you know where I can get some water from?' Eddie's voice was soft, the helpless, persuasive tone Mia recognised from when she didn't want to go into the house at bedtime.

'Sorry. No.' Mia heard the dismissive tones of the girls who walked past the pick-up window.

'I'm stuck.' She heard him say a moment later. Out of the window, she could see a tall, pretty woman had stopped beside the pick-up. 'Where can I get some water from?'

'There's a petrol station, just up the road. Take the second turning on the left, just past the church.'

'Where?' Eddie's voice was quizzical. 'Any chance you'd show me? I'm not from round here. I'm desperate, I have to get my daughter home.'

As Mia gazed out of the window, she saw the girl step away from Eddie, her expression hesitant. 'I... er...' The girl shook her head, hurrying away.

'Stuck up cunts.' Eddie slammed the bonnet down and got into the driver's seat.

'Are we going home now?' Mia asked, gazing out of the window, seeing the dismissal in the girl's faces as they drove away.

When Eddie made no reply, Mia rested her head against the seatback and lulled by the motion of the vehicle let herself drift off to sleep.

* * * * *

Finally, Lindy could bear it no longer. 'You're nothing but a jerk.' Lindy got to her feet, her head spinning slightly from the amount she'd drunk, and from the joint they'd shared an hour or so earlier.

'What's the matter?' JJ got to his feet, his eyebrows raised, as if her outburst was a massive, and uncalled for tantrum.

'You.' Lindy met his eyes. His face showed clearly how unreasonable he thought she was being. 'You're being so obnoxious to me. I'm not an idiot, so please don't treat me like one.'

'I'm not,' JJ's mouth twisted into a patronising smile.

'You are.' Lindy was sick of him, 'I'm going back to the tent. I'll see you later.'

'Wait,' JJ put a hand on her arm.

'Get off me,' Lindy shook his hand off and stalked away across the beach, making her way to and then up the steep path. She emerged on the lane at the top of the path, her fury at JJ bubbling in her veins.

Sobbing, Lindy let the tears of frustration she'd kept in for the last two days finally fall. JJ was a jerk, someone who enjoyed, relished even, putting her down. Never again. They were through before they had even begun.

Miserably, she trudged up the deserted lane. Everyone was at the beach enjoying themselves. She crossed the first field, stumbling over the rutted ground.

* * * * *

'Wake up, we're nearly home,' Eddie reached back to touch Mia's knee, shaking her into wakefulness. Since eating the chips they'd brought from another van in a layby, Mia had dozed fitfully.

She opened her eyes, recognising the last streetlights as they left Penzance, and headed out into the darkness of the countryside.

'The festival.' Eddie slowed the pick-up as he turned off the main road. 'I'd forgotten about that.'

Looking towards the dark outline of the sea, Mia could see the glow of bonfires. There was an explosion of light, as a barrage of fireworks lit up the night sky.

'Lovely, aren't they?' He slowed the vehicle, so it was crawling along.

Mia nodded, watching, fascinated by the bright blasts of colour.

'Can we...' Mia's voice faded. Eddie had stopped the pick-up and was staring down the lane ahead of them. At the very edge of the glow from the headlights, a young woman walked unsteadily along the grass verge.

'What?' His voice had the same distracted edge she recognised from trying to talk to him when he was watching the television.

The vehicle's speed increased, until they drew level with the young woman.

'Are you okay?' Eddie wound down the passenger side window, leaning across to talk to the woman, while steering the pick-up slowly at the same pace she was walking at.

'Yes.' Her voice was snappy, an angry, impatient note.

'Have you been to the festival? Are you staying at one of the campsites? Can I give you a lift?'

'Piss off.' She'd stopped now, turning to face the pick-up.

'I'm sorry,' Eddie's voice was gentle. 'I didn't mean to upset you. I was just worried about you, walking along here. In the dark. On your own.'

'I'm fine.'

'Okay fair enough.' He pressed the button to lower the back seat window, 'Aren't the fireworks beautiful, Mia?'

Mia gazed out at the vivid colours, she met the woman's eyes and smiled. 'So beautiful.'

'Sure you don't want a lift? The campsites are quite a hike away.'

Mia glanced towards Eddie. He had the same persuasive expression she recognised from bath time.

Lindy thrust her hands into the pockets of her jeans her eyes roving over Eddie, before coming back to look at Mia.

'I'm passing Home Farm and Bellmorris, where the camp sites are. It's only a few minutes away.'

Lindy shrugged, taking a step towards the pick-up. 'Okay, sure, thanks. That would be great.'

Chapter Thirty

'Come on. Come on! Get out of the way!' Grace grumbled through gritted teeth, peering through the car windscreen, trying to see around the caravan in front of her. She chanced steering into the opposite lane as the road widened slightly, swerving back as a car came in the opposite direction. 'Dammit.' She sighed. She was going to be late. Very late. But there was no point in killing herself to get to work. She had spent enough time lecturing errant motorists about taking dangerous chances on the roads.

She should have left earlier, but her coaching session at the stables had gone on longer than she had expected. Spurred on by Kaden, she'd jumped her highest fence so far on Sisco.

In the four years she had owned the horse, with Kaden's guidance, they had become a team.

Katia, away for much of the time at university had sold her horse, but for Grace the bug took hold of her more and more. She became firm friends with Kaden, helped by the fact that she fancied the pants off him.

'Why did I ever listen to you?' Kaden had said earlier, patting the horse's neck as they walked out of the arena. 'He's so bloody good. I wish I'd kept him.' But he hadn't. Sisco belonged to Grace, something she was grateful for. Having him meant that she had an outlet for the stress that accompanied her job. In the years since she had been a detective, she'd seen and experienced more than she could ever imagine. Even in such a peaceful backwater as rural Cornwall, crime kept the team occupied.

She squeezed in riding and coaching sessions with Kaden as often as possible, but that often meant that she rushed into the station, hot, with her hair still damp from the shower.

Grace released a long breath of relief as she finally swung her car into the station carpark.

'Hello,' Ollie, the new constable on the desk greeted her. He was a charmer. As Grace hurried into the reception area Ollie flashed her a disarming grin The fact that he was three years younger than her, and that he'd just joined the force, didn't seem to stop him chatting her up at every available opportunity.

'Hi, Ollie.' Grace flashed him a brief smile, her eyes roving over the three people standing at the desk in front of him. One, a dishevelled young man, was in tears, banged his hand in frustration on the reception counter. The couple with him looked uncomfortable, the girl clinging to her partner's hand.

'Sir you need to calm down. Now, if you'll just give me a few details about Lindy,' Ollie, turned towards Grace, mouthing "girlfriend gone missing." Grace nodded briefly, hurrying away, afraid of Steve's wrath if she dared mention anything about missing girls and serial killers to him again.

She glanced back at the three people. They looked filthy, undoubtedly, they'd been at the beach festival that had caused so much trouble over the weekend. There'd been complaints about drunken and unruly behaviour from most of the neighbouring houses. A fight had broken out one evening at one of the campsites. The police had been called to break it up. The cells, Grace knew, were full of hungover lads who would be glad to see the back of Cornwall, and who would not be welcome in the county again. Thank goodness the festival was over, and the more usual peaceful chaos created by unthinking holiday makers and inexperienced caravan drivers would return the area.

She lowered herself into her chair, her hair still felt damp against her neck.

'Grace,' Steve appeared beside her desk. She looked up, glad for the distraction from the seemingly endless mountain of paperwork.

'There's a lad in reception. Been at the festival. Says his girlfriend is missing.'

'I saw him,' Grace sat back in her chair. 'He looked pretty rough.'

'He's with two friends. Ollie on reception has taken the details, but can you go and talk to him? Take a statement.'

'Sure,' Grace got to her feet.

'I know how much you love your missing girls.' Steve quipped, good naturedly. 'Could be another one to put down to your famous Cornish Nasty.'

'Ha ha,' she pulled a wry face, glad of any excuse to get out of the confines of the office.

'I've put him in the green room,' Ollie said, referring to the nickname given to the interview suite. He handed Grace a mug of the infamous station coffee.

'Those his mates?' The couple looked exhausted, their clothes grubby after the weekend.

'Yes, there were two couples. They travelled down together from Weston-super-mare. Seems the girl went missing after she'd had a row with her boyfriend.'

'Okay,' Grace kept her voice deliberately impassive. It didn't do to make assumptions. Perhaps the girl had already gone home or found people who were more interesting to hang out with.

'Hi…Joseph…' Grace let herself into the interview room, balancing the notes Ollie had given her along with the tarlike coffee.

'JJ.' He looked at Grace with red-rimmed eyes.

'JJ.' Grace sat down, relaxing her face into a neutral expression, trying not to breathe the stale stench of unwashed flesh that emanated from him.

He smiled weakly. 'She...Lindy's not gone home. And she's not at the camp site.'

'Can you tell me more about what happened?' Grace waited, pen poised, taking notes as JJ recalled the weekend. 'You're saying there was a row, and Lindy left?'

JJ nodded, hunching his shoulders miserably. 'She was grumpy all weekend. Then, she just stormed off. She said she was going back to the camp site.'

'What happened after she'd gone?'

She watched JJ's face crumble as he stumbled over his words. 'We let her go. She was being a...' The muscles at either side of his jaw clenched and unclenched as he fought to find the words.

'It's okay,' Grace said gently. 'Just tell me how it was.'

'A cow.' JJ spat out the word, as if he'd been chewing on a piece of gristle. His eyes locked on Grace's, his discomfiture at having said something horrible about Lindy clearly written on his face. 'So, when she went, none of us thought much of it.'

'And then what happened?'

'We carried on partying. Wendy said we should go and check if she was okay, but in the end, we didn't. Maybe it was Luke who said that... I can't remember.' JJ shrugged his shoulders, his dark eyebrows almost meeting as he frowned.

'Don't worry if you can't remember.' Grace watched JJ, wondering if he were lying. His memory seemed disjointed, scraps coming back to him at odd moments. Was he telling the truth, or was he a convincing liar, trying to make out he was genuine?

'When we did go back, there was no sign of her.'

'Did you go to other tents to see if she was there?'

JJ swallowed hard, wiping at his sweating forehead with the back of his hand. 'We were all pretty wasted, to be honest. We didn't think about her till the morning. I thought she'd gone into Luke and Wendy's tent. They assumed she was in mine.'

'Okay, so you realised she wasn't there the next morning.'

JJ nodded. 'We looked everywhere on our campsite, and the others. She wasn't there. We rang her home. No sign of her there.'

'I'm going to take some details.' Grace smiled at him sympathetically, 'Then you may as well head home. I'm sure Lindy's just cooling off. She's probably on her way home now.'

JJ's nodded. 'So, we just go…?'

'We'll be in touch if we find anything. And you let us know when she turns up at home.'

She watched as JJ made his way out of the interview suite. Lindy would undoubtedly turn up sooner or later, seething at whatever JJ had done to upset her.

'That one was right up your street, Miss Marple.' Steve laughed good naturedly, when she told him about the brief interview.

Three days later, Grace was just about to ride Sisco when her telephone rang in her jacket pocket.

'Tallis.' The urgency in Steve's voice was apparent, even over the wind-battered noise coming from the telephone.

'Ballmorris Farm. We've found a body. Young woman. You need to get here, now.'

'On my way.' Grace handed Kaden Sisco's reins. 'Sorry, got to go.'

Leaving him to lead the horse away, she jogged back to her car, and was soon hurtling along the lanes towards the destination Steve had given her.

It was obvious where she should go. The field off the narrow lane near Ballmorris Farm was littered with police cars. At the top of the hill, behind a stone wall, an ominous forensic tent had been erected, its sides flapping in the breeze.

Grace checked in with the officer, before hastily donning a white forensic overall and making her way quickly up the hill, feet sliding on the slick muddy surface.

Steve and some of the other officers stood in the lee of the wall, watching her struggle up the hill.

'Good of you to make it.' Steve snapped. Grace glanced at her boss, his face was waxy, an odd, pale-green shade.

When she didn't reply, he continued. 'The farmer found her, behind the wall.' Steve nodded his head towards a middle-aged man his face the same green shade as her boss's, who sat in the passenger seat of one of the police 4x4 vehicles, a collie dog nudging at his hand for attention.

'From the description we have she's out missing woman,' Steve wiped his hand across his mouth, as if determined not to vomit.

Bile, hot and bitter rose in Grace's throat. Lindy. She hadn't gone home. She would never go home. She'd left the festival, and afterwards she had been killed.

'Filthy fucker,' Steve shook his head. 'He's battered her to death. There's a rock... Raped her...'

The detectives surrounding Steve shuffled their feet, staring at the wind whipped grassland.

'Poor kid,' someone mumbled.

'Right. Let's find who did this.' Steve took a deep breath. 'Is this the work of her boyfriend? We'd better get him back in.'

Chapter Thirty-One

Months later, the team were still busy hunting Lindy's killer, something made more difficult by her body being exposed to the elements for days, and her killer seemingly leaving no traces, no blood, no semen. No DNA.

No one at the festival had seen anything. Lindy, it seemed, had left the beach and met her killer. Steve was convinced her boyfriend, JJ, had killed her, but after interviewing him once again, they'd found no evidence to link him with her death. While everyone on the beach was drunk and out of their minds on drugs, they still swore JJ was with them the whole time.

Steve had taken Grace to the mortuary where she had once again looked at the battered corpse of Lindy Walker. On the slab lay the pale, vulnerable looking corpse of the woman, just a few years younger than she was.

'Sorry,' she'd mumbled, as she fainted, her head spinning as stars danced in front of her eyes. Steve had hauled her out into the fresh air. 'Stay there, head between your knees. I'll be back for you in a minute.' He'd returned to the chilled air of the mortuary, to learn how Lindy had met her fate.

'Good to get that out of the way for you.' Steve had said brusquely a while later. 'You'll learn to deal with it.' She took a little satisfaction in seeing his face matched the paleness of her own.

In her short career, she'd seen far more death than she could ever have imagined. It seemed to almost be part of the daily routine; car crashes, elderly people who had lain alone and unmissed in their homes, bodies fished out from the sea. She'd even been part of a team that had collected body parts from the apparent suicide of someone who had walked out in front of an express train.

The frustration at not solving Lindy Walker's murder lay heavily on the minds of all the team, as did the unsolved case of Carrie Anderson, battered to within an inch of life. The search for whoever had hurt Carrie had come to nothing. The horror of what had happened to the two girls was something Grace could not get out of her mind.

There was a heavy air of frustration and helplessness in the station.

'Can I get you some coffee? Tea?' Grace tore her thoughts away from the daily briefing she had just attended.

'I don't want anything. I'm sick of being offered tea and coffee. I want some answers.' The smartly dressed woman glared at Grace.

She held open the interview room door to let the couple pass through.

Ross McDonagh, tall and wiry, glanced helplessly from his wife to Grace, and back again.

'Sit down Moira, hen, will you.' Ross used the Scottish term of endearment. He busied himself pulling out one of the plastic chairs before taking his wife's coat as she shrugged it off.

Grace took the coat from him, wishing, not for the first time, the station had a room more suitable for these kinds of meetings than one that was used to interview criminals. The room was stark, painted in the ubiquitous institution green, the only natural light peeking through a row of tiny windows, high up on the outside wall. The chairs were cheap, hard plastic, chosen for their cost, and for the discomfort they offered to criminal buttocks. It wasn't the right place to interview the heartbroken parents of a young woman who had been missing for six years. There should have been a neat, light-filled room, lined with bright, squashy sofas, with bowls of vibrant flowers, where she could chat to them, gently and reassuringly.

'I'm sorry this is the best I can offer you for a chat.' Grace met Moira's eyes. She stared back, dark shadows staining the skin beneath her green eyes.

'What does it matter?' After her angry outburst when Grace had offered them a drink, Moira had visibly deflated. She looked every one of her sixty years; harsh lines scored each side of her mouth and her forehead.

Grace waited until the couple had settled themselves into the plastic chairs before taking her position at the opposite side of the desk, adjusting her note pad so it was parallel to the edge, a manoeuvre she had found gave her time to collect her thoughts, as well as give them time to adjust to their environment.

'You...' Moira's voice was filled with bitterness, the single word rapping out accusingly.

Ross put a gentle, restraining hand on her arm. Grace watched his fingers move over her skin. His hand was enormous, shaped like a shovel, with short, stubby fingers, and a wide, square palm. A rough hand, one that belonged to a farmer. Grace pictured him working, those vast hands hauling rocks to build walls, and yet still gentle enough to deal with sick animals. And now being used to reassure his heartbroken wife. A similar type of man had found Lindy Walker's body.

'Our daughter, Ayla...' he began. Beside him Moira took a juddering breath, her lips clamping together into a tight line. 'She was studying in Exeter.'

'For god's sake, Ross,' Moira wrenched her arm from beneath his hand and slammed her fists violently down on the table. Grace felt the surface reverberate beneath her notepad. 'We've said all of this before. Over and over again.'

'I know,' Ross whispered, his eyes helpless as they locked onto Grace's. A tear glistened in one corner. He made no attempt to check its slow flow down the side of his nose. 'I know, but she can hear it again.'

'Yes, its fine.' Grace's words sounded trite to her ears. 'I want to hear it again. There might be something we didn't get before.' She opened the slender, blue-covered file she'd unearthed the file when Ollie had announced the McDonagh's were in reception and wanted to talk to someone.

Grace cleared her throat, aware she had been lost in thought about the Lindy Walker and Carrie Anderson. She dragged her focus away from the two young women. The McDonagh's needed her full attention.

'Ayla,' Grace met Ross's eyes. 'Tell me about her. Where did her name come from? It's so pretty.'

'It was my mother's name.' Moira began to speak her voice softening for the first time.

'She was studying at Exeter. She was due to come home, to Scotland, we'd just taken on the farm when Ross's father retired, but according to one of her university friends Ayla decided to do some walking on the coast path. And then she vanished.'

'And there were no problems with her course? Boyfriends? Friends she lived with?'

It was old ground, raked over time and again. The McDonagh's had reported Ayla missing in their hometown of Dundee, in Exeter where she had been at university and then Truro, further west again, as they tried to retrace her steps.

'No. You know all this.' Ross McDonagh's sighed, visibly struggling to contain the frustration he clearly felt at the lack of progress in his daughter's disappearance.

'I know,' Grace sighed, meeting his eyes. 'Sometimes it helps...' How could going over what they already knew possibly help? There had been no progress in the case. Whenever she mentioned it to Steve, he fobbed her off. There was no budget to go chasing after non-existent cases. Nor was there any reason to be certain Ayla had even come to Cornwall. Why would they assume she had come to any harm? Perhaps she had just got sick of everything, her course, her nagging parents, and just upped and left. For all they knew, she could be living happily somewhere else, just as was assumed with the missing young Cornish woman, Glanna Pendrick.

She glanced yet again at the photograph the McDonagh's had given to the police for the file on their missing daughter. Ayla grinned at the camera, her face full of life, eyes dancing with laughter.

'Her hair was different in this one.' Moira reached across the table and gently touched the image of her daughter. 'Longer. She'd started to wear it loose.'

'Any friends in Dundee she stayed in touch with, even from school?'

'She didn't go to school in Dundee. We lived near London until she was fifteen. Ross was working in a bank.'

Ross nodded, a wry smile tilting the corner of his lips. 'Hard to imagine a life more different than now.'

Grace was silent, her mind drifting back to the drunken night with Katia. The girl they'd given directions too, she'd had long, red hair. Grace had a vivid image of it cascading around her face. Could she have been the same person?

Grace ran a finger around the top of her tee shirt, trying to ease the burning heat that had flashed through her. Could the girl they had seen have been Ayla? Drunk, in the dark, she had no clear memory of what the girl looked like. More vivid was the memory of the fear they had felt when the pick-up had driven past them. Had it been a scream she had heard, or just the cry of an animal? But the girl couldn't have been Ayla, she'd walked away, gone to the guest house she and Katia had directed her to.

'What's being done?' Ross demanded. 'We've had no news. Nothing. For years. We keep asking. We won't let this go.'

'I just want her home.' Moira's face seemed to fold in on itself as she gave way to the tears she had been holding in.

As the interview with the McDonagh's ended Grace stood to show them out. She had felt utterly helpless, taking notes, reassuring the McDonagh's she would do everything she could, just as every other detective they had spoken too had done. She'd shown them out of the station, watched from the doorway as they made their way down the street, Ross's arm around Moira's waist, their shoulders hunched with desolation.

As they turned the corner and were lost from view, she'd released a long breath, trying to draw her attention away from their pain. One of the toughest lessons she had learned was that not every case could be solved, the police couldn't provide answers for everyone. Longing for the release of tension she would feel riding Sisco later she made her way into the office. Grace spooned sugar into the coffee she'd made for herself. 'Those poor people, they're heartbroken.' She said as Steve came to stand beside her. He took a mug from the cupboard.

'Of course they are,' Steve poured water over the three spoons of instant coffee he'd heaped into a mug. 'Who wouldn't be?'

He turned, watching her. 'Grace.' His voice was unusually gentle. 'You can't carry this. Let it go. This woman, Ayla. She could be anywhere. There's no sign she came here.'

'It's just...seeing how upset they are.' Grace sipped at her coffee, the hot liquid burning her lips. 'It gets to me, more than anything else. What if she did come here? What if there's some connection between her and Lindy, perhaps Carrie, even? And there's Glanna Pendrick, the local woman she's been missing since the mid 1980's.'

Steve shook his head. 'I'm convinced JJ attacked Lindy. I just can't prove it. Carrie... And Ayla, I don't think she came to Cornwall. As for Glanna...'

'But...'

Steve took a stride closer, 'Let. It. Go.' His face was pressed so close she could smell the coffee on his breath.

Grace met his eyes, seeing the flash of concern there. 'I will.'

She was glad to escape from the station several hours later. Somewhere in the town the McDonagh's were staying in a guest house in town. Driving around, Ross had said. Did they expect to find Ayla walking along one of the country lanes, she wondered, trying, and failing, to turn her focus away from their pain. It was, she knew, a pointless emotion for her. She had to concentrate on things she could change. Like finding out who killed Lindy, injured Carrie or simply proving it was Jem Trevayne who was breaking into isolated farmhouses to steal whatever was lying around.

The radio helped, the banal pop songs blasting out from it drowning out the thoughts that flitted restlessly through her mind. She drove fast, enjoying the sensation of flinging her car into the corners of the twisting lanes, and was at the riding stables a short time later.

'Well timed.' Kaden was leading Sisco out of the stable as Grace got out of her car.

'Thank you.' She took the reins off Kaden and let herself be flung into the air as he gave her a leg up onto Sisco's back.

'Have fun,' Kaden waved a cheery hand as she rode out of the yard.

Sisco pricked his ears, his stride long and jaunty as he strode along the lane. She pushed him into a trot, gathering her reins. A vision of Lindy's ravaged face swam into her mind. Grace released a long breath, forcing herself to focus on Sisco's long ears, pricked sharply in front of her. She had longed for the release of tension riding gave but it was not forthcoming. Steve was wrong, she was sure of it. There had to be a connection between the missing girls, but where was Ayla? If she was dead, why hadn't her body been found? And where was Glanna Pendrick? Regardless of what Steve felt, she was sure Lindy and Carrie had to have been attacked by the same person. There were similarities. Steve seemed so sure Lindy's attacker had been at the festival.

At the end of the lane, she rode Sisco down the track towards the beach, his hoof falls padding softly on the sand blown up from the beach. If it had been the same attacker, then Ayla's body and Glanna's should have been found in the open, as Lindy's had and as Carrie's would have if she'd died. Whoever had caused the horrific injuries was still out there. Somewhere. Maybe the same person. And Steve, convinced of something different, was letting him walk free. Once on the sand, Grace gave Sisco his head, leaning forwards to urge him into a gallop, as if through his sheer speed she could escape her own thoughts.

Chapter Thirty-Two

'Rough day?' Kaden crossed the yard to walk beside Grace.

Grace slid off Sisco, pulling the reins over his head, before leading him towards his stable.

'You could say that.' She unclipped her riding hat and pulled it off, releasing her mane of hair. 'Is it that obvious?' She let the hat dangle from her fingers.

'It was. I could see something was wrong from the moment you got here.'

She glanced at Kaden, seeing the concern in his eyes, but there something else there too. Affection?

'You look better now, though.'

'Thanks. I think I should hose him off. It looks like we've brought half the beach with us.' She glanced at Sisco, sand speckled the lower part of his body.

'I'll give you a hand.'

She brought Sisco into the washing area and held him while Kaden ran the water from the hose gently over him. The big horse stood calmly, used to the procedure.

'There. Finished.' Kaden drew a plastic scraper over Sisco's belly, swishing the remains of the water droplets from him.

'Anything you want to talk about?' Kaden asked solemnly regarding Grace.

She undid the buckles on Sisco's bridle and gently slid it off his head. 'No, but thanks.' She couldn't talk to Kaden, work and her relaxation at the stables must stay separate. The attacks weren't a subject wanted to talk about, the awfulness that swirled through her mind was not something she wanted to share with Kaden. How could she ever tell him about the things she dealt with? While he was engrossed in the peaceful routine of training and looking after the horses in his care, she was up to her neck in the detritus of human life and death.

How could she explain to him about dealing with the pain of the McDonagh's, their search for their missing daughter, and her frustration at not being able to do anything to make that better for them?

What if she shared what had happened to Lindy, her white, still body sprawled in the grass? Or told him about the rock, abandoned beside her, still splattered with her brain matter? Or of witnessing the pain of Carrie's mother, sitting daily beside her lifeless daughter, the only sound between them the clicking and whirling of the ventilator that kept her alive?

Those things had to stay pushed down, deep inside her. She would deal with what it was possible to change and try to let go of what she couldn't. Now she understood the cliché of the drink sodden detective, the broken marriages, the wildness of staff nights out. Everyone was trying to run from the kaleidoscope of destruction they witnessed on a daily basis.

'Would a drink help?'

The sudden invitation brought Grace sharply back to reality. 'Are you asking me to go for a drink with you?'

Kaden had always been the epitome of polite, professional charm. 'Yes, I think I am.' He ran a hand through his dark hair, further tousling his already windswept curls. He met her eyes and grinned shyly, as if surprised by what he had said.

'Okay, then.' She waited, helping Kaden to finish the evening stable routine; feeding the stabled horses, checking their water buckets were full, straightening rugs.

'I'll meet you at the Jolly Sailor, shall I?' Grace named a popular pub close to the stables. Sometimes, Kaden led rides there, after they'd been to the beach.

'First there buys the drinks.' Kaden grinned. Grace's driving speed was legendary: after she had once driven him to a nearby village to buy cans of soft drinks for a group of teenage girls who were helping on the yard, he'd refused to get in the car with her again.

'You lead the way then.' Grace started her car, waiting patiently while Kaden manoeuvred his vast, lumbering Land Rover out of the yard and onto the lane.

The pub's car park was crowded. Kaden steered the Land Rover onto a boggy looking grass verge, while Grace drove slowly along the lane until she finally managed to squeeze her car into a narrow gap between a brand-new Mercedes and a very tasty looking Jaguar.

'Thought you'd changed your mind.' Kaden grinned, leaning on the bonnet of his Land Rover, as Grace hurried back up the lane towards him.

'I couldn't park.' She sighed, glancing at the crowded car park. Vehicles were crammed in at all kinds of angles, double parked, jammed in by their owners in an effort not to have to walk up the lane. It would be fun getting out for whoever had managed to park there.

'Quick. Seats!' Kaden pointed at one of the glass littered tables. The people who had been sitting at it were getting unsteadily to their feet. Grace hurried forwards, sliding into one of the seats just before a red-faced, chubby man, in a shirt whose stripes matched the colour of his face. 'Bugger.' he exclaimed in a London accent.

Kaden met Grace's eyes and grinned. 'Emmett,' he mouthed.

He went in to fetch the drinks, leaving Grace at the table. Was the person who had killed Lindy here? Grace's thoughts turned back to her work. Were they amongst the groups, holding a drink, braying with laughter? A man, sitting on a table opposite, met Grace's eyes, holding her gaze for a fraction of a moment, before returning to play rock paper scissors with the little girl he was with. Was there guilt in his look? Was he capable of killing someone, and then going back to a normal family life, loving, playing with his precious child?

'I got you a half,' Kaden made his way back across the pub garden, easing his lithe body onto the bench seat beside Grace.

'Thanks.' Grace touched her glass to his pint.

'So,' Kaden ventured as the silence between them lengthened, 'work going well?'

'Yeah.' She forced her mind back to Kaden and the pub garden. Normality, real life, seemed to go on without her, as if she were not really part of it. People went about their daily routines, while she and the other detectives waded, up to their necks, through the violence and destruction. What did people talk about? Normal people?

'Do you think I'm good enough to take Sisco to the hunter trials near St. Ives?'

Kaden, if he noticed, did not pick up on the forced note Grace could detect in her voice, as she desperately racked her brain for something to say.

'Maybe. I was thinking I might enter Waterford. We could compete as a pair.'

'If I get the day off,' Grace sipped her drink, glad to have steered the conversation towards safe, easy waters. Gradually, enjoying his easy company, she began to relax.

As they sat chatting, the pub garden gradually emptied. Locals heading home, holiday makers back to their accommodation. The crowded car park was sorted out to the sound of honking horns and shouts of annoyance when people found their vehicles blocked in. Grace and Kaden watched with amusement before the cooling temperatures drove them into the warmth of the pub.

'My turn for the drinks,' Grace said, later, easing her way out of the booth they were sitting in. They'd drunk cider first, and then soft drinks afterwards, neither willing to risk drink driving. They could have another small glass of cider before the pub closed.

'Pint and a half please,' Grace leant against the bar, to attract the attention of the plump, matronly barmaid.

'Won't be a minute, my lover.' She seized the vast jug and expertly poured cider out.

'Thanks.' As Grace took the glasses, a movement at the bar at the opposite side of the room caught her eye. She looked up, straight into the resentful glare of a man she recognised. Jem Trevayne. She had been part of the team that had gone to his home a few mornings previously to arrest him for his part in an aggravated burglary at an isolated farmhouse. The attack had left the man of the house with a fractured cheekbone and his wife a nervous wreck.

Steve had been sure Jem was responsible for some of the nasty burglaries that had been going on around the county. Someone was targeting isolated houses and farms. Mostly sheds were broken into, and power tools taken, although occasionally the homes were entered, and anything of value that could be carried off taken.

They'd paid Jem an early morning visit, getting him and his wife out of bed. The fury had been clearly written across both of their faces, along with their hatred of the police.

There'd been no sign of any of the missing items, either at the shed nor at the small industrial unit Jem rented to build the wooden gates he pretended his income came from. His wife, her arms more covered in tattoos than his, had sworn Jem had been with her the night the farm had been broken into, and had a remarkable memory for his presence on all the other occasions the police mentioned. They couldn't prove otherwise.

'I've marked your card for this one,' Steve had growled, his face inches from Jem's as they made their way out of the house.

Jem had laughed, his dark eyes raking over Steve and those who were with him. 'I know who you lot are too.' She'd felt his anger as his eyes moved slowly over them all.

He clearly hadn't forgotten.

Jem nodded his head in acknowledgment of Grace's presence, his eyes boring into hers. She flashed him a tight smile and turned away, a knot of tension growing in the pit of her stomach. Coming across people she dealt with on a day-to-day basis was inevitable. Most took arrest almost good humouredly, as part of their chosen career, but Jem had looked furious.

'I'd better go after this.' Grace smiled, the feeling of unease settling on her shoulders.

'Yeah, me too. Early start.'

No matter how hard Grace tried, her eyes slid repeatedly back to the end of the bar, and the surly glare of Jem Trevayne. She was glad when she saw him raise his glass in her direction, down the remains of his drink, and stalk out of the pub.

'Thank you. I enjoyed that.' Grace leant against her car door, smiling at Kaden.

'Me too.' An uncertain silence descended. He was gorgeous. Grace longed to step forward and kiss him. Should she let him make that move? Would it make a difference to their easy relationship at the stables? Her mind whirled.

'Gets a bad crowd, this pub.' Jem Trevayne slid out of the darkness to stand beside Kaden, his voice filled with menace.

'Jem. You need to go home. Leave us alone.' Grace said firmly, squaring her shoulders, determined not to show him she was disconcerted by his presence.

He snorted with laughter, making Grace blink at the strong smell of cider on his breath. 'You don't want to be messing with the likes of her.' Jem seized Kaden's shoulder, rocking him slowly.

'Piss off,' Kaden snarled, shoving the bigger man backwards.

'Jem. Go home, now.' Grace forced a cold calmness into her voice as she shoved her way between the two men. Jem towered above her, a seething mass of muscle and hatred. Facing him, Kaden's fists were clenched tightly.

'Watch out for yourself lad.' Jem growled before stalking off into the darkness, his stride unsteady.

'I'm sorry,' Grace smiled uncertainly at Kaden, who stood in the centre of the lane, watching Jem's bulk disappear.

Kaden shook his head, turning to look at Grace. 'You shouldn't be apologising. Occupational hazard I guess. It doesn't matter.'

'It does matter. I don't want you getting hurt because of me. I'm used to dealing with idiots like him.'

'I thought he was going to hit you.' Kaden's face was pinched with tension.

'Kaden, please forget it.' Grace put a hand on his arm, trying to bring his focus back to her.

Kaden met her eyes, 'You should have let me deal with him.'

Chapter Thirty-Three

She was still seething the following morning, angry at Jem for his aggression towards her, and upset at Kaden's reaction to her dealing with the situation. What had Kaden expected her to do? Let him try to beat Jem up? The older man was twice Kaden's size and age. He'd grown up brawling and bullying. It was the only thing he understood. She knew that had been what Jem had wanted. He'd expected Kaden to step in, to defend her, something which would have given him the excuse to attack Kaden.

Jem was on the short road to a prison sentence. He'd already spent the majority of his life inside. It held no fears for him. He'd have had no second thoughts about beating Kaden to a pulp, or even stabbing him. Either of them. She'd been lucky to defuse the situation. Grace knew that.

215

Despite her training, on the way home, her legs had trembled as adrenaline had coursed through her veins. Kaden's reaction had hurt. She hadn't spent years being trained how to defuse aggressive situations only to stand back, like some damsel in distress, and let him take charge. Of course, his manly feelings were offended by her protecting him. Better that than him ending up lying on the grass verge outside the pub, his stomach slashed open with the knife Jem could have had.

'Uggggghhhh!' Grace slammed her hand hard on the steering wheel. Looking up, she met the surprised gaze of an elderly lady waiting to cross the road beside where Grace was stuck in traffic. She tossed her an awkward grin, relieved as the lines of cars began to move on.

Men! The night hadn't gone how either of them had imagined. If things had turned out differently, where would she be now? Still undoubtedly stuck in the line of traffic, but perhaps humming a happy tune, having scrambled out of Kaden's bed. How would he be feeling today, she wondered? Would he have put everything behind him and be merrily going about his work at the stables, or like her, stinging with regret?

Jem, she was sure, wouldn't have given the incident another thought. Avoiding the police and capture was part of his life.

His rage had ruined her night out with Kaden. With her shift pattern, it would be days before she'd be able to go to the stables again. Should she call, Grace mused, or just try to forget the incident and hope that their friendship would pick itself up the next time she was with him?

She steered into the station car park. There was nothing she could do about it now. Feelings, emotions, and personal traumas stopped at the door. She had a job to do.

Hours later Grace sipped at yet another mug of coffee. It was she thought, a pretty soulless job. She glanced around the room, easing the tension in her back and shoulders. Everyone had their heads down, pouring over files, shuffling bits of paper, others watching their flickering computer screens. She was part of the team still investigating the attacks on two girls. Most of the others in the station were assigned to other work, as new crimes came in every day. The burglaries had a new detective, Lawrence Wolfe, on them. He drummed his fingers on his desk, flipping yet another witness statement over. Without more to go on, they couldn't convict the man everyone knew was guilty. Lawrence's frustration showed.

Sometimes, she felt as if the vast tide of crime was going to swamp her. It was beyond her how Steve managed to eke out their budget to make sure each crime was treated with equal importance. The frightened and annoyed people whose sheds had been broken into were treated with as much interest and consideration as someone whose daughter had gone missing. Every day, time had to be split between each crime. A logistical nightmare. Not, like on television Grace sometimes mused to herself, where each crime was neatly solved before another one came in.

The focus on Lindy's death was immense, but much of it revolved around reading witness statements, what festival goers and people in the surrounding villages had noticed. Or more often, what they hadn't.

'Hey!' Everyone looked up, startled as Ollie leant in through the open office door, slamming his hand on the wall to get their attention. His voice was filled with a mixture of excitement and alarm, a heady mix Grace had come to recognise.

'Some bastard has just snatched a girl.'

'Jesus,' exclaimed someone at the far end of the room.

Grace got to her feet, a familiar knot of tension tightening in her stomach. Another missing girl. More distraught parents.

'I'll tell Steve,' Grace hurried towards his office. 'Sir….' Grace tapped lightly on his door before pushing it open. 'There's been a report of another girl being snatched.'

'You're fucking kidding.' Steve shoved his chair back violently and got to his feet.

'I wish I was.' Grace gripped the door frame to stop her hands trembling. 'Carrie, Lindy, dead. Glanna, the local girl, Ayla, the student missing…now another one.'

Steve reached into one of his desk drawers, pulling out a battered looking pack of cigarettes. 'You've always thought there was a connection.' He lit a cigarette, releasing a plume of smoke towards the yellowing paint on the ceiling.

'Yes, I do Sir.' She met his eyes, seeing the raw frustration that lay there.

Steve followed her down to the main office, listening intently as Ollie filled him in. A moment later he was giving out orders, 'Tallis, Rhonda's gone to pick up the girls who rang in. You and her interview them when she gets here. Get everything you can from them.'

She hurried downstairs to the interview room, the sound of Steve's voice following her down the stairs as he organised the team which would deal with the case.

Rhonda arrived with two tearful, white-faced girls a few moments later. Grace met Rhonda's eyes and saw the fear there.

'Come in here girls, we need to get everything you remember about what happened.'

'She just... He just...' The blonde-haired schoolgirl was wild-eyed with panic, dark mascara staining the skin beneath her eyes.

'He just pulled her. We turned around and...' Her companion, a streak of purple running the length of her short-cropped hair looked numb with disbelief.

They let themselves be led into the interview room.

'I just need to get your names...' Rhonda indicated the girls should sit down.

'Do we need parents?' Grace asked.

'We're both eighteen,' The purple haired girl said.

'Names?'

'Liz Byrne. Michelle English.' The girls said, their voices hushed, stunned into silence by what had happened.

'The girl you were with...Sarah.' Rhonda probed gently, knowing the team were already out looking for the girl. Patrol cars would be on the alert for what Michelle had described as a big, black car. Their job was to tease out any information which might help find out what had happened, and who was responsible.

'Take your time girls, tell us what you remember.' Grace tilted her lips into a smile she hoped would reassure the two. Time was vital. If someone had snatched a girl off the streets in broad daylight, they didn't have any fear of being caught. Every moment that passed meant the girl was in more danger and was less likely to be found alive. The fear the girl must be enduring was unimaginable. Steve couldn't deny any longer that someone was snatching young women. The cases had to be linked, the same person was responsible for attacking Carrie, Lindy, and that maybe somewhere out there lay the body of Ayla, maybe Glanna and there could be others.

Slowly they coaxed the information out of the girls. They'd been walking home from school. There had been a group of them, all heading for the bus station. Gradually the group had separated. Sarah, they thought, had been on her own. She was usually in a world of her own, Liz explained, her words fading as her guilt over being unkind about Sarah came to the fore.

A car had come past them, the driver looking at them. 'He looked creepy, angry looking.' Michelle shuddered. Grace felt her breath shorten. Her throat sounded noisy when she swallowed, uncomfortably, remembering with harsh detail the look of the driver who had passed by her and Katia. Time had made the memory recede, yet it was no less frightening when it did come to the fore.

'Something made us look back.' Liz frowned as she tried to remember.

'There was a bang.' Michelle's voice was distant, her eyes unfocused, as she pictured the moment Sarah had been snatched.

'Yes. He'd…The man, he'd got out of the car. He slammed the door.'

'That was the bang. We'd turned around to see what it was.'

'It was all so fast. He had driven on the pavement next to Sarah. He just shoved her…'

'Into the car. Then he'd gone.'

Grace took a deep breath, feeling the panic the girls were in. 'The car, you said it was a big black one. Any idea what kind?'

'Do either of you remember the number plate?' Rhonda probed gently.

Liz shook her head.

'It all happened so fast. I think there was a D in it. Perhaps it was a Mondeo, something like that?' Michelle shrugged helplessly.

'Not much to go on.' Rhonda leant against the interview room door. The girls sat huddled together in the reception area. One of their parent's was on the way to collect them both.

Grace shook her head. It was a waiting game now.

The two women made their way back upstairs to the office, helpless. There was nothing else that could be done.

Grace turned her attention back to her files, but she couldn't focus. Her mind drifted constantly to Sarah, the missing girl, and her plight. Steve had seen the connection. There was someone attacking girls. Someone dangerous, who right now, had yet another victim.

'Woah, everybody.' Steve walked into the office a short time later. 'A bit of news.' He perched on the edge of one of the desks at the end of the room.

Grace fought to breathe. Sarah was dead. Her body had been found. The search had panicked her attacker, and he had killed her straight away.

'Sorry, Tallis.' Steve looked across the room, his face twisting into a wry smile. 'Looks like your serial killer theory has been squashed.'

Grace met his eyes, dropping hers to the heaped paperwork on her desk as she saw the relief in his.

'We've found Sarah. She's safe and well. Seems her kidnapper was her father. Apparently, she'd moved out of the family home to live with some lad, and her dad wanted to make her see sense.'

Grace released the breath she'd been holding.

'Rest up, Miss Marple.' Steve grinned good naturedly. 'No serial killer on the loose.'

Chapter Thirty-Four

'Susie, stop being so boring.' Tanya West flung herself on Susie's bed, lying on her belly. Propping herself up on her elbows she rested her chin on her hands and regarded Susie wryly.

'I'm not being boring.' Susie turned to face her friend, pulling her long, auburn hair over one shoulder. 'I've really got to keep working on this assignment.'

Tanya lifted her feet, walking them in the air, 'You've been doing that assignment for weeks. It must be good enough now.' Sighing deeply to show her disapproval, Tanya rolled onto her back, wriggling across the bed so her head dangled over the edge. Her long, dark hair cascaded around her head and pooled on the floor beneath her.

'It isn't.' Susie extended her long fingers and picked at a ragged cuticle. The sore patch drew her to it relentlessly when she was stressed. 'I've not got all the points in it I need.' A tiny spot of blood appeared beneath the pale sliver of skin. She watched it grow, until it trickled slowly down the side of her finger.

'Does it really matter that much? Who cares? You'll get top marks anyway. Swot.' Tanya flung the words good naturedly, yet there was a ring of truth to what she said. Susie worked so hard; she always had her head in a book. 'Lighten up!'

Susie put the tip of her finger between her lips, tasting the metallic blood on her tongue. It was alright for the rest of the girls in the house. They had no ambitions like she did. No burning desire to better themselves, to get out of the poverty of their childhoods.

She watched Tanya roll backwards off the bed, giggling as she fell in a crumpled heap on the floor, her long limbs sprawling. Tanya had no idea what it was like to be cold, hungry, to spend your childhood afraid of a knock on the door, hiding with your mother when the bailiffs came yet again to take something else out of the house. Tanya and the other girls in the house had grown up in normal homes, where light, heat, and food were taken for granted. Where they had two parents who held down proper jobs, who took them away to Spain or France each summer. They didn't have a mother whose greatest love was cheap vodka, and who thought nothing of selling her body to get it. They hadn't grown up watching their parents lie unconscious on stained, sagging sofas or had to clean up pools of vomit.

Susie wasn't jealous. She had no concept of what their lives would be like. The love, the security. But she was filled with the burning need to get out of the world she had grown up in, and never return to it. Her mother, she knew, was barely aware she wasn't around. She had just smiled blankly when Susie had told her she had got a place at university.

Mrs. Large, the kindly form mistress who had encouraged her during her time at school, had been the only one who had taken any notice. The 'congratulations' card, signed 'Best of Luck, Janine. xx', had become a bookmark used every day to remind Susie of her journey to success.

'Oh, please.' Tanya pulled herself up to sit on the edge of Susie's bed. 'We'd all love you to come out with us.' She lifted her hands to either side of her face in a puppy-like begging gesture, whimpering plaintively. 'It would do you good too. You'll come back to your work a lot fresher.'

Susie shook her head, sighing good humouredly. Tanya was winning her over. It had been months since she'd last been out for a drink. Life consisted of a dull routine of lectures, working on assignments, and regular shifts on the checkout at the local supermarket. She wasn't exactly living wildly.

'Okay,' Susie grinned, cuffing Tanya good naturedly. The two girls exploded into fits of laughter as Tanya pretended to be pushed over by Susie's touch, rolling onto the floor.

'What are you going to wear?' Tanya got to her feet and flung open the door of Susie's small wardrobe.

'That dress?' Susie shrugged as Tanya began to lift the hanging fabric, her face screwed up in concentration.

'How long have you had this?' Tanya disdainfully pushed the red flowered dress back into the depths of the wardrobe.

'I...' It was one Susie had pinched from her mother's wardrobe at home. Susie had no idea why her mother had even brought such a pretty dress. Perhaps one of her many male friends had given it to her as a gift.

'This.' Tanya withdrew her hand triumphantly clutching a short black dress. Susie winced. She'd brought it on a whim from a charity shop, knowing even as she paid for it that she would probably never wear it. The dress was too short, cut too low, exposing far too much of her cleavage for comfort. Looking at it now, as Tanya dangled it in front of her, Susie had no idea why she'd kept it.

'No,' she shook her head, grimacing.

'Oh, yes,' Tanya lifted Susie's hand and put the dress in it. 'Get dressed. I'm going to get changed. The others will be here soon. Hurry up.'

Already regretting her rash decision Susie got changed, taking off her familiar outfit of jeans and sweatshirt, before pulling the black dress over her head, tugging the hemline down, and the top upwards over the swell of her breasts.

'Gorgeous.' Tanya said approvingly, advancing on Susie with an overflowing makeup bag. 'Now, to turn you into a proper girl.'

Three hours later, Susie was regretting her decision. They'd gone from bar to bar, getting sillier and sillier. Susie's feet ached in the stupid high heels Tanya had forced her to wear. She felt cheap and exposed in the tarty dress.

'Celtic Arms next?' Tanya shouted over the roar of noise in the bar.

Fee, who was on Tanya's course shrugged. 'I don't care, just find me A. Man!'

'You wouldn't know what to do with one!' Denise, another of the girls, yelled above the melee, her mouth close to Susie's ear. She winced. 'I'm going to get a bit of fresh air,' Susie tugged on Tanya's arm to get her attention.

'Sure, whatever. We're going to the Celtic Arms when you're ready.'

Susie nodded, and made her way gratefully out of the crowded bar, hating the loud noise and the feeling of the bodies that pressed up against her. Outside, she gasped in the cool, fresh air. After the commotion inside, it felt heavenly. Susie lit a rare cigarette and leant against the wall of the bar, savouring the relative silence. The streets, even at the late hour, were still crowded. People, mostly of a similar age walked, swayed or staggered from bar to bar.

Glad of her jacket, Susie pulled the edges together over her chest and began to walk, longing to be home in the comfort of her room.

She wandered slowly along the pavement, looking in the shop windows. Perhaps she should buy a new dress, she mused, staring at a pale pink one adorning a stern looking dummy. Maybe the next time she got paid. There was one thing for sure: she was not going to ever wear this one ever again.

'Tea,' she whispered, as the bright lights of an all-night café attracted her. It would probably be full of down and outs, but at least that would be better than being in a crowded bar, trying to fend off the countless lads who tried to leer down her cleavage.

The café was relatively quiet. An elderly couple sat at one table close to the counter. Another was occupied by two young lads, one of who had clearly had too much to drink.

'Tea, please,' Susie stood at the counter. Turning, she found the eyes of a good-looking man on her. She hadn't noticed him when she'd come in. He was older than she was, considerably, but handsome, smartly dressed. Caught looking at her, the man smiled guiltily and dropped his eyes. Susie found a table beside the window and sipped her tea, gazing out through the steamy glass at the people who walked by.

'Is this yours?' Susie looked up to see the good-looking man standing beside her table.

She glanced at the brightly coloured blue silken scarf he held. 'No.'

'It was on the floor. I'll leave it on my chair, maybe someone will come back for it.' He grinned disarmingly, then shrugged. 'Sorry, clumsy attempt to talk to you.'

'Ha,' Susie sipped her tea. She hadn't realised how cold she'd been until the liquid began to slide down her throat. 'Good try.'

'I need to improve my chat up lines.' His smile tilted the corner of his mouth.

'Yes.' She returned his smile. The girls would be angry if they knew such a handsome man was sitting in the near deserted café, instead of them having to hunt in the crowded bars.

'Sorry,' he held up his hands in a gesture of surrender. 'I'll leave you to it. You look gorgeous, by the way.'

The door clanged shut as he went out, letting a blast of cold air into the warm fugue of the café.

Her tea finished, Susie glanced at her watch. The pubs would be starting to close now. She'd better find the girls so they could make their way home.

Outside, the streets were still busy, filled with people beginning to flag down taxis, walking away from the centre of the city at the end of their night out.

Susie headed up the street towards the Celtic Arms. The girls were undoubtedly still there. Her uncomfortable shoes clattered on the pavement slabs. She hadn't realised how far it was to the pub.

'Sorry,' Susie skirted past a middle-aged couple who were wandering slowly along, blocking the pavement. It was easier to walk on the road and she made better progress. At the end of the street stood a line of taxis, a group of people separating, getting into the individual vehicles.

'Tanya,' Susie spotted her friends, she hurried as fast as her heels would allow. Ahead, the three girls were getting into a taxi. The last. 'Fuck.' Susie stopped, furious. They'd gone. So had all of the taxis.

Sighing, Susie sank down on the wooden bench beneath the bus shelter that also served as a taxi rank. Shivering, she tucked her hands inside the sleeves of her jacket, pulling the edges of the fabric around herself. It would be a long wait until the taxis had deposited their cargos and headed back into town.

'Hi.' A smart looking pick-up drove into the taxi rank and stopped. 'It's you? The girl from the café?'

Susie glanced up, looking through the half open window at the man from the café.

'Yes. That's me.' She looked down the street, reassured to see the middle-aged couple making steady progress towards her.

'Are you stuck? You look frozen.'

'I am.' Susie sighed. 'There'll be a taxi along in a moment.'

'Where are you going? The university campus?'

'Well spotted,' Susie looked down at herself. She looked the same as all of the other girls around town that night, all legs and tits, her mum would have said.

'I'm sure you'll say no, but I'm going that way…' He shrugged disarmingly, 'If you want a lift.'

Susie shook her head.

'Sensible,' he sucked air in between his teeth making a tutting sound.

'Yup.' She moved along the bench as the middle-aged couple came beneath the shelter.

'Wise,' his voice was filled with wry good humour. 'I look like a serial killer, don't I?'

Susie shook her head, laughing. 'I don't think so.'

'Well, last chance. Cold wait, or a daring lift with a handsome stranger. Go on, live dangerously.'

Susie rolled her eyes. 'Put that way, what choice do I have?'

'If you don't, I will,' the middle-aged lady teased gently.

Susie got slowly to her feet. 'Oh, go on then.' He pushed open the passenger side door to let her in. It was deliciously warm in the vehicle after the bitter cold of the evening.

'Fasten your seat belt. Need to keep you safe.'

Susie did as she was told. That was when she spotted the blue silk scarf.

Chapter Thirty-Five

She watched a trickle of blood run slowly down her wrist. In the dim light it looked almost black against the paleness of her skin. Susie jerked again at the metal handcuff that circled her wrist and secured her to a twist of wrought iron at the top of the bed. That was a mistake. Nothing moved, except the metal, which dug further into her skin. The pain was agonising.

Wincing, she brought her free hand to her face, tentatively feeling her jawline. It ached with a pounding thump as if her heart were directly beneath the skin.

Fuck. She'd actually been flirting with him. She'd got into the vehicle willingly. He was so nice, good looking, charming. Stuck alone at the cold taxi rank, she couldn't believe her luck. She could have sat waiting with the middle-aged couple until the next taxi arrived, whenever that may have been, or get a lift with him. She'd relaxed in the warmth, lulled by the music he was playing. What was that? Scraps of a tune flashed through her mind. Fragile, wisps she couldn't grasp.

'Stupid. Stupid.' Susie hissed, letting the tears she'd been holding in fall freely. Not caring about the pain in her wrist, she jerked at the handcuff, pounded on the bed with her heels, and screamed. The noise made her throat sore. She didn't recognise the sound, the anger, pain, and frustration merging into one single cry.

He'd stopped the pick-up near to the university campus. 'There you go, safe and sound.'

'Thank you.' Turning to open the door she'd paused. Actually paused, hoping he would ask her out.

He must have punched her. Knocked her out. Susie felt tentatively at her throbbing jaw. All her teeth were there, she realised, running her tongue around the inside of her mouth. That was a surprise, her jaw hurt enough that she felt as if each tooth had been lifted out and put back.

She had a vague recollection of sliding towards wakefulness, him pulling her from the vehicle, being lifted, cold air on her skin, and then she'd slid back into the darkness.

Light, a pale glimmer of daylight, was beginning to creep through the tiny window high up the wall beside the bed. Daylight. As time passed, she could make out more of the room. Beside her, when Susie craned her neck, she could see a small table. There were deep scratches, parallel lines on the wall close to where she lay. Someone marking time? Fear jolted though her like an electric current. So many marks. Who had been here? And where were they now? Susie screamed again.

Had anyone noticed she was missing? Thoughts flitted through her mind. When would they realise she wasn't there? Later today? When she wasn't in class? Would it occur to anyone she hadn't come home? They'd assume she was in the library, or studying in one of the cafés, or doing a shift at the supermarket. It could be days before her absence was noticed.

How could she have been so stupid? Accepting a lift with a stranger.

She should have waited. She should have stayed with the other girls. She daren't think about her captor, or what he intended to do to her. She was alive, at least. But was that necessarily a good thing?

The sound of a key being turned in the door at the far side of the room split the silence. Her thoughts froze as she watched, waiting, her heart pounding.

'What do you want? Why have you done this to me?' Words tumbled from her mouth.

The door opened slowly. The bottom of it stuck on the stone slab beneath it.

'You're awake.' He came slowly into the room. Shyly almost. A half smile tilted the corners of his mouth, but it was his eyes that scared her the most. The friendly, gentle look that had shone there the previous night had gone. Something else had replaced it. Something cold. Dead looking.

'Let me go… You must let me go… My friends… The people, they saw me get in your pick-up.'

He put up his hand. 'I don't have to do anything.'

'My friends. They'll be missing me. They'll already have spoken to the police.'

He took a step closer, shrugging. 'I doubt it. They'll be sleeping off their hangovers. Shagging whatever lad they've ended up with.'

Susie shook her head. 'Those people, in the taxi shelter. They saw me get in your pick-up.'

The bed creaked as he sat down on it. Susie drew herself as far away from him as she could, hating the heat of his body against hers. She watched, filled with a horrified fascination, as his fingers began to examine her blood-stained wrist.

'You were just a girl getting a lift. No one takes any notice.'

'But…' the words died on her lips. What he'd said was true. No one noticed anything. No one cared.

'You need to relax.'

Susie's eyes were drawn to his. They were brown, and in the light from the small window she could see flecks of amber in his irises. His lashes, when he closed his eyes, in a slow, almost sleepy gesture, were long and thick. 'I'm going to take care of you now.' He was looking at her in a way she couldn't identify at first. Reverence, she realised with a jolt.

'No, no, no, no,' Susie shook her head, vehemently. 'You have to let me go. I won't say anything. Just let me go.'

His lips tilted upwards. 'They all say that.'

His words made her breath catch in her throat. Her thoughts raced wildly. 'I won't. I promise. I'm not the same as everyone else.'

'What were you studying?'

Susie tried, and failed, to suppress a whimper of horror. 'I'm doing a degree in Maths and Physics.'

His eyebrows rose almost imperceptibly. 'Clever.'

'Yes.'

'Not so clever. You were happy to get a lift from me.'

The handcuff rattled against the metal struts of the headboard as Susie clenched her fist, longing to strike out at him.

'Please,' she was pleading now. 'Please, let me go. I don't want to be here. My friends will be worried.'

His mouth twisted downwards. Susie watched the expression on his face change, thoughtful, considering what she had said. 'You gave yourself to me. You got in the car. You wanted this.'

Susie shook her head violently, fighting the panic that rose within her. 'No. I didn't want this. You offered me a lift. I want to go home.' She wrenched at the handcuff, crying out with the agonising pain as the metal bit into her flesh. Jerking her legs upwards, she lashed out at him, her heel connecting with his leg.

In one swift movement he leapt to his feet, standing over her, his fingers holding her arms, digging into the flesh. 'Don't.' His voice was cold. His eyes, when they met hers, were cold, lifeless. 'Don't make me hurt you.' The threat was clear in his tone.

She forced a breath into her lungs, trying to dull the feeling of hatred and fear.

Abruptly he released her and stood, looking at her. 'I'm going to leave you now. You can think about what I've said. I don't want to have to hurt you. I'm going to take care of you. I'm going to be your life, and you are going to be mine.'

'No. Please. Let me go.'

For a long moment he watched her. 'Think about what I've said.'

With that he backed away, his eyes never moving from her as he retreated. 'Don't go. I need the toilet.'

The corner of his mouth twitched in amusement. Then he was gone. She heard the key turn in the door, his footsteps retreating, and then a silence, broken only by distant animal noises and once, a child's voice.

She watched the shadows in the room change as the sun made its journey across the sky. The light was fading when he finally returned.

'I hope you thought about what I said,' he stood at the foot of the bed, looking at her, a mixture of pity and revulsion in his eyes.

'Yes,' she whispered.

'I've brought clean sheets. There are fresh clothes.' She watched him move around the room, pulling open the wardrobe doors, 'you should have a shower.' He pushed aside a curtain that dangled in the depths of the room. As her eyes adjusted, she realised there was a shower behind it and an untidy heap of towels.

'I'm going to let you go.' He pulled a key from his jeans pocket and undid the handcuff. Susie whimpered as the blood flowed back into her fingers, agonising tendrils of pins and needles swept through her limb.

She should lash out at him, but beaten and weak from hunger, Susie got slowly to her feet, her muscles screaming in protest as she straightened up and walked slowly towards the shower. The damp fabric of her dress clung to her legs. She wrenched it upwards, painfully aware of how low it was over her breasts. He made a snort of amusement at her discomfiture.

Reaching the shower, she pulled the curtain across the shower, turning the water on, shielding herself from him. Feeling vulnerable, she undressed, stepping with relief into the warm water. 'Clean clothes are on the floor beside the shower.'

'Thank you.' While she had been standing in the shower, naked, he had been beside her, separated only by the thin curtain. She dressed hastily, pulling leggings and a sweater on over her still damp skin, desperate to cover herself.

While she'd been in the shower, he had changed the bed. A pretty, floral duvet was neatly folded back over the bed, incongruous in the damp, dingy room.

'I hope we'll be friends,' he lifted the bundle of discarded bedclothes, her clothes tangled within it. 'I'll bring you some food later.'

He regarded her solemnly before leaving abruptly.

As the key turned in the lock, Susie ran to the door, crouching down so she could peer through the keyhole. Beyond the room stretched a long corridor. She could see him, retreating into the distance. There were doors on one side, while on the other were piled heaps of discarded wood and junk. What was behind the other doors? Was he some kind of freak who kept a harem of women, like the weirdo in the film she'd seen a long time ago? She tried and failed to remember its name.

Using all of her strength, she pushed on the door, kicking at it with her heels, shoving it with her shoulder. It did not budge. There had to be some way out of her prison, she reasoned. She wasn't going to die here. Not like this. The captive of some nutter. She circled the room, dragging the table so she could stand on it and look through the window, jerking at the iron bars that were in the front of the glass. They did not move.

She prowled the length of the room, examining the shower, the toilet. There had to be some way out. There wasn't. Finally, she admitted defeat. She picked up the table, pushing against its legs, intending to pull one off, bang him over the head and run. Nothing was loose. There was nothing she could use as a weapon. He'd thought of everything.

'Get back away from the door.' It was almost dark when he returned, bright electric light flooding the room. There must be a switch outside the room that he controlled. She blinked painfully at the sudden glow. He came into the room, locking it carefully behind him. Only when it was locked did he nod in acquiescence that she could move.

He held out a plate towards her. Starving she made a grab for the sandwich.

'Ah, ah.' He pulled the plate away out of her reach. 'You want this? You'll have to earn it.'

Chapter Thirty-Six

Grace's day went badly. Whatever she did seemed to take forever. The mountain of paperwork she had to trawl through never seemed to get any smaller. They were nowhere near finding out who had killed Lindy and attacked Carrie. Even the air in the building seemed to be filled with the frustration everyone felt.

She'd gone to the hospital, with Rhonda, to interview a man who had been knocked over by a car as he crossed the road. What should have taken only a short time was delayed by an accident on the dual carriageway between a caravan and a tractor. Hay and caravan bits were scattered over the road. They'd got stuck right in the middle between two junctions and had no alternative but to wait until the road was clear.

Finally, her shift was over, and she hurried out of the building. 'You okay?' Rhonda jogged to catch up with Grace as they crossed the station car park.

'Yes,' Grace looked sideways at Rhonda, her blonde hair, released from its work-neat French pleat, swirled around her face.

'Oh, right. Sorry I asked.'

'Sorry,' Grace stopped, midstride. 'Is it that obvious?'

Rhonda smiled, shaking her head. 'Yes. You're like the proverbial cat on a hot tin roof. What's the matter?'

'I've got a date.'

'Must be pretty important to have you in this state.'

Grace puffed out her cheeks. 'I think it is.'

'Relax and enjoy yourself.' Rhonda pulled Grace into a hug.

'I'll try.'

'Oh, come on, let me past,' Grace said, through gritted teeth, a while later, as she drove towards the pub. The inevitable tractor was trundling slowly up the narrow lane at a snail's pace. There was no way she could overtake it, and she was already late.

'Thank you,' she waved as the tractor finally pulled into a layby and let her past.

On the lane, near the pub, she deftly squeezed her car into a tiny gap between a new looking pick-up and a bright red Porsche. The driver of the pick-up was engrossed in a pile of paperwork. She hurried into the building, conscious of the taut feeling in the pit of her stomach. She spotted her reflection on one of the decorated mirrors that lined the walls of the pub entrance hall. 'Relax,' she hissed at her reflection, aware of how ridiculous she was being. It was just a drink with Kaden. It was the third time they had been to the pub together, but there had been something different about the way he had asked her. Somewhere, during the time they spent together their relationship had changed from friendship to something else altogether.

'I thought you weren't coming.' Kaden was already halfway down his pint.

'Sorry,' Grace grimaced apologetically.

She loved her job, but sometimes it felt as if her personal life was being squeezed into a tighter and tighter space between the hours she worked.

'Let me get you another drink.' She looked around the crowded bar. It was full with a mix of tourists and locals. No one that posed a threat. The holiday makers stood out in their off-duty uniforms, the men all sporting chinos or shorts, and shirts, while the women were dressed in an array of flowered dresses. The locals on the other hand were mostly farmers, dressed in grubby jeans and shirts, their faces ruddy from the sunshine. There were others too, workers from the town in smart suits, women in neat, soberly coloured dresses. Then aware of Kaden's eyes on her, Grace brought her full attention to him. 'Sorry. I'll just…'

She ordered drinks and returned to the table. Grace took a sip of her drink, relaxing finally.

'How was your day?' As Kaden spoke Grace became aware of a man, at the far side of the room on a stool, his arms resting on the bar. He was listening intently to the conversation of the people beside him.

'Busy. How about you?'

The man, she realised, wasn't part of the group he sat beside. As he took a sip of his pint, Grace watched him, seeing his eyes roving over the room, his expression watchful, assessing. Had she seen him before? Her mind, ever sharp to criminal activity, crackled with interest wondering who he was, and why he was listening to the conversation with such focus.

'Grace?'

'Sorry…' Grace forced herself back to Kaden. In her mind, she'd been filing the face of the man for future reference, recognising that listening to a stranger's conversation was not something normal. Could he be waiting to find out where the people, who were clearly tourists, were staying? Trying to assess their plans, so he could break into their accommodation? The area was full of holiday lets, cottages, converted barns, and gypsy caravans, parked amongst apple orchards. They were easy pickings for thieves. the occupants were relaxed, their sense of security abandoned when they left home. The places were often full of carelessly left out money or jewellery. Catnip for characters who made their living selling the proceeds of a five-minute grab in an empty cottage.

Kaden shook his head wryly. 'I just asked you if you wanted to ride out with a group at the weekend if you are off. We were going to go to the beach and then onto the pub.'

'Yes. I'd love to.' Grace felt her eyes being drawn continuously to the man, who had now got off his stool and was making his way through the crowded bar towards the door. Had he already worked out where the group were staying, and was making his way there now to break in while they were in the pub?

'Love to what?' Kaden's voice had an irritable edge.

'What did you say?' The man had left the bar. Should she follow him?

'Grace, I'm trying to say I wanted to spend some time with you, and you're miles away.'

'Sorry,' Grace shook her head, forcing herself to focus on the handsome young man in front of her.

Sighing, Kaden leant forwards and took one of Grace's hands. 'I've been wanting to see you all day.'

'I'm sorry,' she repeated, 'just, that man. He seemed a bit weird. I was worried he was…'

'You need to leave work behind you sometimes,' Kaden's fingers moved gently over the back of Grace's.

'I know.' She smiled, shrugging helplessly, seeing his expression soften.

'That bloke, the one who went out. He used to be in the police. He does security for some of the holiday cottages.' Kaden met Grace's eyes, his expression wry.

Grace shook her head, sighing. 'I'm spoiling this. I was looking forward to seeing you all day.'

'Come on. I'm going to buy you dinner. Let's start again.' Kaden pulled Grace to her feet, holding onto her hand as he led the way through the bar.

'Sorry mate,' Kaden edged past a tall man.

'No worries,' the man moved slightly to let them past.

'Thanks,' Grace met the man's eyes.

'My pleasure.' He smiled, his eyes roving over her face. Something about him made the hairs on the back of her neck stand up. Creep. She tore her attention reluctantly from the man, back to Kaden. She'd spoilt enough of the evening already without talking about the tall man.

Chapter Thirty-Seven

'What's this idiot doing?' Kaden slid his arm from around Grace's shoulder to change the direction of his driver's mirror, deflecting the bright lights from the vehicle behind them. 'He's right up behind me.' Kaden sighed, adding 'twat,' as the pick-up finally passed them on a long straight stretch of road.

'Idiot,' Grace mumbled sleepily, her head still resting comfortably on Kaden's shoulder. It was unusual to see other vehicles on the normally deserted rural roads, especially in the middle of the night.

It felt like mere minutes since Kaden had gently begun to kiss her in the pub car park, and yet, looking at her watch, she knew it was hours. The kisses had continued, and when it seemed pointless to resist, they'd got into his car and driven the short distance back to his cottage, dinner forgotten.

It had felt like heaven, lying beside him, skin against skin, but good sense prevailed, and they had struggled from the bed so Kaden could drive Grace back to the pub to collect her car and drive home, ready for her early morning shift.

'So...' Kaden steered into the pub car park, deserted, except for Grace's car, alone in the centre of the tarmac.

'So...' Grace grinned. 'Thank you, I had a lovely evening.'

'Me too,' Kaden's voice was husky as he gently slid a hand around the back of her neck and drew her face towards his.

'Damn work,' Grace groaned, easing herself away from him. 'I wish I could...'

'Mmm,' Kaden sighed. 'I wish you could, too.'

'I need to go,' Grace eased herself out of his arms and opened the car door, letting a blast of cold air into the warmth of the interior.

'Drive carefully. See you tomorrow?'

'Definitely, I'll be at the stables as soon as my shift ends.'

She slammed the car door, watching with regret as he drove away, the taillights of his car fading as he drove around a corner and disappeared.

'Home.' Grace told herself decisively, already regretting her decision to leave Kaden. It would have been so easy to stay the night with him, but he left for the stables early, and she needed to shower and get ready for work. There'd be other nights. She grinned, holding the memory of the evening, and anticipating others.

'Shhhhh,' Grace snapped the radio off as it blasted music into her car. Filled with nervous excitement, she'd been singing at the top of her voice to the radio when she'd hurtled towards the pub earlier that evening. Now, she wanted silence. Peace, to let the later part of the evening replay on a loop in her imagination.

Even the sound of her car starting up seemed too noisy in the silence of the country lane. She hoped the engine noise would not wake the pub's landlord. She eased the car into gear and drove away.

She loved the darkness, having the road to herself. Instinctively, she ducked as an enormous owl swooped past the windscreen. The countryside was deserted. The night-time was the time to see foxes crossing the road in the distance, or to catch a glimpse of a badger making his way along the wide grass verge. In the daytime, the roads were clogged with traffic and hikers, but now, in the middle of the night, they belonged to her.

Eager to be in bed, Grace shoved her foot down on the accelerator, feeling her powerful car surge forwards, the headlights arcing into the darkness.

'Fuck,' she stepped on the brake a moment later, hearing an unmistakable thud, and sensing a change in her car's handling. A puncture. The last thing she needed in the middle of the night. She wrestled with the steering wheel until she reached a layby.

Grace glanced at her mobile. The battery was virtually flat. Who could she call in the middle of the night, anyway? Certainly not Kaden. He had a long day ahead at the stables. It was just a puncture. She could change the wheel herself.

A light caught her eye, somewhere in the distance a vehicle's headlights lit up the sky, fading as quickly as they had appeared. There was nothing to do but to get on with changing the wheel.

Stepping out into the darkness, Grace shivered. 'Quicker this is done the better,' she muttered, opening the car boot and unearthing the necessary equipment. The lights from the car and its interior illuminated a small patch in the darkness around the car. Feeling vulnerable, she looked into the darkness. Somewhere close by, an owl hooted. She felt the air move as it flew overhead. Further down the lane, her car's headlights picked up the red glow of an animal's eyes.

Moving hastily, Grace loosened the wheel nuts, and then, crouching on the ground, levered the car slowly upwards with the jack. 'Easy,' she sighed, haste making her movements clumsy.

Getting to her feet, she watched headlights shine in the distance, coming closer, light pooling in front of it. A vehicle came along the lane. Fearfully she held her breath then released it in relief as it passed. In the darkness she was aware of the bulk of the vehicle, the thud of noise from music inside. Despite her growing feeling of unease, she still noticed one of its rear lights and the number plate light were out.

As the vehicle continued, the silence descended. As Grace wrenched at the wheel nuts, the lever slipped from one, banging hard against her hand. 'Dammit,' she winced, instinctively wrapping her other hand around her sore fingers. A moment later she froze. the vehicle, a farm pick-up was reversing back up the lane towards her.

'Do you need a hand?' the driver let down the passenger side window to speak to Grace.

'No, thank you. I'm fine.'

'Okay, if you're sure.' In the darkness his face was shadowed, the features indistinguishable. His voice was soft, with a gentle Cornish burr.

She watched as he drove away. Perhaps she should have let him help. Her job made her suspicious. Not everyone was a serial rapist or dangerous lunatic.

She set to work again, succeeding in getting the deflated tyre off, and lifting the spare out. Crouching beside the tyre, juggling it to line up the wheel nuts, she heard footsteps a split second before rough hands grabbed her shoulders, lifting her bodily off the ground. Grace jerked her body, trying to get her feet onto the road surface, to get a foot hold so she stood some chance against her attacker, her self-defence training making her movements instinctive. His hands were hauling at her arms, trying to drag her away from the car. Grace screamed, her voice echoing in the silent darkness. She fought, using all her strength and skill, trying to claw at him, to hurt him, get something which would identify him, but mostly she struggled to get away.

He was grunting from the exertion of trying to drag her. Stars danced before Grace's eyes as a blow landed on her cheekbone. Nothing existed except the struggle to live, to get away from him. His grip relaxed momentarily as the headlights from an approaching vehicle lit up the lane. He shoved her roughly away. Exhausted from her battle to survive she fell, sprawling onto the tarmac, feeling the surface bite into her hands and knees as she landed.

He was gone as quickly as he had arrived. Sobbing Grace crawled to her feet, watching the man's shape as he vanished into the darkness down the road.

'It's okay, you're safe,' the driver of the car whose headlights had startled Grace's attacker hurried from his car. She half-stumbled, half-fell into his arms.

'Come and sit in my car.' He said gently, helping Grace to her feet. 'I'm going to call the police.'

'I'm a police officer. I'll report the incident,' Grace shook her head, dreading the questions she'd face, everyone knowing she'd been out all night with Kaden, that she'd been stupid enough not to have her phone charged. They'd expect a full report, a detailed description of the man who had attacked her. Grace had no idea who he was, or what make his vehicle had been. She'd driven Steve to distraction talking about the girls who had been attacked in the area, those who were missing. Had she narrowly avoided being one of those girls?

She winced, bringing her fingers to her aching cheek. Already it was swelling. Grace eased her shoulders. If only there were a part of her that didn't ache. Her clothes, in the pale light of the car interior, were ripped and filthy.

'You sit there while I sort out your wheel. Why didn't you ring someone for help? You can't go changing wheels, pretty young woman like you.' The man was still muttering to himself as he left Grace to finish changing the wheel. It was warm in his car. She just wanted to crawl into bed and forget what had happened, longing for the release sleep would bring.

'There. All sorted.' He let himself back into the driver's seat and smiled gently at Grace.

'Thank you.' She fought the urge to vomit. It was hard not to imagine what could have happened if he had not come along.

Her home was in darkness, its bulk intimidating as she drove up the drive, the car headlights illuminating the black silhouettes of the windows. Grace's fingers trembled as she unlocked the front door, after forcing herself to walk slowly from her car, despite every fibre of her body willing her to run.

Once inside, the dark house felt oppressive, frightening shapes lurked in every corner. Grace locked the front door, walking with deliberate slowness up the stairs. Her heart pounded uncomfortably against her chest as she cleaned her teeth, every creak in the old house becoming the foundation of more fear.

Forcing air into her lungs, Grace made her way into her bedroom, pulled back her duvet, and then, her nerves failing her, shoved a chest of drawers up against the door.

The house felt less intimidating in the morning, but her nerves were still frayed.

'Christ,' she swore, examining herself in the bathroom mirror. There was a livid purple bruise beneath one eye, and her cheek was swollen and red where her attacker had punched her.

She dropped the flat tyre off at a garage on her way to work. 'Be ready in a few hours,' the mechanic said, shouldering the tyre.

'Jesus, Tallis.' Steve was the first person she met as she walked into the station. 'What happened?' She met his eyes, seeing the naked concern as he steered her into his office.

Haltingly she told him, later repeating her story to Rhonda who had been tasked with taking an official statement. Grace bit back tears as she related what had happened, clenching her hands into fists to stop them trembling. The memory of the attack was a blur, she had no description, no number plate. Nothing that would help them find out who had attacked her.

'Take time off if you need it.' Steve said, coming to stand beside her desk.

'No bloody way, I want to catch this bastard.'

'That's my girl,' Steve grinned.

Finally, the long day ground to a halt. Grace took another two painkillers, washed them down with a tepid mug of coffee. She longed to go home yet dreaded being alone with equal measure.

The mechanic met her on the garage forecourt, his fingers gripping her now mended tyre.

'What was it?' Grace asked, 'A nail?'

He shook his head, meeting her eyes before saying solemnly, 'No nail. That tyre was tampered with.'

Chapter Thirty-Eight

'Someone, somewhere, knows something.' Steve Cooper let his eyes roam slowly over the assembled detectives, seeing the defeat in their faces. 'We will find whoever attacked Carrie Anderson and who killed Lindy Walker.' As his eyes flickered towards Grace he continued, 'I know there are those amongst you that think the two cases are linked together with a couple of missing students.'

'Could they be?' Paddy picked up a pile of paperwork and shuffled the pages.

Steve shook his head, shrugging. 'My feeling is they aren't linked. I'm bloody sure the boyfriend was involved with Lindy's murder, but until we can prove that we keep going. The same with Carrie. Anderson. It's easy to link cases, throw in every missing person in Cornwall and you've got serial killer. But let's not get excited here, we are a small rural team with a budget most forces would laugh at, we aren't acting out an episode of Luther. Just do what you're trained to do, and we will get the right result.'

Grace gently probed her cheek. It still ached. She reached for another file, easing her back. Being dragged along the ground had wrenched all the muscles in her back and legs. Everywhere still hurt, weeks after the incident.

'Meanwhile we've still got bread and butter cases to deal with, like getting a result in these farm thefts. Tallis, you and Matt go to Blackthorn Farm. I'll get you the address. Have a chat with the guy there, Eddie Hammett. The farm that neighbours him was the last one broken into. See if he saw anything. If anyone strange has been around. Can someone volunteer to check up on what our friend Jem Trevayne was doing that night? He's a bloody tough nut to crack. I'm convinced it was him who attacked Grace, but his wife is sticking to her story. We can't prove otherwise.'

Grace got to her feet, glad to be out of the office, away from the heart-breaking dead ends that both attacks seemed to keep bringing them to. It was frustrating, how someone could have walked away from a crowded beach, and somewhere, on her route back to the camp site met her killer. The thought that she'd been dragged from the road reminded Grace of the night she'd been attacked. It was just a few miles from the windswept field where Lindy had met her dreadful death.

Was Lindy's killer someone local, as she'd thought for so long? Was it true that somewhere in the harsh beauty of the Cornish landscape a killer lurked? Was he a local, and not, as Steve was presuming, a person who had come to the area for the festival? He was adamant her killer was JJ, and seemed blinkered to any other outcome, despite having the team looking into the other leads that came up. He was equally convinced Carrie's attacker was one of the lads she was with.

'Ready?' Matt was beside her desk. 'Okay to go in your car?'

'Sure,' Matt, new to the team, was well known for keeping his car pristine, and the thought of a trip up a muddy farm track would not appeal to him. Matt, tall, with the broad shoulders of a rugby player had joined the force in his thirties after tiring of a job as a hotel manager.

Easy going with a dry sense of humour he had quickly fitted into the team.

Their route brought them past the turn off to the lane where Grace had been attacked. She forced a breath past dry lips, focusing intently on the road ahead.

'You still riding the stable boy?' Matt, sought to ease Grace's tension.

'Yep.' Grace glanced at Matt, seeing the concern in his grey eyes. 'Did you get anywhere with the barmaid in the White Lion?'

She was glad of the distraction. Within the teams light-hearted banter and teasing was part of the life, often stuck in cars together for hours. Dealing with the dross of humanity had to be balanced with good natured chatter.

'This is a fucking wild goose chase,' Matt leant forwards to peer through the windscreen at the long track that led through fields towards a tangle of stone buildings, surrounded by a belt of trees. 'The farm that was broken into is miles away, this guy isn't going to have seen anything.'

'We'll see.' Grace steered around a pothole.

Matt was still under the illusion police work resembled something from the television, and that crimes were solved quickly, and were not the long, plodding procedure they really were.

The track led between two low stone buildings and opened out into a courtyard, surrounded by more buildings. A typical Cornish farmhouse faced them, rectangular, made from blocks of local stone, with a slate roof, built to withstand the ferocious winds that howled in from the sea. Behind the tangle of buildings stood a ruined stone cottage, blackened rafters reaching skywards.

Grace parked the car. 'Ready?' The farmyard was deserted. The place gave her the creeps, the lazy wind that whipped through the branches of the trees was the only sound.

She jumped as a dog suddenly ran from one of the buildings and leapt against the wire mesh fence that surrounded its enclosure.

A curtain twitched in one of the upstairs windows. Grace spotted a shadowy figure; someone was watching them.

'Yes?' The red painted front door opened, and a tall man emerged. 'What can I do for you?'

'Hello. Mr Hammett? Eddie?'

'Yes.' He came forward, wiping his hands on a towel. His eyes moved slowly from Grace to Matt and back again. Grace's stomach lurched. She was sure she had seen him before. She forced herself to speak through tinder dry lips, the man, whatever it was about him, gave her the creeps. 'We're investigating some thefts of farm machinery. Rural farmhouses and cottages, being broken into.'

Eddie sighed, putting his head on one side in a gesture of amusement. 'That's nothing new.' His eyes locked into hers. His gaze slid slowly away as Matt spoke. 'Seems one of your neighbour's sheds was broken into, a knapsack sprayer was taken.'

'We wondered if you'd seen anything?' Eddie returned his gaze to Grace, running his free hand through his hair.

'No.' He smiled, full lips opening to reveal a line of white, even teeth. Beneath the tee shirt he wore, Grace had an impression of a toned, muscular body.

'I've a list here of things that have been stolen recently. Can I give you a look at them, just in case you get offered anything by someone calling here?' Matt shrugged, his feelings of hopelessness about their task clear in his demeanour.

'Sure.' Eddie nodded, folding the hand towel neatly over his arm, as if he were a waiter. As he examined the list, Grace turned slowly, looking at the house and the buildings. From the upstairs window she could feel eyes on them. Someone was inside, watching them. His wife?

'Who lives here with you?' Grace asked.

'Just my mum. My dad's long dead.' He stopped looking at Matt's list, turning his full attention to Grace. There was a darkness behind his brown eyes that tightened a band of tension in her chest. His lips tilted in a slow, lazy smile, that made her feel as if he were assessing her, as if he could see through her jacket, through her jeans, to the nakedness that lay beneath.

She turned away, not wanting to look into the cold violence she could see in his eyes any longer, glad that Matt was with her. Eddie Hammett was a creep. One of those horrible, lecherous men who thought women were only good for one thing. That didn't make him a criminal, though. He was just a farmer, making a living on this wild stretch of Cornish land.

'Is that your pick-up?'

'It is.' Eddie's voice was filled with good natured amusement, fielding yet another of her questions. 'Just got it a few months ago.'

Grace swallowed, trying to bring some moisture into her dry mouth. Her imagination whirled wildly. She'd glimpsed the pick-up driven by the man who had attacked her, was Eddie Hammett's the same model? She couldn't be sure. She was, she knew, so on edge about the incident, even weeks later, that anything, and everything reminded her of what had happened. Of course, Eddie had a pick-up. He was a farmer, what else would he drive?

She stared into the depths of the shed where the vehicle was parked, taking a stride forwards to look closer. 'Had a crash?' The passenger side of the tailgate was dented. The light cracked.

'Reversed into the wall there. Couldn't believe it. Bloody nearly new and I've already damaged it.' Eddie jerked his head towards the low wall that separated the yard from a neatly tended vegetable garden.

'Get that light mended, will you?' Grace met his eyes, holding his gaze steadily, aware of the irritation that flashed through his expression.

'I've been meaning too.'

'Okay, thank you. We'll leave you to it.' She walked away, Matt hurrying beside her, paperwork flapping.

'Fuck.' Grace shuddered, driving away. In her driver's mirror she could see Eddie stood in the centre of the yard, watching them go. 'What a creep.'

'Really?' Matt looked at her quizzically. 'I wouldn't have said that.'

Grace pushed her foot on the accelerator. She couldn't get away fast enough.

Back in the office, she couldn't get Eddie Hammett out of her mind. The way he had looked at her, the violence that seemed to simmer beneath his calm expression. Could he have been the man who had attacked her? Or Lindy, or Carrie?

Surely it had been Jem? The threat had been clear when he had confronted her and Kaden. Cornwall was full of pick-up trucks. It could have been anyone. Unable to think straight, she made her way into the toilets, leaning her aching forehead on the coolness of the mirror.

'Cool it.' She said to her reflection. The night she'd been attacked had changed everything. She saw danger in every shadow, every noise the old house made woke her, leaving her lying watchful in the darkness.

Grace forced a breath into her lungs. She had to relax; her mind was spinning. Just because someone gave her the creeps didn't mean they had been the person who had attacked her, or who was guilty of the terrible crimes that had affected the young women over the last few years.

Walter Upton, the man who worked behind the bar in the pub the local coppers used, gave Rhonda the creeps, she would never go into the pub unless everyone else was going. Grace didn't pick anything like that up from Walter, other than that he was an idiot.

Her training meant she knew how to react to dangerous situations. She was not intimidated by the thugs who crossed her path, but at the bottom of that still lay her own senses. The nose for a villain, that made the difference between being a good detective and not.

There had been something about Eddie Hammett that had made her skin crawl.

And yet...Grace made her way back to the office, picking up the files on Lindy, Carrie, and the missing Scottish girl, Ayla. There were others going back years including one on Glanna, another girl who had gone missing from university. Steve had always been adamant there was no connection, though she had been equally sure there was. Something linked the girls to Cornwall. What if the connection was Eddie Hammett?

There was no proof that Ayla, or Glanna, had been attacked in the area. They'd gone missing from university. Lindy, though, and Carrie, both attacked within a few miles of one another. And now her.

Grace rubbed at her arms, suddenly frozen, despite the warmth of the office. She knew that, without the intervention of the man who had driven past, her attack would have been worse. She'd been putting up a good fight, but the man's strength surpassed hers.

Was that what had happened to Lindy? Grace pictured the girl, walking from the festival, angry at JJ, alone on the deserted road. And Carrie. Were they victims of the same person, or just random attacks?

Had Lindy been attacked by her furious boyfriend? Had the lads that Carrie had been hanging out with been the ones who had caused her horrific injuries, as Steve suspected? His vision was clouded by his belief in what had happened. He had, she knew, wanted to fit the pieces into his opinion.

There had to be a connection. Grace was sure the connection was Eddie Hammett.

Taking a deep breath, she got to her feet, clutching the files, and made her way into Steve's office. It was time. She had to say something.

'Steve, can I talk to you, please?' Grace poked her head around his office door. Wincing apologetically, she realised he was on the telephone.

He held up his hand, first silencing her then gesturing for her to sit down.

'Tallis,' Steve put the receiver down. 'What can I do for you?'

'Gov, Sir…,' Tallis struggled to frame her thoughts, regretting, under his steely gaze, having barged in without knowing what to say.

'Yes?' He reached across his desk and grabbed one of the cigarettes he'd been smoking more and more of recently.

'When Matt and I were at Blackthorn Farm…,' Grace paused, picturing the cold gaze of Eddie Hammett. 'Look, Sir, this is just a feeling, but I'm sure he was the man who attacked me. He had a pick-up, a broken tail light.'

'Can you prove it?'

She shook her head. 'Just an impression, but what if he's the man who attacked Carrie, the lads said there was a pick-up in the boatyard. And Lindy… the festival wasn't far away from his farm.'

'Come on Tallis, I need more than that.'

'You're right. I'm sorry.' Grace gave Steve a wry look.

'Sorry for interrupting,' Rhonda's blonde head appeared around the door. 'Sir, there's been a report of a missing student in Exeter. The last sighting, by an elderly couple, was of her getting into a vehicle. I know this is off our patch, but Exeter have been onto us, they have a partial number plate and a vehicle description which matches one belonging to a local man. Could be nothing…?'

'Who is it?' Steve was already on his feet.

'Eddie Hammett, Blackthorn Farm.'

Chapter Thirty-Nine

She was there again. The little girl. A shadow passed the small window set high up on the wall. Periodically, she glimpsed the girl, her small wellington boots skipping as she passed by the window. It must, Susie had come to realise, be at ground level for the girl. The room where he kept her captive was sunk below ground, a cellar, she assumed. She'd watched, on the occasions he hadn't left her chained, through the keyhole. From there, crouching down, with one eye to the small gap, she could watch him walk away. Beyond the locked door was a corridor. At the end he turned and, she assumed walked up a flight of steps into the light.

Once, during the weeks she had been held prisoner, Susie had dragged the small table from beside her bed to beneath the window, she had made a step from a stool and stood on it gingerly. The surface felt fragile beneath her feet, as if it would collapse at any moment and send her sprawling onto the damp ground. He'd know, then, that she'd been trying to escape.

She'd pulled at the bars beside the window, banging on the glass, trying to attract the child's attention. But if she had heard the noise, she did not acknowledge Susie was there.

Susie sat on the bed, hugging her arms, rocking gently. The knot of fear had become a permanent fixture in the pit of her stomach.

The waiting was the worst, trapped in the damp half-light, knowing he would come eventually. At least once he had been into the cellar and done whatever game he had dreamed up, then she had a respite. He always brought food with him, sometimes a mug of tea or coffee, but by the time he had finished and she had scrubbed her skin raw in the shower, it was always cold.

Susie started as the light in the cellar changed. She looked up and saw the girl. She was crouching beside the window, rubbing at the glass to peer inside. In a flash Susie was on her feet, looking up at the girl.

'I'm here. Can you come and let me out?'

The girl, if she could hear Susie, made no reply, but instead watched her solemnly. Her dark eyes were wide with interest. Her expression changed a moment later, when she was hauled roughly to her feet by a dumpy, middle-aged woman who shook her like a rag doll, depositing her on the ground and glaring in the direction of the small window.

Susie stepped hastily out of sight. The woman's expression had terrified her. There was nothing in her eyes but pure hatred.

'Please, please let me out,' Susie's voice was little more than a whisper in the silence of the cellar. She paced the dank floor, pushing against the door, more through habit than an effort to escape. In her imagination freeing herself was easy. Perhaps one day he would forget and leave it open.

He'd dozed off a few evenings before, one arm circling her neck. She'd tried to ease herself out of his grasp, but he'd woken, jerking her back down beside him. One day though... He kept the key in his jeans pocket. Someday... She'd hit him with something, grab the key, and be gone.

The reality was not so simple. He made her stand away from the door before he entered, never taking his eyes off her. There was never an opportunity to attack him. Weak with hunger and cold, she stood no chance against his fit, muscular body. But, sometime, her chance would come. It was the only hope she had, and she clung to it.

As the room grew colder, she curled beneath the duvet. Its flowered cover was horrifically at odds with the grimness of her surroundings. Closing her eyes, Susie forced herself to focus on her university course, reciting parts of the modules, writing essays in her imagination. Anything was better than seeing the reality.

She froze as footsteps came towards the door, waiting for the sound of the key turning in the lock. Her heart beat a rapid tattoo against her chest. The key did not turn. Instead, from behind the door came a shuffling noise, and a moment later a sheet of paper was slid through the gap between the door and the floor slab.

'Hello!' Susie rolled off the bed, seizing the paper. It was a picture. A girl on a swing, made from what looked like a tyre. Beside the swing a mass of flowers covered the ground.

'Thank you.' Susie clutched the paper, watching it jerk as her fingers trembled. 'Is this… is this you?'

There was a silence. Susie assumed the girl must have fled in fear at being caught by the angry woman.

'Yes. My swing.' The voice was so faint Susie wondered if she had imagined it.

'You're very kind.'

Again, the long silence before the girl's voice came again, softly. 'Thank you.'

'Can you let me out of here?' Susie could hear the pleading note of desperation in her voice.

'There's no key,' the voice was louder this time, more confident.

'It's above the door somewhere.' Susie had heard him place it somewhere close to the door.

'I can't…'

Susie crouched down, squinting to look through the keyhole. The child behind the door chewed anxiously on her bottom lip. The jeans she wore bunched around her feet as if they were made for someone much taller. As Susie watched the girl turned, looking anxiously down the corridor. Long dark hair cascaded in soft waves down the back of her yellow raincoat.

'Please, just reach up and get the key.' Susie pleaded, she wanted to pound on the door, beg the child to let her out.

Behind the door, the child shook her head violently, before turning, fleeing down the corridor.

'Don't go, please.' Susie whimpered. As her legs gave way, she tumbled helplessly to the ground, sobbing.

The girl returned a few days later, sliding another picture beneath the door. Susie seized it. 'Thank you. That's so beautiful.'

She had drawn a bright yellow sun, shining above a field of flowers.

Susie crouched beside the door, one eye at the keyhole. The girl stood uncertainly in the corridor. She wore a different pair of jeans, faded pink corduroy with a brightly coloured sweater that looked two sizes too big for her, the sleeves were rolled up over her slender wrists.

'I love the sun,' Susie racked her brain for something to say, anything which would make the girl stay. 'Is it warm outside today?'

'Not really.' The voice was tentative.

'My name is Susie. What's yours?'

'Mia.'

'Oh, that's so pretty.' Susie bit her lip to stop herself crying out with despair. She was so lonely in the cellar, deprived of any human interaction except for the man. 'Were you at school today?'

'I don't go to school. Nan teaches me.'

'Is that the lady you were with?'

Mia was silent. Beyond the door Susie heard her feet shuffle, as if she were indecisive, wondering whether to stay or flee.

'I'm hungry.' Susie turned to look at the remnants of the sandwich he had brought her the previous night. The thick slices of bread and hunk of cheese he'd put between them had stuck in her throat. Her stomach was shrinking from lack of food. The clothes she'd found in the drawers hung off her. She longed for something decent to eat, a hot shower, the freedom to move without the fear of what would happen to her.

'I brought you an orange.'

'An orange.' The thought of the juicy, sweet flesh made Susie's mouth water.

There was a scuffling noise behind the door.

'It won't fit.'

Susie bit her lip, longing to scream at the girl to open the door. Instinct told her to be gentle, to speak softly, to wait.

'Perhaps if you open the door.'

There was an intense silence. Susie put her eye back to the keyhole. Mia's expression was watchful, filled with fear, one ear cocked to listen for anyone approaching.

Watching her, Susie realised how brave the child had been to even venture down the steps.

'Could you find a way to reach the key?'

She saw Mia move away, half turning towards the entrance to the cellar.

'Please.'

She watched expressions flit across the girl's face, her fear at being discovered fought with her curiosity about the disjointed voice behind the door.

'I'll try.'

Susie watched Mia drag a discarded bucket from amongst the junk and step up onto it. Her body covered the keyhole, but Susie could hear her grunting with the effort of reaching to the top of the door. She imagined her standing on tiptoe, her fingers searching amongst the dirt and cobwebs.

'It's here.' Mia jumped down from the bucket, stepping back from the doorway so Susie could see what she held.

'Can you open it?' Susie got to her feet.

The girl began to insert the key, fumbling.

'Hurry.' Susie pleaded.

Then the noise she recognised, the unmistakable sound of the key turning.

Susie flung herself at the door, stumbling as it gave way, opening outwards into the corridor. She burst through the gap, dimly aware of Mia being thrown to the ground by the force. There was no time to wait. Susie ran, her feet sliding on the greasy ground as she pounded the length of the corridor. At the end, she stopped, pausing to turn up the steps. Glancing back, she saw Mia scrambling to her feet, surprise and hurt shining in her dark eyes.

For a split second she hesitated, wanting to help Mia, but she had to get out.

Susie hurtled up the steps, bursting into the daylight, blinking against its harshness. There was a shout of anger, she didn't wait to see where from. Feet skidding on the muddy ground at the top of the steps, Susie began to run. She was vaguely aware of the ruined shape of a building, tumble down walls, blackened rafters, a farmyard, and beside that, a house.

Her breath roaring in her ears, Susie turned in the opposite direction. The ruins where she had been imprisoned was set amongst trees, short, cropped grass grew beneath them. The shoes she wore flapped on her feet, hampering her flight. Without pausing, she flicked them off and ran on, stumbling over tree roots, sliding on the grass.

Somewhere close by she could hear a vehicle, turning she spotted a pick-up, moving through the trees, parallel to her. There must be a track there. An engine revved. Over the sound of her gasping breath came the sound of wheels, skidding on the rough surface. The engine noise had stopped. Looking back, she could see that he had abandoned the pick-up. He was running through the forestry towards her, she could hear him moving through the trees.

Tripping on a tree root, she fell heavily, sprawling to the ground, breathing in the damp earthy smell. Winded she lay, desperate in her panic to force air into her lungs. Above her, the sun shone through the canopy of the leaves. Somewhere amongst the trees a bird sang, its tune cutting through the silence.

Susie scrambled to her feet, she had to keep going. She plunged up a steep bank, pulling herself up on the tree trunks, her gasping breath the only sound above her scrambling feet. At the top of the bank the trees thinned out, a grassy track ran ahead of her. Chancing a glance back, she paused, watching. No one was there. She whimpered with fright, knowing he could be close behind her, hidden, or up ahead, waiting for her to pass.

Susie stopped, leaning against a tree, terrified of going on, yet afraid of what might be coming behind her. She forced a breath, and ran on, every nerve jangling with fear.

Through a gap in the trees, in the distance she could see the grey ribbon of a road, cars moving steadily along it. She half slid, half fell down a wooded slope, towards the road, cannoning off trees, dimly aware of jolts of sharp pain.

The trees ended abruptly, in a wooden fence, behind which cars hurtled along the tarmac. Fearfully, she climbed it. She waited until there was a gap in the traffic, afraid he might be in one of the cars, that he would stop, force her into the vehicle.

At the far side of the road was a line of houses. She scrambled over a garden fence, dashing towards the house. What if he were there, waiting? Maybe he would know this was where she would make for? He would be coming after her. Susie knew if he caught her he would kill her.

Terror gripping every nerve, Susie plunged headlong into a thick laurel hedge at the side of the house drive. She scrambled into the darkness, whimpering in fear as branches and sharp brambles caught at her clothes, slowing her. She crouched, shivering in terror in the half-light beneath the leaves, afraid to move, convinced that at any moment he would find her.

Susie screamed as a hand touched her leg.

Chapter Forty

Whimpering in terror Susie, kicked out at the hand, as it was withdrawn she crawled further beneath the bush, ignoring the bramble thorns that scraped at her skin. Drawing her legs beneath her she rolled into a tight ball beneath the branches and roots.

'What are you doing? Where have you come from? Is someone after you?' The voice was female, gentle, filled with concern.'

He had sent the middle-aged woman to recapture her. Susie edged further away, panic beginning to set in when she realised her back was against a thick immovable branch. She closed her eyes, waiting for death.

'Please come out. Whatever happened to you you're safe here.' The voice had lowered so it was barely a whisper.

Slowly Susie opened her tightly closed eyes. Through the shining leaves of the laurel bush, she could see an elderly woman. She had crouched down to peer beneath the bushes. One hand, resting on the ground, was stick thin, heavily veined, the skin wrinkled.

'Where have you come from? I'm not going to hurt you.' The woman repeated.

'Leave me alone. Go away. Please.' Susie hissed. The man would be coming. She raised herself on one elbow, eyes darting furiously as she searched for a loose branch, a rock, something she could use as a weapon. He couldn't be far behind, perhaps he had seen where she had hidden.

Susie's fingers scrabbled in the dry earth, working at a rock, frenziedly trying to lever it from the ground. The soil was cool against her fingers as she dug them in, further and further down, pulling, until finally the rock came free. It fitted in the palm of her hand, resting heavily there.

'I want to help you. My name is Eileen. I live here.' As Susie watched the woman eased her hand, wincing as ancient muscles and ligaments protested. Eileen moved to a kneeling position, resting her bottom on her heels.

Susie opened her lips, her mouth working, desperately trying to speak, but all that would come out were puppy-like whimpering noises, sounds of utter terror and desperation.

'Please come out.' Eileen lifted the outer branches and moved forwards.

'No!' Susie's cry was animal like, ferocious. Gathering her reserves of energy, she lifted the rock.

'Okay,' the elderly lady put her hands up in a gesture of surrender as the leaves fell back into place, once more darkening Susie's hiding place.

He was going to come soon. He'd come into the bush and drag her out. He'd hurt her again. Worse. There would be punishment for escaping. Susie's mind flitted briefly over the little girl. She hadn't meant to hurt her when she'd slammed the door back. Mia had been trying to help. Where was she now? Had the woman locked her into the cellar?

The branches lifted. Eileen peered into the gloom. 'I'm not going to hurt you. I promise.'

Her eyes, when they fixed on Susie's, were kindly, full of concern.

'Wait there.' Through the branches, Susie watched the woman get ponderously to her feet.

Susie huddled into the depths of the bush She should run again, get to safety. But where was safe? Now her breathing had slowed, she could hear traffic. Could she run? Get to the road. Flag down one of the cars? She daren't. He could be in any one of them.

Through the waxy leaves she spotted Eileen returning, spindly legs outlined beneath a black skirt as she hurried across the grass.

'I've brought you a blanket.' Crouching down the elderly woman lifted the waxy leaves of the bush. 'You might like this.' Eileen pushed a pale pink blanket through the branches towards Susie who made a noise of agreement and nodded once, her eyes never leaving the woman's face, watching for any sign of aggression. Susie tightened her fingers around the rock.

Slowly, Eileen inched forwards, pushing the blanket in front of her.

Susie inched her free hand forwards, her other gripping the rock. Ready. Her fingers, they were filthy, unrecognisable, the nails were black-rimmed, bitten, the skin around them raw and torn.

She took the blanket. It felt light, so soft beneath her skin, and smelled... Susie brought the fabric to her face, breathing in the scent of clean washing. After the damp, cheap, flowered duvet cover, it smelt divine.

Susie pulled herself into a crouching position, letting the rock drop from her fingers.

Eileen's eyes followed it as it rolled, coming to rest against one of the exposed roots.

Susie eased the pink blanket around her shoulders, an aching cold seemed to be lodged deep inside her.

'Will you come out?' Eileen shifted uncomfortably, easing her knees onto softer ground. 'Please, no one is going to hurt you. What's your name?'

'Su... Susie.' Her lips moved awkwardly over her name. 'Susie. I'm Susie.'

'Come out from here,' Eileen's voice was soft. 'Please, I want to help you.'

Susie shook her head. She felt safe in the bushes.

'I've some food inside. Some clothes... although,' Eileen paused. 'Perhaps I shouldn't do that... Evidence?' She mumbled half talking to herself. 'Please, love. You're shivering. You need to come inside. It's safer there.' Eileen frowned. 'Is someone chasing you?'

Susie nodded.

'Hurry. You'll be safer inside.'

Susie scrambled for the rock, its weight in her hand giving her confidence.

Slowly she eased her way out of the depths of the bush, pushing the branches out of the way.

'There you are.' Eileen smiled gently as Susie finally emerged into the light.

Susie levered herself upright, the grass felt soft beneath her feet, the sunlight warm on her face.

'Let me...' Eileen put a hand on Susie's arm.

With wild animal strength and a cry of fury, Susie lashed out, lifting the rock.

'Sorry. I won't touch you.' Eileen released Susie's arm, stepping back out of the way.

The rock tumbled from Susie's hand, as the final reserves of her energy were used up. Defeated, she watched it hit the ground and roll slowly away, before coming to rest at the edge of the grass.

'Oh my god, what has happened to you?' Eileen's eyes were wide with horror.

'My name is Susie. Susie Carne. I've been held prisoner. Somewhere up there,' Susie pointed to the hillside at the opposite side of the road. As the words tumbled from her, she glimpsed herself, seeing her filthy, tattered leggings and top. There were tears in the fabric through which her mud-blackened, torn and bloodied skin showed through. Her feet, bare, were black with mud, one red toenail, incongruously bright, shone out of the dirt.

Eileen moved slowly ahead of Susie, her shoes crunching on the gravel drive at the side of the lawn. The stones felt smooth beneath Susie's feet. Her soles ached from running barefoot.

As they walked towards the house a movement on the hillside caught Susie's eye. She turned. He was there. He had seen her. He was plunging down the hillside through the trees towards her. Susie screamed, watching fixated, helpless as he reached the bottom of the hill. Beside her she was aware of Eileen turning to look, her expression filled with fear.

And then he turned away, vanishing into the trees. He had gone. Over the sound of her sobbing Susie realised she could hear sirens, when she turned in the direction of the noise there were blue lights flashing in the distance.

Chapter Forty-One

'That's Blackwater Edge.' Grace leant forwards to peer through the windscreen as the countryside flashed past. High above them soared a wooded hillside. 'Blackthorn Farm is next left. About another mile there's a long drive.'

'What the hell…' Steve stamped on the brakes as ahead of them an elderly lady hurried out into the middle of the road and stood, legs planted firmly, waving her arms.

'There's a girl here. Her name is Susie Carne she's been abducted, held prisoner,' Her face was flushed with excitement. 'Eileen Moore,' she stuck her hand through the open window towards Steve. 'She's terrified, poor thing.'

Steve hurtled up Eileen's drive, scattering gravel in every direction in his haste. He was out of the car as Grace radioed the station for help. He jogged across the lawn towards Susie who was wrapped in a pink blanket her face a mask of terror. 'Susie?'

'No!' Susie flailed wildly, as he got close to her. 'Don't touch me.'

Steve held up his hands. 'Okay, sorry, Susie I won't. Tallis...' He glanced towards Grace. 'Your call...'

'Hi Susie,' Grace having called for backup, crossed the lawn towards Susie, she inched forwards, smiling gently. 'You're safe, we just want to help you.'

Susie's eyes swivelled to look at Grace, her white face a mask of naked fear. 'You did so well to get out.' Grace continued.

Susie nodded once, her eyes slowly focusing on Grace.

'Do you remember where you came from? Where were you held?' Grace glanced at Steve, seeing impatience in the taut line of his shoulders.

Susie took a juddering breath, one hand slowly emerged from beneath the blanket to point in the direction of the woods opposite the house. 'Somewhere up there. I ran through those trees.'

'Was it a farm?' Grace probed gently.

Susie closed her eyes, whimpering softly.

'Eileen,' Steve said. 'Will you look after Susie just for a few more minutes. There's help on its way.' He turned his focus to Grace. 'Come on. Let's put a stop to this bastard.'

Leaving the two women, Grace followed Steve as they ran across the lawn towards the car.

'Down here, Blackthorn Farm,' Grace directed, a moment later, sliding in her seat as Steve flung the car around a corner and onto a narrow, rutted farm drive. During the bumpy journey Grace had relayed Steve's instructions to the rest of the team. An ambulance and patrol car to care for Susie, and reinforcements to help them.

'He'll know we're coming for sure.' Steve looked at the tangle of stone buildings set half-way up the hill at the end of the long driveway.

'If he's even there, now Susie's gone. He could be anywhere.'

The car stopped in the yard in the centre of the buildings. A red pick-up stood in the centre of the yard, the driver's door flung open, showing the haste in which the occupant had abandoned it. From the bottom of the valley, Grace could hear sirens.

'Eddie!' Steve yelled, his voice echoing around the silent buildings.

A moment later an angry looking middle-aged woman emerged from the house. 'He isn't here.' She fixed them with a steely glare, her lips clamping shut into a tight line.

'You are?' Steve faced her.

'Elizabeth Hammett. Nan. Mrs Hammett to you.' she spat coldly, glaring at them.

Steve thrust his jaw forwards; a gesture Grace recognised as gathering his patience. 'Where has he gone? We need to know.'

Nan folded her arms aggressively across her chest, regarding him through lowered brows, like a bull about to charge. She was silent, watchful, emotions flickering over her face, until finally she spoke. 'That way.' She jerked her head in the direction of the woods, a field away from the back of the house.

'Thank you.'

'Fuck you! Bastards!' Nan's shout of anger followed them as Grace and Steve ran out of the farmyard in the direction Eddie had taken. Boot prints led across the muddy field, beside them were smaller ones.

'Jesus.' Steve panted. 'He's got a kid with him.'

They reached a gate at the edge of the field and looked into the depths of the wood. A churned, muddy track ran parallel to the woods, scored by deep tyre ruts. 'Where's this go?'

'It comes out at Blackwater Edge at one side, and onto the old railway line on the other.' Grace replied, recognised the surrounding land, she'd ridden Sisco at a hunter trials nearby.

'This is where Susie ran.' Steve glanced back at the farm. 'I've never seen anyone so terrified. What the fuck has that bastard done to her?' He shook his head, before scrambling over the creaking wooden gate and plunging into the woodland.

'Come on!' Steve yelled, reaching into his pocket for his radio, speaking into it as he ran. 'Rhonda, get a car to Blackwater Edge and another to the old railway line. We've got to get this bastard. He's got a kid with him...'

Grace ran alongside Steve, her breath roaring in her ears.

'No idea how old she is. Or if he's grabbed her. Any calls about missing kids? Getting her to safety is going to be paramount.' Steve shouted into the radio as he ran.

Their footsteps were dulled by the thick layer of pine needles that lay on the ground. Grace breathed in the earthy smell of the peaty ground. High above them, the sun shone through the canopy of branches, sending shafts of light onto the woodland floor. Somewhere ahead was Eddie Hammett, thrown into panic by his captive escaping.

'Need. To. Give. Up. Smoking.' Steve panted, pausing for a moment to bend double, gasping for breath.

Grace ran on as fast as she could, ducking beneath the branches. She wondered about his mindset. Where was he heading? He could have always anticipated this would happen and have a hide somewhere, or a vehicle ready to get away.

The girls, Carrie, Lindy, Ayla, Glanna, was he responsible for them all as she believed? The thought gave her no pleasure. If they had done a better job, he wouldn't have been free for so long as to continue to capture and hurt young women. The sooner they had him caught the better. Eddie Hammett had a lot of questions to answer.

They plunged up a steep slope, legs scrabbling for grip on the slippery surface.

Grace scrambled up, clinging to tree branches and exposed roots to propel herself upwards. Steve had got his second wind and bounded up beside her.

'Railway line is just up here.' Grace panted, breathlessly, spotting a ribbon of bright green amongst the trees.

Side by side, they emerged from the trees, blinking as the light changed. Ahead lay the grassy track of what had once been an old railway line, taking tin and copper away from the Cornish mines.

Somewhere up ahead, Rhonda and another team of uniformed officers were hurrying towards them from the opposite end.

A movement caught Grace's eye. Ahead of them on was the old railway viaduct which spanned a deep valley. Eddie Hammet, clutching the hand of a terrified looking young girl, stood on the viaduct. Wild dark hair billowed around the child's face blown by the wind that whipped down the valley, battering the viaduct. Sensing their approach, Eddie turned to look at them.

At the far side of the viaduct, Rhonda and two uniformed officers emerged from the trees.

'Where's my armed response?' Steve yelled breathlessly into his radio.

'On their way, Boss.' Came the reply.

'Fucking hell. I've a bloody potential hostage situation here. And no armed response.'

'They are on their way.' The officer repeated.

As they watched Eddie released the girl's hand, pacing the short distance between the tall wrought iron barrier that spanned the edge of the viaduct. He moved to the edge, leaning against the barrier, looking down. The viaduct spanned the valley, its faded red-brick arches soaring hundreds of feet into the air from the river below. The sound of the rushing water, far below them was deafening.

'Eddie!' Steve took a stride towards the bridge. The man turned, resuming his pacing, from one barrier to the other. The girl, her sweater whipping around her thin frame, watched, her fearful gaze moving from Eddie to the police at either side of the bridge, before returning to him.

'Eddie, you need to give this up. Now.'

At the far side of the bridge, Rhonda was inching forwards.

Steve held his hand up, indicating Rhonda should stop. 'Last thing we want to do is panic him. I don't want him going over there,' he said quietly to the team surrounding him.

Grace forced a breath into her lungs, they all had to keep calm, wait until Eddie was ready to walk off the viaduct, with the girl, and get them both to safety. Facing Steve Eddie shrugged, holding his arms out from his sides in a gesture of surrender. 'Give me a minute.' Eddie's voice was strong over the noise of the water.

It was over. He was giving himself up. She closed her eyes, feeling relief wash over her.

She opened them to see Eddie crouching beside the little girl. Gently he pushed the mane of hair off her face.

'Come on, Eddie.' Grace whispered. He looked calm, resigned, ready to walk towards them. Soon they'd learn about the horrors he'd inflicted, discover once and for all what deaths he had been responsible for. Get him into prison, where he deserved to be. As well as the vile woman back at the farm.

Eddie straightened up, taking the girl's hand. He turned, looking in the direction of Rhonda, then slowly swivelled his head to look at Steve. His eyes flickered briefly over Grace. A slow smile spread over his face.

In one fluid movement, he released the child's hand, vaulted over the barrier, and was gone.

'Shit.' Steve spat as they dashed onto the bridge, leaning over the barrier to look at the shallow river-bed below where the broken body of Eddie Hammett lay.

Steve had almost knocked the small girl over in his haste to look over the barrier.

She stood alone, white faced. The wind whipped at the strands of hair Eddie had pushed back, they billowed around her face once more.

Grace held out her hand, feeling the girl's icy fingers as they slid into her grasp. 'Come on love.' She said gently. 'Let's get you somewhere safe.'

THE END

Thank you for taking the time to read this book. I hope you enjoyed it, I certainly enjoyed writing it. Each time I sit down to write – and that is every day – I realise just how lucky I am this is my job. I can only keep this job because people like you enjoy my books and buy them. No words can express how grateful I am for that.

If you would like to find out more about my other books, please visit my web site.

www.louisebroderick.com

I love to hear from readers so please feel free to contact me on via my Facebook page or email. The details of these are all on my web site.

It would make my day if you would take the time to leave a book review on Amazon. Positive reviews really do help to sell a book, so if you would do that for me you are helping me to continue creating my books and continuing as a fulltime writer.

Can I just say a huge thank you in advance to anyone who takes the time to do this for me. I know very well how precious time is and am hugely grateful for anyone who cares enough to spend some of their valuable time helping me. Thank you.

My Other Books:

Writing as Louise Broderick
Trainers
Winners
Millionaires Are A Girl's Best Friend
After – Sometimes The End Is Just The Beginning
Plot. Write. Sell.

Writing as Jacqui Broderick
Pony For Free
The Unwanted Pony
The Cat's Whiskers